THE DETECTIVE

The Primrose Path

Jayne Stennett

Copyright © Jayne Stennett 2021
The right of Jayne Stennett to be identified as the author of the work 'The Detective' has been asserted by her in accordance with the Copyright, Designs and Patents Act 1988. All rights reserved. No part of this publication may be reproduced, stored in a retrieval system, or transmitted, in any form or by any means, without the prior written permission of the author.
All rights reserved.
ISBN-13: 9798774386826

The author wishes to acknowledge that this is a work of fiction, so any resemblance to the characters in this book, to anyone living or dead, or to the places mentioned, is purely coincidental as they are all fictitious.

*For Jess, my beautiful daughter, supporter, and muse.
Thanks for always being there to offer advice, doughnuts, and tea.*

CONTENTS

Chapter 1 .... *1*
Chapter 2 .... *6*
Chapter 3 .... *13*
Chapter 4 .... *19*
Chapter 5 .... *23*
Chapter 6 .... *28*
Chapter 7 .... *34*
Chapter 8 .... *40*
Chapter 9 .... *47*
Chapter 10 .... *52*
Chapter 11 .... *58*
Chapter 12 .... *66*
Chapter 13 .... *72*
Chapter 14 .... *78*
Chapter 15 .... *85*
Chapter 16 .... *91*
Chapter 17 .... *98*
Chapter 18 .... *105*
Chapter 19 .... *112*
Chapter 20 .... *121*
Chapter 21 .... *129*
Chapter 22 .... *136*
Chapter 23 .... *143*
Chapter 24 .... *150*
Chapter 25 .... *157*
Chapter 26 .... *166*
Chapter 27 .... *173*
Chapter 28 .... *184*
Chapter 29 .... *190*
Chapter 30 .... *198*
Chapter 31 .... *205*
Chapter 32 .... *213*
Chapter 33 .... *220*
Chapter 34 .... *227*

Chapter 35	233
Chapter 36	238
Chapter 37	246
Chapter 38	252
Chapter 39	257
Chapter 40	265
Chapter 41	270
Epilogue	279
Author's Note	281

"Do not as some ungracious Pastors do, show me the steep and thorny way to heaven.

While like a puff'd and reckless libertine; himself, the primrose path of dalliance treads."

Shakespeare, *Hamlet*

CHAPTER 1

"Guilt is rooted in actions of the past, perpetuated in the lack of action in the present, and delivered in the future as pain and suffering."

David Roppo

Steve placed his arms around Meg and pulled her close. She was just stirring, whereas he had lain awake for hours, and watched as the dawn's orange glow had crept over the windowsill, making shadows on the wall behind him. She turned to face him and smiled. Kissing him she snuggled back onto his chest. She didn't see how fleetingly the smile played upon his face or how his hand raised to feel the deep grooves that ran down both cheeks. He had gained the scars just a few months ago from a serial killer whom he had fought, when he had tried to stop her from harming Meg. He could still feel her nails tearing into his flesh and the burning green eyes that glared back at him. The Diabhul was in the reflection and showed the depths of her insanity. Those eyes haunted his nightmares and, to make matters more complicated, the killer had turned out to be his long-lost sister. She had been responsible for the death of Meg's parents and brother and the attempted murder of Meg's teenage daughter Romany and several other innocent people that had gotten in her way.

He didn't mind the scars that much, but he did mind what had brought him to have them in the first place. Meg didn't know about the guilt that he felt after discovering the abuse that his sister had lived through; whereas he had a loving mother and father and the most idyllic childhood on a farm in rural Ireland. Ahh … Bally-Bay where the nightmare began; he thought now of his mother back on the farm on the outskirts of Bally-Bay. His thoughts drifting to the grave of his daddy whom he now knew wasn't his birth father; high up on the hill under the Faery-thorn. He knew that he was struggling with his feelings towards his mother; he also knew that his life had been completely turned upside down by the revelations about his birth. He had confronted her at the time to learn the truth but had not returned since his visit with Meg straight after the capture and internment into a mental health facility of his sister.

Gently putting Meg's head onto the pillow so as not to disturb her, he wriggled out from under the covers and headed to the bathroom. Today he had a meeting with his boss and his old friend Sean O'Dowd who was flying in from Dublin. He had been tying up all of the loose ends in Ireland from the victims' cases; left by Bree, or Magda as his mother had told him she had named her at their birth. He didn't want to call her Magda even if it was her given name as Meg's mother had been called Magda which had led to the killer believing that she was her mother and the revenge that she exacted had devastated Meg and her family. She had called herself Bree and that is what Meg knew her as. Not that he spoke of her to Meg but if he did it was to address her as such.

Climbing out of the shower he looked into the mirror; he had decided to grow a beard to try and cover at least some of the scars and he scrubbed at his face and smiled. He looked at the white streaks in his beard that had appeared practically overnight and matched the ones now residing in his hair. Forty-seven years old and he looked at least ten years older now; the trauma had definitely aged him. At least beards are trendy at the moment, he thought, and although Meg had asked him not to grow one he had decided to grow it anyway. They had even rowed about it, not that Meg disliked the beard per se but she had accused him of hiding behind it emotionally and he knew that she was right.

He had always been stubborn but now he realised that he wasn't ready to face the world yet. Even his decision to move into the house with Meg had been worrying him. He knew that he loved her and Romany but he needed time to come to terms with what had happened and didn't feel that he could give her what she deserved. All that he could offer was a broken copper with a lot of issues to resolve. She loved Steve and had told him numerous times that they would work it out together; but to be honest he had felt that he needed to do it by himself so found himself pushing her away and withdrawing inside himself more every day.

Shrugging on his suit jacket and adjusting his tie he slipped out of the front door, hoping to escape before Meg realised that he had gone. Instead she had watched him leave from the bedroom window; a tear tracking down her cheek as he drove away.

She turned and headed for the shower and to get dressed, ready for her day teaching at the local primary school. She used to love her job and had worked very hard to help her students, mostly with special needs, or anxiety issues, to achieve the little steps that they needed, to function in an unforgiving world. Maybe it was because of her training that she knew how much Steve was suffering and she longed to help him too, but she also knew that life wasn't as forgiving and neither was Steve. For the meantime she had to sit back and watch her gorgeous man torture himself with guilt, blame, and frustration, and suppress his anger to the point where she was worried if he, or even their relationship, would make it through. Sighing she called out to Romany to get up as she headed for the kitchen. She had to smile as she entered the room and the smell of coffee assaulted her senses; her good man as always was thinking of her and had put the coffee on for her before leaving. He knew how much she needed her coffee in the morning to set her up for another difficult day.

'Romany, will you get yourself up and moving, I will be leaving in twenty minutes,' she called up the stairs.

Her beautiful daughter was still recovering from the injuries inflicted on her by Bree, who had caused her to fall from a horse and put her in a coma for weeks. She had suffered a fractured skull, back and pelvis as well as internal injuries so a few months down the line she was still recovering, slowly. Meg knew that they were all lucky to still be alive and it was all thanks to her darling man. She smiled as she heard her daughter clopping down the stairs at a rate of knots and shouting out about some lost homework. Her mother stood in the kitchen doorway with the homework held tightly in her hand. Romany moved to take it from her and shove it in her bag, but her mother moved it out of her reach. 'Ah, ah, young lady, not until you have eaten at least a slice of toast.'

'Aw Mum, I will be late!'

'No you won't, I will drop you off if you hurry up.' Meg watched as her daughter reached for the buttered toast waiting for her on a plate on the kitchen island.

'Thanks, Mum.' She turned and smiled at her mum, shoving the piece of toast into her mouth at the same time as snatching the papers from her mum's hand. Meg laughed and hustled herself and her daughter out of the door to the car. Once inside the car she pushed a sandwich box into her daughter's hand. "I made you some lunch too."

'I'm not a baby, you know.' But she still smiled as she pushed the box into her backpack.

'I know, love, but you need to take care of yourself.'

'You mean *you* need to take care of me. What will you do when I go off to uni?'

'You need to finish school first and then college so until then indulge me.'

Romany laughed, Meg looked at her daughter, saw the shining blue eyes and soft dark curls that framed her heart-shaped face and she knew that no matter how old she got, after nearly losing her for good, she would care for her as much as Romany would allow. Kissing her cheek she pulled into the school car park and watched her long legs stride off into the building without a care. Sighing she reversed the car and drove off to her work, pleased that her daughter didn't seem to be having any after effects from the trauma she so recently had endured. Her memory of events was still very foggy and Meg was glad that at least Romany had been spared the worst of it.

She made her way into work and her mind soon became filled with everyday minutiae. Her thoughts with Steve and his meeting today; running alongside thoughts of what to have for dinner tonight, just like millions of other women. But she wasn't the same as millions of other women; they hadn't been the one to escape the clutches of a serial killer; and almost lose everything.

CHAPTER 2

"When all the dust is settled and all the crowds are gone, the things that matter are faith, family, and friends."

Barbara Bush

Steve pulled his car into the parking space and stopped, unbuckled his seatbelt, and turned to pick up his briefcase, then the pain hit him suddenly; throwing his arm across his chest he doubled over; his breathing became laboured, and he wondered if he was going to pass out. Putting his head down he tried to concentrate on his breathing, willing it to return to normal. Was he having a heart attack? He could hear his heart beating fast and feel it nearly jumping out of his chest. Just as his breathing began to return to normal and he had gained some control, a tap at his car window reminded him that he was still in the car park and had yet to even make it indoors.

He looked up into the sparkling blue eyes and huge grin of his friend Sean. Pulling open the car door Sean looked down at his old friend with concern, he could clearly see that he was distressed.

'Well now what do we have here, too much to drink last night? We are not as young as we were. It will finish you off so it will; why do yer think I gave it up.'

The lilting Irish brogue of his best friend brought Steve back to the present and he tried to smile. Rubbing his hand across his chest he laughed at his friend and, not quite able to meet his eye, he muttered, 'I am fine, just some indigestion, that's all. I really need to stop eating those hot curries. It's good to see yer; did yer have a good flight?'

Climbing out of the car he held out his hand and felt his own hand encased in the firm grip that Steve remembered. Sean, pulling him into a brotherly hug, whispered quietly in Steve's ear, 'Are yer really alright, man?'

'To be sure it's just the Diabhul in the chicken Katsu.'

'Talking of devils, I have finally closed the last investigation from Dublin concerning the murders of Collum, Phoebe, and her parents and thought I would bring the paperwork over personally and pay you a visit at the same time. Sadly, we have been unable to find any evidence connecting her to the young doctor and his children in the car accident. Everything points to it just being an accident. If she hadn't confessed we would never really have looked at it as anything else. I will hand over what I have and leave the rest of the murder investigations over here in England in your capable hands.'

Strolling to the entrance of the police station, Steve acted as if nothing had happened but not quite meeting his friend's eye. Sean decided that he would drop it for now but certainly have a word with Meg to see if things were ok. The look of concern for his friend lingered on his face as Steve pulled open the door and a cacophony of sound hit their ears.

'I hope you are staying over; you can stop with Meg and me for the night, it will be good to catch up over dinner.'

'I was hoping you would say that! I haven't booked anywhere to stay.'

The handover went smoothly and Steve showed Sean what evidence had been gathered so far in the investigation of Meg's brother Jonathon and her parents Magda and Andrew Callahan, who had all been killed by Bree. Before they knew it, the day had gone and they headed out of the door for home.

'Please don't talk shop when we get home, Sean. I have been trying to protect Meg from the worst of it and Romany, thank God, doesn't remember any of it; so I try to keep work separate. Even though it concerns Meg's family it will never come to trial as Bree is clearly insane,' Steve cautioned.

'Of course, buddy, no problem, as long as we can find five minutes in private to talk about what was happening earlier; and I won't take no for an answer. I have known you for a long time, Steve, and since way back when we were young garda's, we never had any secrets from each other.'

Steve sighed and they drove off, heading towards Meg's house. After meeting and greeting Meg they settled in the living room with a beer and Sean admired the amazing house. 'Yeah about that … no way could I ask Meg to move in with me, after all what could I offer her and Romany except a semi detached on some housing estate if we were lucky. The way house prices are going around here we probably couldn't even afford that.'

'She didn't choose to be with you because of your wealth or lack of it, Steve; it is clear to even me with a terrible track record with women that she cares for you deeply. I know you and it's not about what you can offer Meg; what exactly is going on?'

Steve sighed and shrugged his shoulders, not wanting to burden his friend. 'How are the kids, do you get to see them much? Have you met anyone new yet? The last time we spoke you were telling me about a girl that you had been talking to at your A.A. meetings,' Steve questioned, hoping to steer the subject away from himself and his feelings of inadequacy.

'The answer is yes the kids are well and I have been seeing them on a more regular basis now. I am still making amends to them and things are still difficult between my eldest and me but hey!' He shrugged his shoulders and looked sadly at Steve.

'But we are not talking about my problems; I thought we were talking about yours. You know that you can tell me anything and it won't leave this room. After all, you have been through an awful lot the past year; nobody would blame you if you were finding it tough. I wish that I had talked to someone when I was at my lowest ebb until waiting till it was pointed out to me. Just promise that if you need to talk to someone that you get help. Don't be so bloody macho.'

Steve rose from the sofa and made his way to the kitchen to help Meg with dinner and Sean knew in that moment that he had lost the battle. All he could do was hope that his friend could find no shame in getting help and, by the look of what he had witnessed earlier, the sooner the better. After all, he had survived hell twice before so he should make it again.

After a great meal cooked by Meg and Romany, they all headed off to bed. 'I will thank you for your hospitality now as I have ordered a taxi to get me to the airport in the morning, I will be up and gone early. Let me know if you are coming over to Ireland anytime soon and we can meet up. Take care of yourselves and, Steve, if you need any help with that little work problem just give me a call.'

Steve hurried into the shower and when he came out Meg was asleep. Good, he thought, I won't have to fob her off again tonight. He climbed wearily into bed, kissed her on the cheek, and fell into a deep sleep. He awoke from a nightmare a couple of hours later to the sound of his own scream. Meg had been covered in blood, he was sure that she was dead. The Diabhul stood over her and Steve couldn't move, no matter how hard he tried to get to Meg, he was rooted to the spot. He looked down at his own hands and they were covered in blood … Meg's blood; he knew he couldn't save her … or maybe he had killed her? Suddenly the Diabhul turned its face towards him and he saw that it was the face of his own mother.

Meg's face swam before him as he entered the waking realm; she had been shaking him and calling his name for an age, becoming increasingly concerned that the nightmares were becoming more frequent, and it was taking longer and longer to wake him up each time. Steve tried to push her away and make light of the fact that he had been so distressed by the images in his head that he had screamed. Meg on the other hand decided to take the bull by the horns and stroking his face she begged him to talk to her to no avail. He flung back the covers, the clock said that it was almost time to get up so he headed for the shower and, as he stood under the water, the images from his nightmare crowded his mind and he felt his chest tightening and his breathing changing. Hearing the noise of Steve falling and the crash in the bathroom, Meg rushed through the door. She ran to Steve who was laid out on the floor, the noise had been the shower rail falling from the wall and crashing on the floor as he fell.

'Steve, Steve.' Rushing to him, Meg lifted his head onto her lap just as he started to rouse. As soon as he tried to focus his eyes he vomited all over himself and the floor. Meg ran into the bedroom and lifting the phone she rung for an ambulance. By the time she came back into the room Steve was trying to stand. 'Wait, darling, please, an ambulance is on its way.'

'I am fine, please, just let me clean myself up first.' He pushed her away and she recoiled at the look in his eyes. Unsure of what to do she decided to get dressed and left him standing under the hot running water. What was she to do? She knew that the man that she had come to love was suffering and needed help; if only he could accept that. Just as she was using these few minutes to think, so was Steve; confused and feeling helpless he waited as his heartbeat and breathing returned to normal before he felt comfortable to leave the bathroom. As he entered the bedroom he heard the ambulance arrive. Meg by now had dressed and ran down to open the door before Steve could protest. Leading the paramedic upstairs they found Steve sat on the bed trying to put his socks on.

'Hey buddy, my name is Lewis. I hear that you had a bit of a fall, do you mind if I look you over?'

'I'm fine, I just tripped that's all, sorry your time was wasted.'

'Not wasted at all, I love a trip into the countryside, it sets me up for the day. Can I just check you out anyway? I might as well now I am here.'

Grumbling under his breath Steve acquiesced. After checking out a few vitals and finding nothing, Lewis started to ask a few questions about how Steve had felt before he fell, did he feel dizzy or sick? When it came to the question about whether it had happened before he watched Steve glance over at Meg before shaking his head in the negative.

'Hang on, Meg, is it? Do you think that you could fetch me a drink of water if it's not too much trouble? I didn't have time to get a drink before the call and I'm dying of thirst.'

Turning to Steve as soon as Meg had left the room he asked him again if he had any of the symptoms before. With a big sigh Steve knew that he needed to tell Lewis about yesterday, as today it had scared him very much. After listening quietly while Steve explained the feeling of pain and tightness in his chest and how he was trying so hard to breathe, Lewis asked a couple more questions about work and his relationships. Steve, fearing the worst, asked him straight out: 'Come on then, tell me the worst, is it my heart?'

'No actually you are fit and fine for your age, blood pressure is up a bit but that is to be expected after the mother of a panic attack that you have just endured.'

Steve looked at Lewis in shock. 'Panic attack? Are yer pulling me leg?'

'I can assure you that you are fine physically and panic attacks are not a laughing matter, or something that we should take lightly, but a nasty symptom of something else going on. With your job I am not surprised that you are stressed; but you do need to speak to someone. I can recommend a fantastic Psychiatrist; she will help you to make sense of everything that is happening to you and maybe prescribe something to help with the symptoms. Everyone needs a little help now and then you know, there is no shame in asking for some.'

Lewis started packing his items away in his bag, as he was writing a note to hand to Steve with the name of the doctor on it. Steve's hand shot out, and grabbing his wrist he begged him not to tell Meg. As she entered the room Lewis stood up, passed the piece of paper to Steve, and said; 'Please do as I suggested and make an appointment with your GP.' And he left.

Meg by now was very concerned; setting the glass of water on the dresser she ran to Steve and flung her arms around his neck. 'What did he say? Are you feeling ok now, darling? What did he think was wrong?'

'Ah don't panic now I'm fine, he thinks it's just a tummy bug that's going around.'

'Well if that's the case why did he say to visit the GP?'

'Oh that was if it didn't get any better in case I need some antibiotics,' he lied.

Kissing Meg gently on the lips and holding her face in his hands, he looked her in the eye. 'I promise you, I am fine, a *mhuirni'n.*' He knew she didn't believe him, but how was he supposed to explain a bloody panic attack? He couldn't understand any of it himself, for god's sake! Letting her go, he stood carefully. 'I must get on, I will be late for work.' Pulling on his shirt and tie he quickly made his way downstairs and out of the door, calling out as he went, 'See you later; I will pick up pizza to save you cooking.'

Meg was still on the bedroom floor on her knees, bewildered by Steve's behaviour and questioning everything. At first she was tearful and now she was downright angry with him as she heard his car pull out of the driveway. No, Steve Ryan, you don't get away with it that easily, I have had enough of lies from the men in my life and whether you like it or not we will talk about this tonight, whatever the consequences.

CHAPTER 3

"Realising that the one person who you told everything to, was actually hiding everything from you."

Unknown

Balling her fists she stood and went to call Romany and then headed for the kitchen. Her coffee this morning needed to be large, strong, and black. Soon Romany made an appearance, totally unaware of the drama that had occurred only that morning, so Meg left her to her peace and headed off to work.

Later that day Steve had a meeting with his boss, and then his team to discuss Sean's visit and the information contained in the case files that he had brought over with him from Ireland. Laying out the pictures of the victims on a white board from their own case files, he surprised everyone by handing over everything to his Detective Constable Jason Short. Something that he had discussed with his boss earlier. He knew that the rumours abounded in the station about his relationship to some of the victims and the perpetrator and rather than leave them to fester, as rumours were wont to do, he had asked to be removed from the case and to take some leave. He stood before his team a pale shadow of the Strong Detective that they all knew. Speaking to them briefly he began to explain.

'As most of yer are aware I have personal connections to the people involved in this case. I will be very clear and blunt with you all and I hope that you will respect my privacy and I do not expect any questions from anyone unless they pertain directly to the case and are relevant information. It turns out that through information received and D.N.A. results, the perpetrator of all of the crimes in Sean's files from Ireland, and the open cases that we have been working on concerning the murders of Andrew and Magda Callahan and their son Jonathon Callahan and attempted murder of Romany and Meghan Cross, **is** my twin birth sister. I am also in a relationship with Meghan and am a friend of the family. I will just say thank you for all the hard work that you have put in and I know that as I hand everything over to the very capable hands of DC Short and DS. Dyson; they will tie up any loose ends. As you all suspected the case will not come to trial but a plea of insanity will be entered on the behalf of the person now known to be Magda Reilly, known as Bree. I shall be taking some well-earned leave with my family from tomorrow and, as stated before, I do not wish to be disturbed unless absolutely necessary.'

He left the room before all the hubbub of noise from mutterings and questions could start. Once outside the door he heard Detective Sergeant Sara Dyson call them all to order. She was a great colleague and friend and he knew that he could trust her to wrap things up efficiently and quickly; with the greatest of diplomacy. Leaving the building, he wasn't ready to go home and face Meg; he knew that sooner, rather than later, a confrontation about his behaviour would come, and just for a few hours he wanted to forget everything. He parked outside the Rose and Crown pub and settled himself on a barstool. He called for a pint of best ale. He smiled as it appeared before him on the shiny wooden surface of the bar. Even though he was an Irishman, he never could quite take to Guinness. The rich dark stout was too bitter for his tastes and although not a great lager fan either, he loved a pint of real ale.

Taking his time, and several pints later and whisky chasers in between, he felt himself relaxing a bit; maybe also because he was slightly drunk. He had always felt that he had to have tight control over his actions in case the demons of his past were released. So he was renowned for leaving the pub after a couple of pints, never more than that. Today however the barriers were down, he called for a whiskey and thought to himself you have done your worst, so bring it on. The afternoon crept on into the evening and Steve was getting drunker by the minute. Having not eaten all day again he was feeling nauseous. Slipping from the stool he made his way to the toilets, swaying fiercely from side to side as he went. From the corner of the pub someone had been watching him all the time and he slipped out and followed Steve as he stumbled his way to the other side of the room. As he passed in front of the open door of the pub he stumbled and a hand on his back shoved him hard outside. He staggered as the fresh air hit his lungs, it seemed to make it harder to focus on anything and the need to pee became more urgent. A face loomed in front of his and as he tried to focus a voice that he thought he recognised shouted in his face.

'Well, well, if it isn't the great Detective Steve Ryan. A bit worse for wear, are we? That's a bit naughty for a copper, isn't it?'

Steve tried to speak 'Jaak … Jake.' He had recognised the voice as belonging to a small-time scumbag drug dealer, Jake Regan, whom he had scared away from Romany last year. He knew that he held a grudge and, the state that he was in, it wasn't going to be Steve that came out of this confrontation very well. He felt himself fall as the first blows hit his stomach and he watched as he spewed air and beer in equal measure onto the floor of the car park. Once he was down the kicks and blows rained upon him, but thankfully he passed out long before a passing motorist pulled over to intervene.

For Meg the day seemed to be extraordinarily long, and the hours dragged. Returning home at four thirty she found a note on the kitchen island from Romany reminding her mother that she was going to a movie and a Macdonald's with her friend. Sighing, she put the kettle on for tea and decided that Romany being out was a good thing and would leave her time to talk to Steve without interruption. Six p.m. came and went and still no sign of Steve. She tried his phone and it switched to messenger straight away, leaving a message she asked him to call her back and let her know if he was bringing pizza and what time he was expecting to be back. She paced the floor and as the time ticked on she went through a variety of emotions from worry that something bad had happened, to guilt that she had pushed him to talk to her about what was wrong, and anger at his behaviour. Anger seemed to win out at the end, as nine p.m. came and went, and when Romany made an appearance at ten, she was desperate to know what to do.

Romany, seeing how distressed her mum had become, sat her down and made her a cup of tea. Handing it to her mum she picked up her phone and Googled the local hospital's telephone number. 'Just like mammy, you always know exactly what to do; thank you, darling.' Meg stood and hugged her daughter.

'I am sure he is ok, Mum, he probably is working late.'

'I am sure you are right.' Romany looked at her mum, unaware of the morning's health scare for Steve she couldn't understand her mum's smothering attitude and calmly stated her intention to go to bed. Meg, not wanting to worry Romany unnecessarily, decided that she wouldn't ring the hospital after all. Steve was probably sulking and in a mood. So, making herself a bowl of soup from a tin, she sat at the island in the kitchen wondering how she could have been so wrong about Steve. After all, she was one hundred percent sure that he was a good man, but she had been wrong before.

Just as she was placing her bowl in the dish washer, a car pulled into the drive. Running to open the door with angry words on her tongue, ready to lash Steve with, she hesitated as she saw a taxi driving away and a very unsteady man covered in blood and stinking of beer and vomit walk into the hall.

'Steve,' she gasped when she saw the injuries on his face. Holding him and carefully helping him into the house she at first was distraught at the injuries to her lover, but mostly she was full of withheld cross words and hidden emotions of anguish and hurt.

Steve looked in to Meg's face and could clearly see the conflicting emotions as they flittered across her features. If nothing else, his beloved Meg was an open book and he knew that he would never get anything other than honesty from her. Why was he feeling like this and why for god's sake was he hurting the ones that he loved? He had no words of apology for Meg; as nothing he could say would make any sense, or even begin to explain his behaviour.

Meg, waiting to hear an explanation, realised that nothing was forthcoming and her words stung as she flung them at him.

'Steve Ryan I am not sure what it is that you are going through at the moment, but I do know that the man I know and love would never ever treat me in such a despicable way. I don't wish to know where you were, or even what happened, as it is perfectly clear to me that you felt that you couldn't share whatever is happening to you, with me. I love you and I plead with you to go and get yourself some help, for your own sake, not for mine. I don't want or need someone in my life that lies and doesn't love me enough to give me the same respect that I give them. I have had enough of that from one man, I will never take it from another. I am going to bed. you can bloody well sort yourself out seeing as that's what you want to do.'

Meg's fury hit him harder than any punch that Jake had given him that evening. He knew that he had behaved like an absolute shit and the problem was he didn't know how to fix it. He didn't know why, or how to explain what he had been feeling lately. Guilt lay like a blow to his stomach and he ran to the sink, heaving with emotion and sick with contempt for himself, he vomited. Falling to the floor he sobbed, was he going insane? Was it hereditary? Why was he behaving in this way? The questions, along with the feelings of inadequacy, guilt and hysteria, built inside him and he felt himself laughing and crying at the same time. Oh Jesus, Mary and Joseph, he thought, am I going crazy like her, just like Bree, my sister?

CHAPTER 4

"This is not about guilt or innocence, the point is it's time to turn a page."
Charlie Luken

Steve opened his eyes; the bright light hurt his head and blurred his vision. He felt a cool cloth being placed on his forehead and it felt wonderful, as did Meg's voice, soothing and comforting. He closed his eyes and as he tried to move, he groaned, his ribs and stomach protesting at the movement and sore from the beating that he had taken.

'Steve I am so sorry; I didn't mean any of it. I love you so much. Are you able to get up from the floor if I help you?'

He jerked his head up and groaned as the nausea overtook him, but he persevered and could see that he was on the kitchen floor where he had fallen last night. He didn't remember anything else, but it was obviously morning as the sun shone in through the window. Blinking fiercely he focussed on Meg's face and the anguish that he saw on it told him everything he needed to know.

'I am so sorry, a mhuirni'n, I am so sorry.'

Meg, ever practical and taking control of the situation, realised that they could talk once Steve had been cleaned up and she had checked him over. Helping him up the stairs she gently stripped his clothes from his body, she saw the bruises around his rib cage and thought that she would have trouble getting him to the hospital to have them looked at, in case they were broken. She helped him into the shower. The warm water soothed his tired mind and body; she left him standing under the stream of water while she went to get clean clothes.

After he was dressed and the majority of his wounds were cleaned and dressed properly, he tried several times to speak. 'Please Steve wait until I have got Romany off to school and you have eaten something, I think you need to rehydrate as well; then we have the rest of the day to talk. Ok?' She kissed him gently on the lips, trying to find a spot that wasn't sore or cut. Helping him onto his feet she led him to the kitchen; sitting him at the island she poured him a glass of water, and then pushed a couple of paracetamols in his direction. He gladly accepted them and swallowing them down he realised just how thirsty he was, gulping the full glass down quickly, he asked for more. Romany popped her head in the door and called a good morning, rushing to escape before her mum could push unwanted sandwiches into her hand, not realising that her mum had more on her mind this morning than breakfast.

Once Romany had left the house Meg turned to Steve; holding two cups of coffee in her hand she nodded her head at the door to the small sun room off of the kitchen. 'Shall we take these in here? It will be more comfortable while we discuss what we need to do.'

Pulling himself carefully from the stool, he was grateful that Meg had taken charge of the situation. It didn't look good though when he saw the steely determination in her eyes and the set of her chin. He knew that sorry wouldn't cut it this time and that he would have to try to be as honest as he could with Meg. Although he knew that talking about what he was actually feeling would distress her too much; some things just needed holding back. Settling him comfortably on the sofa propped with cushions, Meg sat opposite him on the armchair. She took a deep breath before speaking and he could see how difficult this was for her as much as it was for him.

'Well Steven Ryan, will you at least tell me what is going on? Or if you can't will you promise to make an appointment this morning with the doctor and at least speak to them? I refuse to sit back and watch whatever is happening destroy you and our relationship; if there is anything that I can do to save us from this bloody train wreck, I will do it.'

Steve, taking her hands in his, apologised again for last night, but seemed reluctant to discuss with her what the issue was.

'Come on, Steve, you owe me the truth. Do you not love me and don't know how to tell me, is that it?'

'Ah a mhuirni'n no, no you are the best thing in my life. I know that I am not everything that you wanted and I am so sorry that I have disappointed you, I can't offer you all of this.' He put his hand out and gestured at the house. Meg was becoming angry now and she looked at him in disgust.

'Do you really think that I am that shallow, Steve? All I can say is that you don't know me at all, but I do know you and that is **not** the problem.' Her anger dissipated as fast as it had arrived and dropping to her knees in front of Steve she looked him in the eyes and pleaded with him to tell her what he was going through. He knew in that moment that he would lose Meg if he didn't at least explain some of what was happening to him. Taking a deep breath he at last spoke.

'I think I am going crazy. I thought I was losing my mind, yesterday I had a panic attack … and it wasn't the first time. I thought I was going to die. Am I mad? Just like her? Am I losing my mind?'

'Why would you think that, my love? You are the most grounded person I know. You are nothing like Bree.'

'I am having the nightmares again, the ones from when I was young. I saw what she did to the priest and I found her there laughing … Meg, she was just laughing. How could my mother have lied to me for all of those years? Why did she leave her behind? That animal of a priest deserved what he got, but so many others have suffered too because I didn't stop her.'

'How could you have stopped her? You didn't even know she existed and yes what she did was terrible; I should know that, more than anyone, but what happened to her was a tragedy and it had nothing to do with you. You are not like her, my love, not at all. If you think it might help, why don't you see if you could visit her and lay those ghosts to rest? After all, you saved me and stopped her before she could kill again. You are not responsible for what she did.'

It was as if a dam had broken. Steve sobbed into his hands, he felt ashamed that Meg should see him like this but it also felt good to finally share some of his feelings. It didn't take them away, as he didn't think anything could ever do that. In the back of his mind he could hear her taunting him with her laughter, but he did know that he would get some proper help. Something that he should have had years ago but because of rigid societal and moral codes he had refused to even acknowledge that he needed it. He saw it as a weakness, something that he had to deal with in his own way. But he knew in his heart the opportunity to stop his sister had been his long ago and he had failed. Meg lifted his tear-stained face and asked about what the paramedic had really said yesterday. Fumbling in his pocket he produced the piece of paper that Lewis had given him with the name Dr Evelyn Watson, Psychiatrist, written on it, with a telephone number.

'Now, my beautiful man, I am going to scramble us some eggs, something light for your stomach, and you are going to give her a ring and see if she can fit you in today. Is that clear?'

Steve, feeling like a chastised child, nodded his head and pulled his phone from his pocket as Meg returned to the kitchen clutching their used coffee cups.

CHAPTER 5

'The difference between shame and guilt is the difference between, 'I am bad' and 'I did something bad.'

Dr Brene Brown

Meg placed the cups in the sink and started to gather the ingredients she needed to make some scrambled eggs for them both. She had earlier rang in sick and spoken to her head teacher about a couple of days off, and was surprised at how supportive she was; recognising that Meg was still healing from her trauma and that it would take time to adjust. Meg herself had wondered at times how they would all get through and whether or not they would arrive whole, or even together. She had no doubts that the journey ahead was going to be difficult and she loved Steve enough to help him as much as she could. She made the eggs whilst listening to Steve's voice murmuring on the telephone in the sun room. Good, she thought, he must have managed to get through, and she hoped that he had also managed to get an appointment quickly.

She was just setting plates onto the table when he tentatively reappeared in the doorway. 'Come on, darling, don't let it get cold, we can talk whilst we eat.'

'I managed to get an appointment this afternoon at four p.m.'

'Oh fantastic, I can drive you and we can pick up your car when you have finished. I need to get a little shopping so I can do that while you are in seeing the doctor.'

The rest of the day was taken up with mundane tasks to fill the time till Steve's appointment. Both he and Meg were avoiding the subject for a while, allowing each other to adjust to the huge step that they had both taken by admission of needing help. For Steve's own sake and sanity, also for the difficulties in their relationship. Sometimes both being caused by specific behaviour of one or the other, but also from a conflicting victim-policeman attitude as Steve had battled to be both. His strong desire to protect the ones he loved had been in conflict with his role of a criminal investigator.

Steve became quieter and more withdrawn as the time to see the doctor drew nearer. He was unsure if he would be able to open up to a complete stranger and was worried that he would have another panic attack and embarrass himself. Meg had noticed him becoming quieter and felt the need for a pep talk. 'It's ok, love; I know that my big Irish man is finding this so hard to deal with; but you have been brave enough to get this far, it is only one more step to take. I am right here for you and there is no shame in doing what you need to, to keep your body and mind healthy.' Meg held him gently and kissed him slowly. He knew in that moment that he would go through hell for her and if that meant admitting to and accepting help, then that is what he needed to do.

They left the house and Meg drove them to town, she dropped Steve outside the building that the doctor worked from. It was an old Regency Georgian with a couple of worn stone steps and a wrought iron handrail on either side of the steps leading up to a heavy wooden door painted in a deep, navy blue. There was an old metal boot puller set in the stone at one side to enable gentlemen to pull off their boots when a servant wasn't available. In times gone by before tarmac, when the streets were made of earth and cobbles, mud was everywhere. It had probably been a house once upon a time but had in recent times been turned into several offices, their bells on a discreet plaque beside the entrance doorway. Meg watched him ring and enter the building before she drove off and sighed with relief.

She parked easily and hustled inside the supermarket; Steve would message her when he had finished his session. She prayed that it went well but she also had no illusions that it was just a first tentative step on a very long ladder.

Later, as she picked him up, she watched him walk towards the car with not a spring in his step as such, because his injuries prevented that, but at least a tilt of his head and an uplifted chin. She smiled and was pleased that she could see inside this broken man the loving, kind, and gorgeous man that she had fallen in love with.

Helping him into the car she drove him to the pub where he had left his car the night before.

'Are you sure that you will be able to drive it home, Steve? If not you can leave it and I will arrange for a friend to give me a lift to collect it.'

'I will be just fine now, don't yer fuss me; I need to apologise to the landlord anyway, after brawling drunk in his pub.'

'Well not exactly his pub really, his car-park,' Meg laughed. 'You are lucky he didn't call the police or the ambulance, I still wish you would have those ribs checked out.'

He climbed out of the car as Meg dropped him at the entrance. 'Shall I wait for you?'

'No need, I will call if I need help.'

With that he turned and entered the pub. Seeking out the landlord he apologised and explained that the kid had caught him at a weak moment and that he held a grudge because he had arrested him before. The landlord patted him on the shoulder and reassured him that as long as he was ok, that he was good. He also told him that he was aware of Jake and his grubby little reputation, and had warned his staff to make sure that he wasn't served again, he didn't want his kind of trouble upsetting his clientele.

Steve left the pub and climbing into his car he drove to the chemist on the corner of the high street. He didn't want Meg to know that the doctor thought that it was a good idea to put him on some medication, to help relax him and to help with the panic attacks. He collected his prescription and drove home. As he entered the house the smell of dinner cooking reminded him that he hadn't eaten since breakfast with Meg hours ago and his stomach growled in protest. He slipped off his jacket and, coming up behind Meg, he slipped his arms around her waist and kissed her neck. Not noticing Romany sat at the table, her schoolbooks laid in front of her, he felt his passion stirring as Meg leant back into his arms. They were brought to a halt abruptly as Romany gathered her books with a loud crash and said, 'Eww you two get a room purlease!'

Steve and Meg turned towards the retreating back of their disgusted teenager and both burst out laughing, the sound releasing any tension from before, and with their arms around each other they continued their kiss. Pulling away he turned to Meg, still enfolded in his arms and, as she turned, he let out a breath and she laughed.

'Ribs a bit sore now, Steve Ryan? Well, I have no sympathy for you, brawling in the street like a kid.' Laughing she tickled him and squirmed out of his reach and they both started laughing, light-heartedly, like lovers, Steve grimacing at every intake of breath. Once he had managed to quiet down he made his way to the bathroom, popping two tablets from the foil pack he swallowed them down. He didn't feel right keeping things from Meg, especially as she was involved in the aftermath of Bree's killing spree too, but he felt that there were things he wasn't ready to share with anyone yet and she had enough to deal with without him adding to it. He was glad that he had taken a few days off from work. He could probably get things sorted quickly and he need never tell a soul. Or maybe he was being naïve; either way he would never let it affect his work; he was a professional through and through.

Joining the girls he entered the kitchen just in time to help carry the plates and food through to the dining room where Romany was busy laying placemats and glasses. Turning a jug of water towards her mum she asked hopefully with a smile, 'Can we have wine?' Steve, not wanting to drink on the top of his tablets, thought it was a good excuse to explain his no drinking. 'Ah water's just fine for me.' Romany looked at him with a disappointed face and Meg thought that he had too much the night before anyway. After their meal, and Romany had returned to her room, they snuggled up in the lounge. Steve went to put the television on. Meg stayed his hand.

'Wait, love, are you not going to tell me how your session with the doctor went?' Steve sighed, he didn't want to discuss it anymore today, he was feeling relaxed and a little drowsy. After all, he didn't get much sleep last night and was thinking of just chilling in front of some David Attenborough and having an early night. Meg, however, was like a dog with a bone; she would never be satisfied with a no but would keep digging for answers. He decided to tell her a half truth as he wasn't ready to tell anyone everything but also as not a lot had happened. 'Well we didn't really talk yet, the time whizzed by, we just talked about what had happened briefly; she explained that it will take a while to feel comfortable enough to open up and that was it.'

'Well I hope that you feel better for seeing her, darling man, was it an early night you were thinking of?'

Steve smiled at her but it didn't quite reach his eyes. She didn't notice as he pulled her towards him.

'I don't know how much use I will be to yer, me ribs are killing me.'

'Serves you right, Steven Ryan,' Meg teased.

CHAPTER 6

"The Diabhul and I get along just fine, as this is a place of lost souls and evil thoughts."

Unknown

Steve nearly tripped as he skipped the bottom two steps of the doorway. Forgetting that he wasn't quite healed, the jarring had sent a sharp pain up into his ribs. He bent over, trying to catch his breath. The session with his psychiatrist had not gone well. She felt that it was too early to see Bree and that it wouldn't accomplish anything and could possibly set him back. Any progress that they had made over the last few weeks could be forfeited and he would be back to square one; or possibly worse than that. He felt that the answers that he sought would be found from a visit to Bree. What he had failed to tell the doctor was his own fears and doubts about his own sanity and because he wasn't used to exploring his own feelings he had shut them in. He was not only seeking answers, but understanding. He was afraid to look into the dark place, where he had stored all his thoughts and feelings concerning his family; especially how he felt about his sister and his mother. He was worried that he wouldn't like what he saw.

Meg had been watching him and she nearly rushed out of the car and ran to him, but she had been struggling herself with the way that he had been shutting her out. Maybe she needed to step back and let him heal at his own pace. She would be there when he felt ready to talk, that was all she could do. It hurt her as much as him to watch him everyday pretending that he was fine, as he fought with his own demons. She also knew that those demons were mostly the same as hers; fear, pain, and loss of faith. Somehow though, because of him, she had also found hope, love, and gratefulness. All she wanted to do was give him the same back.

Steve had returned to work after a week off and luckily no-one had questioned him. The notes had all been filed away and new cases awaited him on his desk. He was grateful for the mundane routine cases that he was dealing with; a couple of burglaries and a case of fraud which he was in the process of passing over to a colleague in the fraud squad. So he was very surprised to get a call into the chief super's office. Knocking on the door he entered when he heard the call to come in.

'Hello sir, you asked to see me?'

'Yes Steve, I just wanted a catch up to see how you are doing? It's been a few weeks now since the incident; I hear that the case concerning your family has been turned down by the crown prosecution service and has been put to bed; good news I am sure you will agree. You did a great job catching the killer and I am proud to have such a good detective on my team. The circumstances must have been extremely difficult for you and I know that you are dealing with the trauma in a positive way. But if you need a bit of time off or psychiatric help via the department to help with what has happened there is no shame in asking you know. I can easily make a referral if you wish and no-one else needs to know.'

Steve was quite touched by the concern in the chief's voice but also knew that all he wanted to hear was that he was fine and nothing would come back to effect his department. Also that he had dealt with any feelings he had on the subject, as was expected of him, quietly and discreetly, as a copper should.

'I am fine, sir, I am glad that it's all done and dusted; although the press were a little difficult to deal with at first, once they found that there was a link between myself and the killer. Really I'm fine.'

'Fine is such an easy word, Steve, and I am glad to see you well; don't forget what I have said and if you need anything just let me know.'

Steve was relieved to be dismissed and returned to his desk. Prick, he thought to himself, he just wanted to make sure that I wasn't as crazy as my sister. Talking of which, he had decided to make an appointment to visit her. Finding the number of the mental health facility where Bree was being held he dialled the number. Asking for the doctor in charge of her case he explained that he wanted to speak to her if possible. 'I actually thought that the police were not going to question Magda. I am not sure that she is mentally fit to answer your queries and as her physician I don't recommend it unless absolutely necessary; as I explained to your chief constable.'

Steve didn't want the doctor to know about his relationship with Bree and thinking on his feet he explained that some relevant paperwork had been discovered and it could even help Magda (he stumbled over her name and nearly called her Bree) and that he just wanted to take two minutes to run a couple of names past her. After getting his agreement to a two-minute meeting, he replaced the telephone. He felt relief but also was scared that his lies would catch him out. He would keep it to himself and hope that he wasn't discovered. He wasn't happy with himself, it went against all of his beliefs as a detective, he had never before used his power as a policeman to get him anything. The shame of using his name and reputation was outweighed by his need to see Bree again. He made an appointment to visit the next day and with so much to think about he decided to call it a day and maybe, to make it up to Meg, cook her a nice dinner with a glass of wine or two. He was scared but also very excited to be going to see Bree. After picking up some chicken and vegetables from the deli on his way home; he had decided that a nice sweet potato and chicken curry was the way to go. With a little lift to his step he hoped that something else was on the menu too. One thing that had suffered over the past few weeks was their sex life; guilt and pain were not conducive to good relationships. He had not felt so happy or relaxed for so long and for once he felt a little normal. He also felt that the pills that the doctor had prescribed, that he had been taking secretly, were helping his mood. Instead of spiralling into great troughs of pain and anger he was beginning to see the light.

Meg stepped through the door and inhaled; the smell of something delicious cooking made her mouth water. With a smile on her face she stepped into the kitchen and was swept up into Steve's arms. After thoroughly kissing her, he slipped her coat from her shoulders and her bag from her arms and sat her on a stool with a glass of very chilled wine. She didn't understand quite what was going on but if she was greeted like this every night she would never complain. After putting her bag and coat away Steve returned; he kissed her again and asked 'Are you ok, a mhuirni'n? I just wanted to say sorry for everything and to tell you how much I love you.'

Meg was speechless and as she watched her gorgeous man dish up a meal made with love then call Romany to join them, and pour her another glass of wine, she knew in a wink of an eye that this man had not only taken her heart but her soul too. After settling for a movie they snuggled on the sofa. Steve had made coffee and Romany had disappeared upstairs as most teenagers do. The evening wore on and Meg, drowsy and comfortable, realised that the movie had finished and they had both fallen asleep. She looked at the sleeping Steve, he seemed so peaceful, she placed a blanket from the end of the sofa over him and she went up to bed. A few hours later she was woken by the sound of a scream dying away, followed by another echoing around the atrium of the hallway. Rushing out of the door she almost bumped into Romany on the landing.

'It's ok, love, I think Steve is having a nightmare. I left him asleep on the sofa.' Clambering down the stairs as fast as she could, she was eventually confronted by Steve standing in the living room, arms wheeling, as if he were fighting a demon. She rushed forward only to be knocked to the ground and before she knew it Steve was on top of her, eyes blazing, trying to grasp her around the throat. Meg realised in that moment that he wasn't really awake and that his night terror had overtaken him. Screaming his name over and over, she saw Romany approaching with a vase raised above his head. She brought it down just as clarity appeared in his vision and then disappeared again, under the force of the vase breaking on his skull. His full weight collapsed on top of her and Romany, sobbing, tried to pull him off of her mother. Meg heaved and between them they managed to move him enough for Meg to wriggle out from underneath him. He came to moments later to find Meg trying to soothe a sobbing Romany and chaos strewn around the living room. Meg turned a tear-filled face towards him as he tried to understand exactly what had happened and the gravity of the situation. 'Oh my god a mhuirni'n what have I done?' He looked around him at the devastation and his eyes tracked to the marks on Meg's neck and understanding dawned. He felt the back of his head and when he looked at his fingers blood covered them. Leaning towards the girls, now curled into a foetal position together, he reached towards them only to be met with fear in their eyes. 'Please let me help you, I am so sorry, are you both alright?' He reached out again and this time Meg let him take her hand and pull her upright from her position on the floor, bringing Romany with her, she flinched when he tried to take her into his arms.

'Please let me clean up and then you can tell me what happened … what I did.' Confused, he started tidying up the broken pieces of the vase, placing the cushions and upturned coffee table back in place. 'Let me settle Romany in her room and I will be back to sort out your head, please sit down in that chair and don't bloody move.' Meg's anger was by now palpable and expected as they were all in shock. Walking Romany upstairs, Meg took a few moments to think what she was going to say to Steve. Tonight he had scared her like no other time. The only thing that she could relate it to was the night that Bree had tried to kill her. She shuddered as the picture of Bree and Steve merged into one, their eyes blazing out at her with such hatred that only the Devil or someone insane could have ever done.

Meanwhile, Steve had gathered his coat, left a note for Meg, and ran out of the door. He flung himself into the car and drove off into the night, with no clear idea of where he was going. The road wound its way through the flat marsh of the fens and he drove until, exhausted, he pulled over as the sun began to appear above the horizon. He sat and watched as dawn broke in its glory of orange and yellow and thought to himself, Oh god forgive me, what have I done?

CHAPTER 7

"Who hurt you? My own expectations."
Six word story

Meg tried to go back to sleep but she lay holding Romany in her arms. Her beautiful girl had eventually calmed down and fallen asleep, but sleep had eluded Meg. She had heard Steve leave and was unsure if she felt relieved or upset that he had gone. Maybe that was something to think about whilst she lay there. She knew that she loved Steve, that wasn't in doubt, but she was unsure if she could make a life with him if things didn't change. She had seen how frightened Romany had been and she never wanted her to experience that ever again. The solution was staring her in the face but she was refusing to see it. Perhaps this had been the slap in the face that was needed to make them all wake up and admit that they all needed help with what Bree had done to them.

Steve, meanwhile, made his way to a café that he knew opened early; after downing his second cup of strong coffee, he was ready to face Meg. He had decided that it would be best for everyone if he moved out for the time being; the last thing he needed was to put his loved ones at risk. He was frightened about what had happened and the fact that he was unaware of his actions made his fears about his own mental health a reality. No matter what Meg said he refused to put her in any kind of danger. Heading out of the door he returned to Meg's house. He noticed that her car was gone and looking at his watch he realised that she had left for work. Also, he only had time to throw a few things in a bag and head off to his appointment with

Bree. He caught sight of his face in the hallway mirror as he headed out the door. The shock of the stranger staring back at him halted him in his steps. He looked like shit and he felt like it too. The sad reflection of the man that stared back at him was unrecognisable as himself; a few months of hell had taken its toll. Leaving Meg a note he arranged to meet her somewhere away from the house in case she didn't want him near Romany; he would understand if she never wanted to see him again. He left for his appointment.

He drove up the long sweeping drive towards The Lawns Psychiatric unit, his pulse raced, and he was still unsure what he wanted from the visit. Parking in a gravelled carpark he made his way to the forbidding front door and rang the bell. As he was waiting for the intercom to answer his eyes strayed to the perimeter fence. Rose flower beds laid out in a formal pattern across the lawned front area gave a deceiving impression of a serene and peaceful setting. Having the eyes of a detective he saw past it all to the perimeter wall beyond, topped with razor wire, the guard at the gate, and the barriers across the gateway. All evidence pointing to a high-security facility. He gave his name and also the doctor's name that he was to see, then the door made a loud mechanical click as the nurse buzzed him into a waiting area. No sooner had he settled in one of the chairs available than Dr Phillip Jones appeared, hand held out towards Steve, ready to shake in a firm grip.

After introductions had been made, the doctor led Steve through a number of secure doors until eventually they stopped in front of one; one of many similar doors in a very long corridor. The cries of patients and shouts of alarm burst out of the air every now and then, but no sound emanated from the room where they stood.

'I am unsure what you expect from Magda, her condition has deteriorated since she was arrested and her ability to function on most levels has been seriously affected by the drugs that we have to use on her. We have to sedate her or she continues in a state of high hysteria and will self harm or harm others. You will find her quite subdued but she is able to understand and reply to questions. I will give you five minutes to complete your interview but if she becomes distressed at any point I will stop it at once, do you understand, Detective Chief Inspector Ryan?'

Steve nodded his acquiescence and opened the door. His eyes roamed the room until they alighted on Bree sat by the window, her hands resting in her lap demurely. He wasn't fooled however and his senses were on high alert. His voice sounded strained, even to himself as he walked towards another chair to sit opposite her and said, 'Hello Bree, I hope that you are comfortable here and are being well looked after. I have some questions that I would like to ask you if you feel up to it, concerning what happened with Magda's family; and I may have some answers for you about our connection to each other.'

The doctor lifted his eyes to the detective as he said this and realised his mistake in allowing access to his patient. He also missed the small smile and acknowledging lift of her head as Steve spoke. Before he could stop any more interaction, she looked up and he was fascinated to see a warm smile appear on her face. He had seen no reaction before to any kind of stimulus so decided to see where it led.

Steve sat down and looking directly into her eyes he said simply, 'I am sorry for your suffering, Bree, and I can understand the pain it caused and the consequences of the actions that you took towards the priest and sisters, but can you tell me why you killed the others? The young garda, the doctor and his wee children, they were all innocent, Bree.'

She waited awhile before turning her green eyes on him. He was startled for a moment and leant back, as the resemblance to his darling Meg was so obvious.

'Innocent ... no-one is ever innocent, dear brother, are we not all born of original sin?' She watched his face change. 'Ah so you want me to accept your guilt and understanding. The simple answer is I don't, and the others just got in my way, dear brother, as I would have killed you eventually, for the same reason.' She turned cold green eyes towards him and started to smile. 'Ha ha but that's not what you want to know, is it? Come on now, Steve, ask the one question that you really came to find the answer to; our dear mother couldn't give you what you need, so you turn to me. The Diabhul is in all of us, but well fed Diabhul's behave better than famished saints, so I have been told, and I can see that you have been feasting with yours, a veritable banquet I don't doubt. We are the same you and I, we were made by the Diabhul and torn from our mother's womb together; so yes you are as much his son as I am his daughter.'

The laughter started then and Steve stood abruptly as he looked at his sister's face, he could swear that it had transformed into the Diabhul himself; her green eyes blazed fire and he backed his way out of the door. Hands on knees, trying desperately to control his breathing and bent double, the doctor found him. Leaning against the wall of the corridor Steve felt the pain across his chest and felt his lungs tighten. He knew that he was passing out and welcomed the blackness, then bliss … he heard, saw, and felt no more.

He came to in the doctor's office, a glass of water was handed to him and he looked up into the doctor's expectant face as he waited for some answers.

'Sorry Doc, I have been having these panic attacks and I think that is what happened.'

'I think you are correct, Detective Chief Inspector Ryan, but I was waiting for an explanation of your false information given for the reasons to see Magda. I noted that you call her Bree and that she seems to think that you are her brother; is that true, or another fantasy?'

'No Doc it's true, and a very long story. I apologise for my deception; I didn't think that you would let me see her if I told you the reasons. I don't even really know myself why. I just felt the need to see her and to find out if … if … I am insane too.'

The doctor smiled at this last statement as he had heard it so many times before. Especially from men who were brought up by women of strong faith. He wished that societal boundaries surrounding mental health, especially in men, were broken down and perhaps he wouldn't be in the place he was right now, with someone whose mental fragility was teetering on the edge alongside his machismo.

'Well I think it's time to tell me everything. If I don't have the whole picture, I will never be able to give Magda the treatment that she deserves.'

Steve looked up into his compassionate face and related to the doctor the whole sorry story including how he had found out from D.N.A. that Bree was his sister. Explaining how she had called herself Bree and this is what he had known her as, and that it was only after his mother had confirmed her birth and name, was it officially known as Magda; as no records were made of her birth, or even of her existence. He also went on to explain that he had been suffering with panic attacks since the case and had begun to doubt his own sanity as a result. With a sigh he sat back in his chair, the words had tumbled out and it was a relief to pass on all of his fears and emotions.

Folding his arms across his rather portly stomach, the doctor took a breath and decided that now was not the time for patient confidentiality and perhaps Detective Inspector Ryan's visit had given him an insight that he would never have gained into Magda's mind.

'Well Detective Inspector I should be angry at you for coming here under false pretences but I am glad that you have, as it may have helped me. Let me just reassure you first that no you are not insane; neither is your sister. Magda suffers from multiple personality disorder, as a result of the trauma of the physical and sexual abuse inflicted on her in her childhood. She also has some psychopathic tendencies which led her to seek revenge on those that she felt were responsible for her situation. The hysteria is her way of coping with the horror of the situation and sadly if she had received help when the incident happened with the priest, instead of more torture and abuse, she may have made a full recovery. I don't expect her to do that now, but I do hope to enable her to address what has happened and the resultant behaviour from her afterwards. I don't expect her to want to atone for what she did but to understand and accept why she did it. That is where you come in; she has reacted to you in a way that was totally unexpected. She has been near catatonic since her confinement here and today she was a princess awoken. Would you consider visiting her regularly to see if it helps her?'

Steve was stunned by what the doctor had to say but he had seen Bree in action, and he knew how she could manipulate a situation to her own ends. He wanted to discuss it all with Meg, but he didn't even know if she would have him back. Plus, he was in a very vulnerable state himself and felt that he was teetering on the edge of an abyss. He certainly didn't want to join his sister in her dance with the Diabhul. He knew what he had witnessed, and no reasonable explanation could be given for it.

'May I ask you a personal question, Doc, are you a religious man, a spiritual man … a man of faith?'

'I am a scientist, Detective Inspector, first and foremost, so I will always seek the most reasonable explanation first. I think I know what you are referring to and yes, I have witnessed many strange and unexplained behaviours in people, in highly traumatic situations; but do I think that Magda is possessed by the Devil? Then the answer to your real question is no.'

CHAPTER 8

"The moral dilemma is to make peace with the unacceptable!"
May Sarton

Steve had rung and left a message on Meg's phone, hoping that she would meet him at the little tearoom in town. A place that he knew she loved to come to for a natter and a coffee with her friends. He wanted most of all for her to feel comfortable in his presence and it was the perfect place for a talk, away from eyes and ears. He sat in the seat by the window, eagerly searching the street for her approach. Every time the small bell that hung over the door rang, when anyone entered, he jumped. Until suddenly his beloved Meg was stood in front of him. He stood abruptly and pulled out a chair for her to sit on. Placing her bag on the floor next to her she slowly sat down. Steve kissed her cheek and the waitress appeared to take their order. After their tea and coffee arrived, they both started to speak at the same time; laughing, Steve gestured with his hand for Meg to continue. Bracing himself, he sat back, expecting a tongue lashing and to hear the words that he dreaded most of al, that he wasn't wanted in her or Romany's life again. Instead, his hand was grasped in hers and her gentle voice told him, 'I have done a lot of thinking since last night, Steve, what happened was beyond your control, but I have Romany to think of and she must come first. I know that I can't bear to be without you, and I love you so much. All I want is for you to be well again and us to be happy. I want some kind of re-assurance from you that you will seek help; as I can't allow what happened to re-occur; it wouldn't be fair to you, me, or Romany to have to deal with the aftermath of what happened last night again.'

Steve was shocked. He couldn't believe what he was hearing, his beloved Meg was reaching out to him; giving him a second chance. Did he deserve it? No. Did he want it? Yes! Looking into Meg's tired eyes he could see the damage that he had caused, and the long hours that she had spent thinking things through. He loved her even more for it, if that was humanly possible. He decided there and then that he didn't want to lose her, that his only option was to tell the truth, no more lies or deceit.

'I love you, a mhuirni'n, I cannot imagine how I must have frightened you and Romany last night, all I can say is that I wasn't aware of my actions. I have not been honest with you about my mental health, and I am so sorry. The doctor gave me some tablets and I didn't tell you I was taking them. Apparently, I shouldn't drink alcohol with them, and I did. To admit that I needed tablets to even function, I felt was a weakness; what I now realise is that the weakness is in trying to behave as normal and not taking action. Denial led to my behaviour last night, all I can do is ask for forgiveness. There is a lot more that I need to tell you, but I don't want to do it here. I would understand if I wasn't welcome back in the house and, if you would prefer it, I will move out.'

He looked at Meg questioningly and she returned the look before kissing him so thoroughly that he was left in no uncertainty.

Picking up her bag she held his hand tightly as they left the café, he brought hers to his lips and he knew everything would be alright. They arrived home and Steve sat Romany down to apologise and explain his behaviour. The medication responsible, now sitting in his jacket pocket, he held it tightly in his hand. He withdrew it and showed it to her, promising that he would never be so foolish again. And that he deserved much more than a whack on the head.

Looking at him warily she smiled and kissed his cheek. She knew that this brave man had saved her and her mum from a maniac, so she could easily forgive him now that she knew why. She also understood that he needed some response from her to show that she understood, and shoving him in the arm, she made a face. 'Well, that face would scare off any intruders so it might be useful to keep it around, sorry if I added another scar with the vase.' Hugging him quickly she left her mum and Steve to talk. He had been more of a dad to her in the last few weeks than her own father had in sixteen years; she definitely didn't want her or her mum to lose him now.

After coffee had been made, Steve started to explain to Meg the whole sorry story from when as a young man the nightmare of his first meeting with Bree had never left him. It still tortured him, and he had allowed it to interfere with any relationships that he had ever had; including the one with his parents as he had not returned to visit them because of the memories of that night. And the guilt he felt when his father died, and his mammy was left alone. The anger that he felt towards her too, just recently, when the whole horrible, sordid, situation of his and Bree's birth and the subsequent lies that it perpetuated. He held nothing back; honesty is what he promised and that is what Meg deserved. For hours he sat head held in his hands; at times in tears and others striding around the room, arms flailing in near hysteria, when he explained how he had felt when she and Romany had been put in danger. How the feelings of helplessness, and fear that he would lose her drove him to a near breakdown. The revelations from his mammy; that Father Benedict was his real father and Bree his twin sister and finding that what he had always believed his whole life was all a lie. Last of all he told her how his doubts about his own mindset had led to him using his role as a police Detective to allow him an access visit to Bree. And his joy and his pure relief that what he had been feeling was his own fears and inadequacies and not inherited mental illness, as he had convinced himself he had. And not, as he imagined, a spiral into a dark pool of insanity, where his sister waited with the Diabhul for him to join them.

Meg sat and quietly listened to everything that Steve had told her.

She loved him more, but was also exasperated with the male mentality of his need to hold it all in. Especially how he felt that it was somehow unmanly to admit that he was struggling, which then made it impossible to not conform to straight and strict gender roles. Those which he had grown up with which were the norm, and a given, in his Irish upbringing. She wanted to acknowledge the pain that this had caused him and especially to his mother and family in the past and how it reached, even now, into his present. She was so sure of one thing; that she would not allow it to transfer to his future, if she was still in it!

Lastly, he told her what he had found when he visited Bree and how the answers that he hoped for and expected to find were not going to be found there. He explained how he had, had another panic attack after seeing her again and explained Bree's reaction to seeing him, as if she had been waiting for him to join her. The doctor's explanation of all of her multiple and complex conditions and that he had asked Steve to continue the visits as he had caused a reaction that they had struggled to make in her behaviour. Something that he himself recognised was not advisable in his present condition. He held back his thoughts of any weakness, or that his strong faith had led him to believe that she was possessed by the Diabhul.

They had talked for hours and both were very weary. Meg had decided that tomorrow would be soon enough for her to put her emotions on the table and any decisions would be better made in the clear light of day. Hoisting him up from the sofa and arms around each other, they made their way to bed as the first light of dawn was creeping above the horizon. Even though they were exhausted they made gentle love, as if it were a healing to the open wounds and scars that had been revealed; a salve to quiet the hurt and pain of the last two days.

They slept on till late morning and Meg was relieved to see that Romany had got herself up and off to school. She sometimes forgot how much of a woman her daughter was becoming and she fondly thought how proud she was of her. She glanced at the family photo on the wall of her parents and brother Jonathon's smiling faces looking down at her. She wished that they could see how beautiful she was becoming, and she knew how proud her mammy would be of her granddaughter's creativeness and art. Romany had certainly inherited her talent from Magda, her grandma.

Steve placed his arms around her shoulders. 'What are you thinking, a mhuirni'n? I am sorry that I couldn't save them too. I had great respect for Jonathon, and I know that we would have been good friends if he was still here.'

Meg quietly wiped a tear from her cheek and smiling brightly she turned towards him. He held her tight before saying, 'Now who is hiding their feelings, my love? It was a great loss when they died and I know that it is a large hole to fill in your heart, but I did promise Jonathon to protect you and I failed, so I apologise again. Perhaps together we can remember them with what I have been mulling over for a while?'

Meg turned questioning eyes on to him, an eyebrow raised in expectation of an explanation. 'I will explain after I have poured some caffeine into my system, either that or I think I might need a jumpstart.'

After they had settled at the table, and Steve had drunk two cups of best Columbian, Meg's curiosity got the better of her and she poked him hard in the shoulder. 'You needn't think that you can leave that hanging in the air, Steve, now spill."

He laughed and taking a deep breath he came out with it. 'You know that Jonathon and I were working together on an article about county lines drugs as it is called, where vulnerable people are targeted by drugs gangs to sell drugs for them. They do it under threat or coercion, sometimes gangs take over their homes and money too, leaving them with nothing and no-one to turn to, so they have to sell drugs for them. I have wanted for a while to set up a unit to deal solely with this issue but because of budget cuts etc it hasn't happened. I was thinking of leaving the force in the next couple of years. I am nearer to fifty and I have looked into accessing my pension early and I would like to do some work with young addicts and help them get clean and get help. Set them back on the right road. After what has happened with Bree, I think maybe the time is right to do it.'

Meg was utterly astonished; this was the last thing that she had expected to hear and was speechless! Curiosity led her to ask, 'This is not something new, is it; how long have you been waiting to do this?'

'It seems like forever and a few years ago I was involved with a voluntary youth group, which is where I first met Jake. It has been a regret of mine that he wasn't helped, and I have watched over the years as he has spiralled out of control and further into drug use. I have had to arrest him a few times now, but I know that is not the answer to the problem for these kids. But first I want to concentrate on sorting my own life out.'

Meg looked at the determination set on his face and with a worried frown she asked, 'Does that last statement concern you continuing some kind of relationship with Bree? Because, if so, I think that I was wrong to suggest it in the first place, Steve, she is evil and I don't like the effect she has on you or our relationship.'

'But she is my sister, and she went through hell. The doctor thinks that I can help, so I must.'

'Do you not see that she is already using your feelings of guilt for her own ends? Please Steve, she manipulates and destroys everything that she touches in her path, and that includes you.'

Exasperated that they were rowing yet again, Meg grabbed at her keys and said, "I need to pop to the school. I have some books to mark. I will see you later."

Steve understood her feelings about Bree, after all she had been responsible for devastating her whole family and nearly killing her and Romany, but he had to do his duty, didn't he? But at what cost?

CHAPTER 9

"You are unsure which pain is worse, the shock of what happened or the ache for what never will."

Unknown

Slamming the door behind her she was as cross with herself as she was with Steve. Yet again it had been about what others needed emotionally and not herself. She had always had to accommodate what Barnaby her ex-husband wanted. She had put aside any ambition, job satisfaction, or emotional attachments about where they lived and how they lived. Everything she did was to advance his career. She was just beginning to enjoy her job through her own efforts and support from her parents and, as Romany had gotten older, she had hoped to have more freedom to do as she wished. She wasn't blind to her marriage difficulties but had chosen for her daughter's sake to ignore them. She also knew now that had been the wrong thing to do, and she wasn't prepared to compromise her own needs, ever again, for anyone.

She decided that a long overdue visit to Becky and the boys, her brother Jonathon's family, was on the cards as she had the rest of the day free. They had always been more than just sisters-in-law, more like friends, and she had neglected them since Jonathon's death, something that she now needed to put right. Knocking on the door of her childhood home that Jonathon had moved his family into following her parent's death, she was overcome with a feeling of dread. Was she ready to face this now? How selfish she had been not to come when Jonathon's family probably needed her the most. She had allowed herself to wallow in her own grief and had got caught up in her feelings for Steve, which had overwhelmed her senses. All of this was forgotten as she found herself wrapped in a pair of sisterly arms and two happy little faces flung their arms about her legs.

'Aunty Meg, Aunty Meg have you got Romany with you?'

'Hi Bradley, Joseph, I am sorry she isn't here, she had school today but I don't, and I wondered if Mummy and you two would like to come to MacDonald's for a treat, but only if mummy agrees?' She looked expectantly at Becky as the two boys danced around their legs with excitement. Becky smiled and she looked up at Meg, quite exhausted, and mouthed 'life-saver'. Grabbing their coats and bags they all climbed into Meg's car and headed into town. The MacDonald's restaurant was situated on the outskirts, as they usually are, with a few department stores surrounding it and a leisure complex with a skating rink, bowling, and a multi-screen cinema. Many a time she had brought Romany here when she was smaller, and they visited the cinema to see the latest Disney film. Afterwards they swallowed milkshakes and burgers before bouncing in the ball-play. 'How about we go see a film afterwards too?' She whispered this last bit to Becky in case they had other plans.

'That will be great! It's been so long since the boys had any fun, I have not been so good at fun lately.' Flinging her arm around Becky, she drew her into a hug and the boys skipping ahead with excitement ran off into the play area. 'I know exactly what they want so I will go and get the order; what can I get for you?' After giving Becky her order of food, Meg made her way over to the area where the boys had run to and peering through the window she saw them happily disappearing underneath a heap of plastic balls. Smiling, she found a table nearby and settled into the booth. Before she knew it Becky was back and as if by instinct two hungry boys appeared; after eating their fill they ran off again to play.

'Thank you for this, Meg, I can't tell you how much we all needed this! A little piece of normality is just what the doctor ordered. I have missed you so much, how are you and Romany doing now? Is she fully recovered, and how is that handsome detective?'

The last thing that Meg wanted to do was burden Becky with all of her problems as she had enough of her own and she felt guilty enough for not being around more.

'We are all fine, love, but how are you and the boys coping?'

'We have good and bad days, as to be expected, the boys are still suffering from nightmares but gradually things are returning to a bit of normality. Everything is settling into a routine. I am glad that you have come today, I was going to call you … I don't know how to say this, but I want to sell the house. I just can't live there anymore, there are too many memories of Jonathon. I wanted to tell you all so that you could have first dibs to buy it. I really didn't want it to go out of the family.' She wiped a tear away as it rolled down her cheek and, pushing her chin upright, she looked into her friend's face. 'I will let you tell the others for me.'

'Of course, love, we all understand.' Meg looked at her thoughtfully. 'I would love it, but I can't afford to buy it on my own; but I will let the others know. Mind you, I haven't spoken to Talley since I found out about her and Barnaby; but it doesn't bother me anymore. In fact, I should thank her … she is welcome to him.'

'Oh, I did forget, I am not thinking straight, sorry Meg.'

'No really we are all grown-ups and I can honestly say I really don't care anymore.'

The boys came back, and they headed off to the cinema; all thoughts of loss, houses, and grief forgotten inside the buckets of popcorn and the laughter of the afternoon; a blissful respite before reality kicked in again later. After helping Becky to get the boys to bed later on, Meg left; hugging her friend and sister as hard as she could she promised to return very soon. The sun had set a few hours ago and she didn't want to spoil the happy feeling that she had gained from seeing Becky and the boys, so she decided to take the long route home through the fens. One thing about her house, the only thing she loved was its setting; it was beautiful! When she had seen the plot her first thoughts were to imagine lots of children playing outside watching the diverse array of marsh birds nesting and watching their chicks hatch in the spring. Messing about on boats up and down the long ditches that formed the drainage and flood defences of the flat land. She loved the changing colours of the reed beds and the farmer's sheep nestled with their backs to the sometimes harsh winds that blew.

Sadly, this had been only a dream and her life changed completely as she spent more and more time with Romany at her parent's house. She had never liked the house that Barnaby had built, she had felt so lonely in it; it was large and echoing, like a show house, but never a home. For him it was a status symbol; a look at how far I have come. That is why she liked her parents' home, it was always cosy and warm and filled with laughter. Maybe if her home had been filled with children, she mused. Barnaby had signed it over to her as part of her divorce settlement and she had been wondering what to do with it. Suddenly she had an idea. If Becky was agreeable, perhaps they could swap. Becky had always loved her house and it was worth more than her old family home, but that didn't matter, maybe that was a solution for them all. She knew that Romany would approve as she had loved her grandparents and they had practically lived in their home most of the time, whilst Barnaby was away on business. She hurried home to discuss it with Romany and Steve.

She hadn't realised just how late it had become and as she stepped into the hallway Steve pulled her into a huge hug. 'Where have you been, Meg? I have been so worried about you.'

She looked up and saw the fear in his eyes just receding. She had been so carried away having fun that she hadn't thought to ring him and just assumed that Romany would pass on where she was. She had texted her earlier to tell her that she would be late home. Obviously there had been a mix up and she could see how worried Steve had been; after all, they were still feeling so vulnerable, she should have thought about him sooner, but she was still angry with him from earlier.

'I am sorry, love, I was only with Becky and the boys, I have been neglecting them lately and I thought Romany would tell you where I was. We took the boys to the cinema for a treat. I just didn't think.'

'I am sure Romany would have told me, if she had been home,' he seethed. 'What were you thinking, Meg; didn't I warrant a phone call or a text? I can't take any more worry, I didn't know if something had happened to you or Romany as she was missing too.'

'Well you could have texted me, I would have told you where I was,' she replied angrily. 'Missing! Really Steve … missing?'

'If you look at your bloody phone you would see all my missed calls and texts. I can't do this, Meg, I can't live with the thought that I could lose you all over again. I can't be with you like this.'

He grabbed his jacket from the hall rack and slammed the front door behind him as he left. She sighed, fished her phone out of her bag and turned it on. It bleeped and flashed as at least twenty texts and missed call messages pinged up. 'Oh god I'm sorry, Steve,' she said out loud, then went through to the kitchen and put the kettle on. What the hell was going on? It seemed that they were both determined to wreck any sort of relationship that they may have, or any kind of future together. She was tired … so tired of fighting … it seems Bree has managed to get her wish; but she is killing me slowly instead. She lifted down a cup and flung a teabag into it before wiping away the tears that had gathered at the corners of her eyes. 'Fuck you, Bree … fuck you!'

CHAPTER 10

"One of the hardest parts of life is deciding whether to walk away or try harder."
Unknown

Steve returned to his own flat; he was glad that he hadn't given up the tenancy, he still had a few months left to run on it. Meg had asked him to move in with her and although at the time he was delighted, he was now beginning to regret that decision. He turned the key in the lock and entered the flat. Everything smelled a bit musty, and he opened a few windows to let in some fresh air. Filling the kettle, he looked through the cupboards for some coffee. He wasn't going to make the same mistake that he had the other night and have a drink with the tablets he was taking. No, he had learnt his lesson now; but he had to admit a glass of whiskey would go down nicely just at this moment; but black coffee would have to suffice instead. He would need to get some shopping in tomorrow as the cupboards were bare. He hadn't been there for a while. Pouring himself an instant coffee as soon as the kettle boiled, he took it and plonked himself on the sofa.

What the hell was he doing with his life? How could everything go so wrong, so quickly? After his last session with the psychiatrist, he had been able to cling on to his feelings for Meg and they had both seen it as a positive in his life; now he was not so sure. He wasn't stupid and sometimes policemen and victims in their cases did fall in love; there was a name for it … wasn't there? Maybe … some strange syndrome? He had heard of secondary and primary victims in trauma cases and that was what was happening to him and Meg, according to his psychiatrist. She had explained that there was a thing called the nightingale effect which was very similar where a nurse would fall for a patient. She had also told him that relationships formed in this way very rarely came to fruition. He had always felt that their love for each other would see them through, now he wasn't so sure. Everything had been turned upside down and he wasn't sure of anything anymore.

He sat for a while just thinking about how his life had changed for the better as soon as he had seen Meg's face at Jonathon's barbeque last summer. Was it only a few months ago? It seemed a lifetime away. Maybe that was what was wrong? He and Meg were rushing things. After what had happened to each of them, they didn't want to miss any moments or time with each other. Their losses allowed them that secret knowledge that only comes to those that have suffered to find it. Don't wait, as sometimes tomorrow doesn't come.

His life before Meg was empty and lonely, he was just forcing himself to survive one day at a time. He had shut himself away from the world and any attempts at a normal relationship faltered, and he just let them go, not willing to fight, drifting and unable to acknowledge that the root of his problem was connected to the incident years ago in Bally-Bay where he first encountered Bree. It had always been Bree, even up until this point in time it was about bloody Bree. Some days he wished that he had killed her on that day and others he just longed for the sister that he would never have. It must be because they were twins, he always had that connection. Meg understood it as her and Jonathon were twins too. He felt something that day all those years ago as he had encountered her in the church screaming in hysteria and covered in blood. Even when he saw what she had done to Father Benedict he had felt drawn to her. A bond had been made, a connection that still wasn't broken. Maybe the only way to survive what was happening to him was to walk away from her completely, as Meg wanted him to do. Perhaps she was right all along.

He wrestled for hours with the questions in his mind. He had looked clearly at his relationship with Meg. It had been bordering on the obsessive and he understood this to be a reaction to what they had been through and how close he had come to losing her. Coming to terms with what had happened was harder than he had at first thought for both of them, but more so for himself. He was trying to be honest and clear about his own feelings. Feelings that he had buried under heaps of debris, of past relationships and emotional baggage that he had dragged along behind him for years. Acceptance, that is what Dr Watson had said; accepting that he couldn't change anything, or alter what had happened before, only that it had been out of his control and he had just been an unwilling participant. He had tried to put it all in a box and move on. He now realised that is what he had been doing with Meg; playing happy families and not looking at the disgusting and dirty mess that was his life; full of secrets and lies. Afraid of what he would find underneath the surface if he dug too deep.

He went into the bathroom and, stripping off for a shower, he climbed in. The hot water pounded his shoulders and massaged all of the tightness away. He hadn't realised how much the situation had been taking its toll on his body. He was determined about one thing, he was going to get up early and go for a jog. His fitness had been going downhill since he had been with Meg. He realised now that if he wanted to get through this then he needed to get back to some form of fitness and hopefully his physical health would help his mental health. Climbing into bed he fell asleep immediately, awaking only when the alarm on his phone played the sickly sweet tune that he found so annoying, knowing that he had to get up to turn it off, that way it ensured that he didn't turn over and go back to sleep. Plugging in his ear buds he bounded out of the door and headed to the local park. Ten laps around the lake was his usual exercise routine and he was determined to do it today even if it killed him, which it very nearly did after only five laps; he felt the lactic acid building up in his muscles. He knew that if he pushed himself he would completely seize up. He had suffered with a bad back a few years ago after receiving an injury whilst chasing a young kid through an alley way. He wasn't getting any younger and decided to be sensible. He slowed his pace and gently plodded around the last lap and finding a bench he sat down upon it. Looking up he admired the view across the lake, and the ducks and water birds just awakening. He sat and slowed his breathing as he watched the sun rise high into the sky. His head was clearer now than it had been for a long time. He knew what he needed to do but he didn't know if everyone else would agree with him. For a start he needed to get back to work. Perhaps having something to take his mind off of his problems would help. He had decided that he was partly responsible for Bree, and he needed to do everything possible to help her. If visiting and talking to her is what was needed, he was duty bound to do it. He was her only family and she needed him. You never know, he thought, it might even help me. He got back, showered, and after throwing his kit into the wash he made himself a coffee and sat down to message Meg. He rang Dr Watson, his psychiatrist, and made an appointment to run everything by her before coming to any decisions. He thought that she wouldn't approve of him visiting Bree and so he needed to come clean about his reasons for doing it, but how could he describe the feeling of living life with a part missing? Finally, when he had met Bree properly, and knew for certain that she was his sister, no matter what she had done, he had felt an affinity, a completeness that had been missing for so long. He messaged his mother. Perhaps it was time to visit her and explain how he was feeling, he owed her that at least. She had loved and cared for him and he for her, for all of his life. He couldn't allow what had happened to destroy that.

He felt good now that he had made some decisions and he hoped that he could talk it through with Meg later, he had invited her out to dinner and hoped that she would reply to his message this afternoon. With a spring in his step, he headed in to work. He had a session with

Dr Watson later at four and he hoped that his boss would be more understanding of his need to quit and be supportive of his decision.

Meg meanwhile had rung Becky and they both had agreed to swap houses. Becky thought it was a brilliant idea and felt it would be a new start for them both. After promising to arrange an appointment with the solicitor to deal with any paperwork, Meg told Becky to start packing up, as the house was hers whenever she was ready to move in. She had glanced briefly at the text from Steve, but she wasn't interested in replying yet; for the next few weeks she wanted to concentrate on making a life for herself and Romany. Steve had not been the only one that had done a lot of thinking lately and she was certain that she needed to do this on her own. She didn't doubt that she loved him, but she hadn't realised how deep the issue with Bree had gone. She had been naïve in thinking that out of sight meant out of mind. Maybe it was the best thing for them both that they left it for a while until they were both in a place, mentally, to deal with a relationship and all the complications that brings, especially when her child was involved. Her need to protect Romany was as strong if not stronger that Steve's to protect her. Sadly, perhaps they were unable to overcome their problems, but she hoped with all her heart that they could. Maybe she would take a holiday to see Aunty Sian and her cousins? Summer school holidays were coming up and she could do with a break from everything. Bally-Bay could be the answer; a nice rest at the seaside with family. She was missing her mammy so much that Aunty Sian would be a great substitute. Just to hear that Irish lilt again brought shivers to her spine and goose bumps to her skin. She hoped that it would not always make her think of Bree.

At first, she had encouraged Steve to visit Bree, thinking that it might help him, but then her anger had kicked in. That woman (she refused to call her Magda and ruin her own mother's name) had killed her parents and brother and nearly destroyed her life; now she realised that letting her into their lives in any way, shape, or form, would be folly. In fact, she was still playing a huge part in what was happening to their relationship. Usually mild mannered, Meg wished that the bitch would rot in hell; she didn't deserve their compassion. She had practically roasted her parents and brother alive, on the yacht and Jonathon in his car; none of them stood a chance because they had trusted her. She deserved to be punished for what she had done. Yes, hell was where she belonged with her father, the Diabhul.

CHAPTER 11

"Those who need help the most, run the farthest from it."
Jonathon Kellerman

Steve was disappointed that Meg had not rang or messaged him back, one thing he was glad of was that he had gone back in to work and talked to his team. It was so good to be back, sometimes the mundane can have more healing power than any pills. He had talked to his boss and decided that for the time being he would stay on. He could always volunteer with any youth groups in the area and perhaps his decision to leave had been rash and made whilst he was over-wrought. One thing was certain, he was feeling a bit more positive. He hoped that his appointment with his psychiatrist Dr Watson went as well this afternoon. Maybe he would pop out for a sandwich and give Meg another message, she might not have got the other one or had been too busy to reply. After sending a message to Meg he grabbed a coffee and a sandwich and headed back to his desk for a couple of hours paperwork before his appointment at four. Meg had received the second message from Steve but decided that she needed a bit of space and would talk to him later.

One thing that Meg's father would have said about his little Sidhe was that she was stubborn, determined, and always fair, but she never suffered fools gladly, as did the little people that he named her after.

Steve found that his colleagues were tiptoeing around him; although they all welcomed him back, he was still catching them whispering and glancing his way. He soon discovered that he found their interest a bit disturbing. Maybe he was being oversensitive and he had decided to ignore it, to duck his head down and pray for a new case. He longed for something that they could get their teeth into as a team; something to bring them back together. He longed for the old camaraderie and the shared work ethic that teamwork involved. God he even missed the tiredness from the late nights and early mornings, at least then he would fall asleep and not toss and turn in nightmare moments all night long.

Later that afternoon he was sat in Dr Evelyn Watson's room telling her how his dreams had become more vivid and colourful of late; but the one that always stayed with him more than any other, the same one that he had had for many years, had been worse. She listened patiently as he described the church entrance that loomed large in his dream and he would find himself entering, no matter how reluctant he was. The sight of the priest lying across the altar and the blood that pooled beneath his body seemed so much brighter and redder. Not just the blood, but the light in the room and the colour of the stained-glass windows. The gleaming gold leaf on the statuary of our lady, and of Jesus on the cross shone so brightly, almost blinding him. The altar cloth, which was covered in a deep red, an almost black stain as the blood seeped into it. He could smell the metallic scent of the blood and almost taste it. His senses seemed to be enhanced in his dream-state; he could certainly hear the scream that reverberated around the church, it was almost tangible and he felt it as well as heard it from inside of his body. The scream emanating from himself mixed with the hysterical laughter from a young girl that stood in the aisle covered in blood, who he now knew had been Bree. Above all of this, he thought that he heard the heartbeat of the priest, pumping, in his eardrums; gradually becoming slower until it eventually stopped. At which point he explained that he usually awoke, bolting upright with sweat clinging to his body. He always felt that the laughter lingered on in his head even though he knew he was now awake. And he always then felt his own chest, listening and feeling for the reassuring beat of his own heart.

When he had finished, she had asked him to look at the dream, as he had described it in a very specific way. It was not a dream that his imagination had plucked out of the air, but a real memory which was a different scenario. She also asked him to explore how he felt as he entered the church. His feelings of helplessness and fear were what would be expected from an inexperienced and very young garda with a sheltered upbringing.

'Going into an unknown situation for any human being will trigger a basic, animal, fight or flight reflex, until we can assess the situation for hidden dangers. Once we recognise this feeling for what it is, we learn to control it, as you have done as you have gotten older as an experienced adult and detective. The dream memory had bypassed this control, because it took you back to the same scene where you, as a young garda, had not learnt this control; so you experienced all the emotion as if for the very first time,' she explained. 'The rest of the memory is your reaction to the horror of the situation and what you were seeing and hearing. The trauma of that night has not been dealt with and because you tried to bury it along with any emotional tie to it in a bid to forget, it will continue to resurface. It is like trying to stop a flow of water with your hands, eventually the water will seep through the gaps.'

Dr Watson paused, allowing Steve to take on board what she had just said.

'I don't suppose that you would recommend that I visit Bree then. I have a confession to make, I already have and it wasn't pleasant.' Steve continued to tell the doctor about his huge panic attack when he had spoken to Bree and Bree's reaction to seeing him and the consequential request from her psychiatrist for him to visit her again. He also explained how the visit and all of the other issues had impacted his relationship with Meg.

'Thank you for your honesty, Steve, you could of course have easily kept this to yourself, but it can only help your recovery to be honest with me and yourself. If you are waiting for me to approve or disapprove of your visits to Bree, it is not my decision to make, but yours. From what you have told me I do believe that you have some doubts yourself about how that will affect you and your own mental health. I can only make professional observations and recommendations. For the present time I would suggest that you concentrate on your own health, and I will give you some exercises to do for the times that you feel anxious, or out of control of your own feelings. These will hopefully help you to eventually take control of any panic attacks as soon as you feel them start to begin. They may resurface whilst you explore your feelings, and this should help you to deal with any situations that you are not comfortable in. Use these breathing techniques to help as soon as you feel that tightness in your chest or your breathing changes. If you can get on top of the attack before it takes control and starts to overwhelm you, you are halfway there.'

'I want to get well, Doc, and I promised that I would be honest with you from the start and I am a man of my word, if nothing else.'

Dr Watson smiled and standing she asked Steve to make another appointment and handed him a booklet with tips to control anxiety written on the front. She liked this detective, he was kind, honest, and true; sadly, just the sort that ended up in her office, sat in that chair, opposite her.

Outside he pulled his phone from his pocket, as he slid his thumb across the screen, he could see at first glance that he had no messages from Meg; maybe he should give her more time, maybe he should just bloody well ignore what he felt for her, then perhaps the Diabhul would be satisfied. He knew that would never happen as she had entered his world a long time ago and she had no intention of leaving quietly. He decided to leave another message and hope that she would feel ready to talk to him to decide if they had a future together or not. In the meantime, he was going back to work for a couple of hours and then he would grab a takeaway on the way home. He wasn't ready to face an empty flat just yet.

As he entered through the double doors, the room silenced. He felt all eyes turn towards him and follow him as he made his way to his desk. He would probably need to get used to this, after all, having a maniac, psycho, serial killer for a twin sister was quite a novelty. He smiled quirkily as he looked up and all of the eyes turned away from him quickly. Except one. She headed towards him, Detective Sergeant Sara Dyson; her eyes locked onto his and he could see within them empathy and pity.

'Sir,' she called to Steve, 'we have had a call from Bristol force whilst working on a case of a murdered John Doe; they found a connection to a case we were working on. Theirs was the body of a drug addict found in an alleyway; it wasn't pleasant he had his eyes poked in and was terribly beaten. They thought they had some rival gang, turf war going on, but no other incidents have since occurred. Then when the D.N.A. from the scene came back they linked it to our case. I think that you had better sit down, sir, the results were for … Magda Reilly. I'm sorry, sir.'

He saw real concern in her eyes as she looked at him, but also a little fear too. He knew that he hadn't been himself but he had never lost it at work, ever! Perhaps the fear was for him? He thought then said, 'Get us a coffee will you please, Sergeant? Extra strong; I think I will need it.' She passed the paper with the Bristol detective's number on it and turned towards the room. If any of them as much as smirked or even bloody blinked she would put them on cell cleaning duties for at least two weeks. She was proud to see all of her team going about their normal business, answering their phones and turning their attention to their work. Steve had earned his respect from them all, she needn't have worried, and they were a good bunch. She smiled sadly as she looked around the room, her eyes coming to rest on Steve who now had the phone to his ear and his head in his hand. How much more can he take, she thought, before he breaks?

After coming off the phone to the detective in charge of the case in Bristol, he decided to head home anyway. He stood abruptly and rushed out of the door just as Sara Dyson appeared with his coffee.

'Your coffee, sir,' she called after his retreating figure. He didn't even glance back as he practically ran out of the building. He could feel his breathing starting to quicken and black dots were forming at the corners of his eyes; he knew he was either going to vomit or pass out, one or the other if, he couldn't get himself under some kind of control. He leant his body against the wall of the parking garage and gulped in huge gasps of air. He knew that rationally he just needed to breathe and get a rhythm going for the feeling to abate. Concentrating as hard as he could he managed to stop himself from blacking out. Gradually he got himself under control enough to get to his car, opening the door he threw himself in and leaning his head back he closed his eyes. He didn't see the figure watching him with great concern from the doorway that led to the stairwell and the upper floors of the carpark. Once she had reassured herself that Steve was safely in his car, Detective Sergeant Sara Dyson returned to the building.

Steve turned the key in the lock and headed into the hallway of his one-bed flat. It opened out into an open-plan kitchen/living area with a bedroom and bathroom off of that. He had hardly been home so space had meant nothing to him. All he had really needed over the years was a place to lay his head at the end of the day. There had been a few one-night stands over the years but nothing serious till Meghan. He thought about her now, and looking around his home in dissatisfaction he thought to himself, 'What can I even offer her that she doesn't have already? A great house, a job that she loves, a life … I can't even offer her that at the moment as I can't seem to sort out my own life.'

He flung his keys and phone onto the kitchen worktop and headed into the shower, after a pummelling under the spray he felt a little better. He could now think a bit more rationally. His thoughts as always turned to Bree. Why did she keep popping up into his life like a bad omen? Every time he thought that he had dealt with it and made a decision, something else reared its ugly head that concerned her. The detective on the case of the unidentified drug addict found in the alleyway in Bristol had asked him if he could interview Bree about it on his behalf as he had been denied access, whereas he had a connection via the other case which he believed was connected. In other words, he had passed the buck well and truly into Steve's hand. Steve was sure that he didn't know his connection to Bree as he probably wouldn't have asked him. But it rested now firmly in his lap. Tomorrow he would ring and get another visit with Bree arranged, but for now he was going to order a pizza, get himself a beer and slob out in front of the TV.

The doorbell ringing woke him from the doze that he was in on the sofa. He had drifted off whilst watching the news. He still had the towel around his waist, and he made his way to the door. Expecting his pizza delivery, he was quite shocked to see Sara stood on the doorstep. He grasped his towel to him and stepped back to invite her in.

'Can I get you a drink, a coffee or tea?' he queried.

'No thanks I was on my way home and I thought I would check in to see if you are ok? I know that the news and shock of the latest bombshell about Magda must have hit you hard. I think you have been so brave, and I know you have been through a lot … I just wanted you to know that I'm here for you … you know, if you want to talk … or anything?' She leaned into him and, pulling his towel towards her, she kissed him. Steve didn't know what to do, he was overwhelmed for a moment and started to return the kiss. It was a simple solution to how he was feeling; just to lose himself for a couple of hours and just go with his urges. And as the kiss deepened and he felt himself beginning to respond, the towel fell to the floor between them. Sara could see the reaction that she had caused and smiled. Encouraged by his reaction she leaned in further and started to remove her clothing. Grasping at each other, the world forgotten; they were interrupted by the doorbell ringing again. This time it really was the pizza delivery and as Steve slowly returned to his senses, he had never been so glad to see it. Suddenly he pushed her away from him. Grabbing his towel, he wrapped it securely around his waist.

'Detective Sergeant! S–Sara I apologise … I can't … I can't do this. No, I don't want this! I love Meg. I am sorry if I led you to believe that there could be anything between us. Please forgive me you are great and—'

'No don't do that to me, Steve. I have felt like this about you for a long time and I somehow thought that I could be the one for you too tonight. Please don't tell me how great I am, that would just be insulting. I'm sorry I misread the situation … err sorry!' She opened the door and raced past the startled pizza delivery man and Steve let her go, turning to pay the man. He gave Steve a wink and whistled, grabbing the money as he disappeared too into the night. Turning back into the room he had suddenly lost his appetite; how could things ever be the same between them at work? He trusted and respected Sara as a colleague, nothing more … until tonight he had not thought of her in that way. She was certainly pretty, and she understood the working hours and life of a copper, but he loved Meg with his heart and soul; that he couldn't change.

He threw the pizza in the bin in disgust, he suddenly felt sick. What the hell had he been playing at, how the bloody hell could he explain that one? Meg must never, ever find out.

CHAPTER 12

"We are each our own devil, and we make this world our hell."
Oscar Wilde

Steve woke next morning with a thumping head, dehydrated, and feeling sick. Obviously shouldn't skip meals on these tablets either, he thought as he tumbled out of bed and into the kitchen. Perhaps he should down a glass of water before he started on the coffee? Rubbing his stomach, he felt very hungry too. Looking through the fridge he found some eggs and settled on some scrambled with toast and he fished last night's pizza out of the bin. It would be fine, it was still in the box; shoving a slice into his mouth, he was glad Meg couldn't see him. Putting on the coffee pot, he drank down a glass of water before heading for the shower. An hour later he was fed, caffeined up, and ready to face everyone, including Sara. What he was going to say to the poor girl he had no idea. but he wasn't going to shy away from his responsibility, and he was as culpable as she was last night. Thank god for the pizza delivery as he was unsure, to be honest, if he would have stopped. It was nice just for five minutes to forget everything, but the price he would have had to pay would have been unbearable. He drove into the car park just as Sara arrived too and as they both climbed the stairs he broached the subject of last night, pausing on the landing she turned to him. 'I'm a little embarrassed, boss, can we forget that it ever happened?'

'Sure to be sure, as long as yer are ok?' His Irish brogue was more pronounced with his nerves. He reached out to touch her hand and she expertly twisted away before they touched and bolted up the stairs.

He was relieved but he was sure that Sara was unhappy that he couldn't give her what she wanted. The thing to do now was as he had always done, behave like a professional and just get on with his job.

Heading to his desk he shut the door and picked up the phone and rang The Lawns Psychiatric unit to speak to Dr Jones and make an appointment to see Bree again. Confirming his appointment for the afternoon, he settled down to his paperwork and kept busy. At lunch time he went out and grabbed a coffee and a sandwich. He sat himself outside in the sunshine and finished his food before deciding to try and ring Meg. He looked at his watch, damn, he had missed her lunch break at the school and so he decided to text her again.

I am sorry, a mhuirni'n, forgive me please? Just talk to me. I shan't give up on us. I am lost without you my Sidhe. Xx

He was surprised when a few minutes later his phone pinged, and it was Meg.

I know and I am missing you too, but I need to know that you are not going to see Bree again. I am sorry, Steve. Xx

Oh fuck! What could he do now? Through no fault of his own he had to visit her, and it was planned for this afternoon. Could he lie to Meg, or should he not go to see Bree? If he was honest with himself, he was looking forward to seeing her ... he wanted to see her more than anything. As if he was compelled to ... Oh god, he needed to. He decided not to reply to Meg for the moment, maybe in the back of his mind he could make it right by pretending that he hadn't read her text till after the visit. After all, he was going for work-related purposes, wasn't he? She need never know, if all goes well then after today he can make her that promise.

The doctor watched through the small observation window in the door. He could see that Magda had become very animated since he had told her that her brother was going to visit her again. She had been walking around the room talking to someone that only she could see. She smiled every now and then, but he observed how it never quite met her eyes. Her fingers grasped at the material of her gown, and she pinched and twisted it, winding it around her fingers. She would suddenly let it go and smooth the material down, only to start all over again. He observed her carefully for any signs of distress but apart from the expected reactions to being locked up she seemed quite happy that he was coming. She had returned to her quiet state of mind after DCI Ryan had last visited her and she had been no longer engaging with anyone on any level. He had been just as surprised as all of the staff to see the agitated state that she had gotten herself into and he was considering some sedation before her brother's visit, or before she worked herself into a state. He found the case fascinating and wanted the visits to continue so that he could study the effects on his patient. He was also curious to see how the twin relationship connected them together; even though they had only really known about each other for a few months. He was unsure at this time whether that would prove useful in her treatment, but he certainly knew that even the mention of the detective's name animated her and caused a huge reaction. He was also under no illusion just how dangerous she was. She had already been responsible for several staff attacks, and she had shown no remorse at all for her actions before or since her incarceration. He was looking forward to seeing the relationship develop between the two siblings.

The knock on Steve's office door made him jump, he had been in deep concentration going through all of the notes that pertained to the investigation and interviews with Bree before she was transferred, she would only speak to him and the trauma was still very raw for him but being the professional that he was he had taken all the statements from her at the time before handing it all over to his team, once she had been transferred to the psychiatric facility for assessment. He looked up; Sara stood in the doorway with some files in her hand.

'Here are the last statements before transfer,' she said, handing a plain brown folder over. 'I hope you don't mind me saying, Steve, but is there something in particular you are looking for and secondly is it something that you should be still looking at? For your own sake I don't think that you should.'

'It's ok, Sara, thanks for your concern. I was just trying to find something that Bree … I mean Magda may have mentioned about the Bristol murder. I am sure that she mentioned something; I just can't seem to find it.'

Sara turned on her heel and left as he opened the folder and. scanning the pages, he found what he was looking for. Yes, just as he thought, she mentioned someone attacking her in an alleyway in Bristol before catching the train. It was after she had found out that a person she had tracked down to Bristol, thinking that she was her mother, had died. He remembered now how angry she had been and her words still chilled as he read them again. The only reason she had mentioned it was because she had been so furious with the man; he had ruined her new sweatshirt that she had just brought. She said she had to dump it in the bin by the station because she had his blood all over the sleeves, before catching the train to Cambridge to find Meghan's family and their mother Magda Callahan, who was on her list of women that she thought might be her mother. But it was her words that rang a bell; he remembered thinking at the time how odd that she was leaving him with a riddle, but it all made sense now. Through gritted teeth she had expressed her feelings for the attacker in what Steve had thought, at the time, a strange way. "After all, we are only as blind as we want to be" and she had laughed harshly, the glee evident in her face.

This information and the fact that she had been detained under the mental health act as unfit to stand trial, meant that he could safely pass the statement over to his Bristol colleagues without the need to visit Bree at all. He was relieved he wouldn't have to lie to Meg which at this moment in time he had decided was more important to him than some crazy psycho sister. Although, as he admitted to himself, he continuously felt drawn to her in some inexplicable way. Picking up the telephone he rang Dr Jones at The Lawns and told him that he would not be coming to see Bree and didn't expect to do so anytime soon. His own health and relationship had to come first. He actually felt a sadness and loss, but he realised that to get well again it was what he needed to do. Then he emailed Bristol and scanned in the statement highlighting the description Bree had given of the location of the attack.

Dr Jones was just leaving the room after giving Magda the news that her visitor was not coming and behind him you would think a wild animal had been captured. The only way to describe the noise emanating from Magda was animalistic. She howled, a deep guttural sound, it rumbled around the room, echoing off of the walls, until suddenly it stopped. Only to be replaced with the sound of the hysterical laughter of old. The doctor knew that he was at fault, but he had wanted time to study her reaction to the news of DCI Ryan's return visit. He was hoping to use her as a study subject for the paper he was writing. He had never come across in his career quite such a complicated and difficult persona and she was worthy of study, but now, who knows? 'Give her a bigger dose of sedation, nurse,' the doctor said as he brushed past. 'I think we are going to be starting back at the beginning again. Damn that detective.'

Steve picked up his phone and quickly sent Meg a text

I am sorry, my love, I have been so foolish. I promise I am not going to see Bree again. I have decided that she needs to be removed from our lives for us to have any kind of a relationship. Please meet me to talk tonight. 7 p.m. at the George?

His thumb hovered over the screen, he hesitated before finally pushing send. What if she refused to see him? What if this was the end of their relationship? Would she even turn up? They had been through so much together in such a short space of time and the trauma inflicted on them from Bree was bound to have some after effect. He wasn't naïve and he realised that Meg had lost so much more than him and he felt her loss as his own, because Bree was his sister and he felt responsible. He witnessed her grief and he saw how strong she had been, Romany too, whereas he had just been weak in putting his own feelings first without thought of the effect that might have on Meg. He was also a daily reminder of the terror that she had put her through so how the hell could they have a relationship with all of that shit?

He sighed, gathered up his jacket off of the back of the chair, and headed out to go home, shower, and shave before meeting Meg at the pub later. He was no longer going to hide these scars behind a beard, why should he feel ashamed? That was the problem with his culture, everything was shameful from feelings to actions, so you were buggered if you did or didn't, he thought, smiling. Especially if you were a man, secrecy and silence were expected, not an acknowledgment of any emotion. He felt lighter somehow, maybe it was a sign of hope or just because he felt that he was finally making the right decision.

CHAPTER 13

"Do not give your past the power to define your future."
Unknown

Steve looked at his image in the mirror. He didn't recognise the face staring back at him. He had lost weight, his cheekbones were more defined, and the long scars that ran across them were less red and angry looking and had turned a silvery grey. Matches my hair, he thought, and he ran his fingers down the sides and noted the colour change. He had shaved for the first time since Bree had attacked him, and it felt strange to have no beard again. In just a few months he had aged years; but at least he was alive and breathing. He hoped that Meg would still look at him the same way as she had before Bree had taken her toll of their lives. She sure demanded a hell of a payment, not just physically, but she also wanted your soul too. He turned, grabbed his keys, and rushed out of the door, he wanted to get to the shop to buy Meg some flowers. Damn! He was kicking himself now, why the heck hadn't he thought of that before? Now she will have to make do with some over-priced bunch of bland blooms from Waitrose. Oh well, he could make it up to her later, when things were more settled … he hoped.

He settled nervously at a table in the corner by the window, so that hopefully he would see her coming. He wished she would turn up. He needed all of his Irish charm and luck tonight. He didn't want to think about life on his own without Meg. He hadn't realised just how insular and lonely he had been; cut off from family, friends, and even colleagues at work. He had been functioning, but only just, for a long time, and now it was his time to live.

He turned to the sound of the door opening and saw her step into the room. He could swear, as they say in the movies, that the world stood still as he looked at her. She was beautiful! All that he ever wanted or needed was stood in front of him; she was his life, his universe, his soulmate.

Meg approached the table tentatively, unsure of Steve's reaction, or her own. She had made some changes since she last had seen him. Her gorgeous red hair that he so admired, which used to hang down her back in waves, was now cut in a chic shoulder-length bob. She noticed some changes in him too and was surprised to see that he had shaved. He was thinner too, she noted, probably due to the stress she thought. But overall, he looked well. Looking up into his blue eyes she didn't care, she realised just how much she had missed him, and her heart gave a sigh as she fell into his arms. 'So much for being strong and holding my ground,' she murmured against his shoulder.

'You are always the strong one, a mhuirni'n, I just hope that you can forgive me for being so weak when you needed me.'

They were lost in each other's arms and kisses for a long time until the landlord called out laughingly, 'Do you two want a room? I have a few empty.' The whole pub whistled and catcalled as Meg tried to hide her blushes. 'Is it champagne you are wanting? Or will a pint of ale suffice and a glass of wine for the lady?'

Steve looked towards the landlord whom he had known now for years and nodded his thanks. He had seen Steve at his best and his worst and he was glad that he had saved his blushes; he had told him that tonight was important to him when he had commented on the flowers. Suddenly he felt very awkward, like a teenager unsure what to say. Breathe, he thought, compliment her, and relax man, for God's sake.'

'I love what you have done with your hair, you look beautiful.

Have you eaten yet, Meg? They do a mean steak and ale pie here with triple cooked chips to die for.'

She nodded her head, shy too, and suddenly he was very hungry. They enjoyed an evening like their first date. Both of them determined to not touch on the subject that they knew was in the back of their minds. They just wanted to relax and enjoy an evening of flirting and small talk without any dramas. The landlord called time and reluctantly they made their way to the car park. Holding hands, he turned to kiss her goodbye, not expecting anything else from the evening. He knew that he needed to give them both time to re-adjust to being together again; so he was surprised and grateful when she whispered in his ear, 'Well your place or mine? Romany has a sleep-over at a friend's and won't be home till morning.'

'Only if you are sure and ready, Meg, I will wait for as long as you need for you to trust me again.'

'Oh I'm sure, you big Irish lug, oh I'm very sure, I don't know if I can wait to get you home.' He laughed as she snogged his socks off, he couldn't wait for his pants to do the same.

They tumbled through the door of Steve's flat and then tumbled into the bedroom and onto the bed. His place had been the nearest and seeing as there was some urgency they walked to his flat. Their lovemaking had been passionate, urgent, and forceful. Laying now an hour or so later, sated and snuggled in each other's arms, he was beginning to be tempted to start all over again. Meg felt his body stir and she felt the excitement of another bout of lovemaking run down her spine. 'Now what shall we do for the rest of the evening?' he queried and she watched as the devil danced in his eyes and she shivered in anticipation, lost in his kisses.

He woke the next morning to the sound of his tuneless alarm. Trying not to wake Meg he slid out from under the covers, pulled on his joggers, and grabbing his trainers he slipped out of the door for a run. At first, he was full of energy and after a few laps of the lake he slowed his pace. Everything around him seemed brighter today. The water, the trees, the flowers in the grass, and mostly the sky, it was a clear cloudless day and the sun had just begun to rise up into the brightest shade of blue.

Steve breathed deeply, the fresh air tingling in his nose and throat. Jesus but it was good to be alive. He walked back to the flat, taking in deep breaths as he went, the smile on his face as wide as the scars on his cheeks. He was totally unaware of the figure that had been watching him from behind a tree. She had also seen him meet Meg at the pub the night before and seen them kiss and hastily push their way through the front door, almost indecently hurrying, undressing as they went. She knew that given more time she would have him to herself but now that bitch was back on the scene! She sighed. He was only with Meg because he felt sorry for her, after what she had been through. She didn't understand him like she did, as only another police officer could. They had been a team for the last two years and she had wanted him from day one. Her love for Steve had grown over that time, she had known that he had no—one else in his life; so it was just a matter of time before she could make her move. That was until Meg came along and had bewitched him. Now all she could do was sit back and watch and suffer the embarrassment and rejection that he had given her the night before. She had very nearly been with him, just a moment away, damn that pizza delivery.

Oblivious to everything around him, even the undercurrents from Sara, he ploughed through the day with only one thought: for it to finish as quickly as it could so that he could get back, to be with Meg. He felt quite giddy, as if he was experiencing his feelings towards her for the first time. Probably, he thought, because he had freed himself from Bree and he was able to offer Meg a relationship unencumbered by the emotional ties of the case. This was the real thing, the raw and exposed self that he was offering Meg. That was all he had and that was all she wanted. They had agreed last night to take it wherever it led them, with no expectations or ties to what had gone before. He was happy, yes! For the first time in a long, long time he was happy. For once he felt he had a future to look forward to and Meg was going to play a huge part in it. He shrugged his shoulders and smiled. Just at this moment in time life was good.

That evening Meg had invited him around to the house. They had agreed to take things slowly and to let them play out as it was meant to. Romany came in and he was relieved and ecstatic when she fell into his arms and gave him a hug.

'I missed my Irish dad, don't go away again.' She looked up into his face and he could see how much she meant it and the fear of losing him completely showed in her eyes.

'I am sorry, love, hopefully your mum has forgiven me, and I can try and make it up to you both.' Steve held her away from him and gave her a wink.

'Has she told you about the house yet? Apart from a new haircut, she has been having a life change. I think it's her age,' she whispered loudly enough for her mum to hear.

'Oi, you two, I can hear you, yer know, and no I haven't had a chance to talk to Steve about any changes I am making yet.'

Steve looked at Meg and raised an eyebrow. 'Am I included in these changes, a mhuirni'n, or is it exclusively for you and Romany?' he asked.

'You are included if that is what you want but there is no pressure to move back in.'

Meg quickly explained the situation to him; how Becky and the boys were finding things hard in the house where they had lived with Jonathon. 'It's understandable; she wanted to sell up and make a new start for herself and the boys. So, we have decided to swap houses. I couldn't afford to buy her out and as you know it was my family home.

Romany is happy too, so it solved everyone's problem to simply swap.'

'What a fantastic idea, I know that you have never felt happy here so will it be the house where I met you at the barbeque? If I remember rightly, it was a stunning old arts and crafts house.' Steve remembered that night and her gorgeous green eyes as she turned, as they first met, and it was as if he knew then how special Meg was and what a huge part of his life she was going to be.

'That's right, I grew up there with Jonathon, Talley, and Finn. That reminds me, I haven't seen Finn for ages and I need to tell him what is happening about the house; would you come with me at the weekend, Steve? You haven't seen the stables yet, have you? Now have yer true Irish blood in yer and would yer know a good bit of horse-flesh when yer see it?' Meg joked as she put on her best Irish accent.

'I do actually, you forget that I was brought up on a farm and I love to ride, and your bloody cheeky accent is rubbish.' He chased her and caught her in his arms before kissing her thoroughly.

'Yuck you two, get a room.' Romany made gagging noises as Steve turned and chased her too. They all collapsed in a heap in the kitchen and once they had all got their breath back Romany asked, 'Can I come too? I haven't been to the stables since er ... you know. I think it would be good for me, I just don't want to ride yet.' Meg, realising that Romany was taking a huge step to want to come to the stables, was pleased. Steve, realising what a brave thing she was doing after her terrible accident caused by Bree making her fall, and the subsequent weeks of injury and coma that she had endured, wanted to be as positive as possible.

'Whenever you are ready, love; I will willingly come ride with you and even lead the horse till you feel comfortable. What do yer say?'

He hugged Romany in one arm and pulled Meg into his embrace on the other side. 'One step at a time for us all but we do it together ... that's a promise.'

CHAPTER 14

"Life is really simple but we insist on making it complicated."
Confucius

The days slipped by and Steve, true to his word, led Romany on a very gentle ride around the paddock whilst her mum talked to Finn.

'I hope that you don't mind, Finn, about the house swap. It seemed the best solution for all of us, and this way the family home stays in the family,' Meg explained.

'Of course I don't mind, god it is so good to see you. I have missed you so much.' He pulled Meg into an embrace and held onto her tightly. 'I never thought that we would ever be so broken apart, as a family. It's not just losing Mammy, Daddy, and Jonathon, but everything else too. I am so pleased to see Romany overcoming her fear. Steve is a good man, Meg, definitely a keeper. Talking of good men, I have met someone that I care for very much; he has been supporting me through all this hell. I was just going to tell everyone about him when everything kicked off, so I didn't get the chance. His name is Jack, and I would like you all to meet him.'

'Oh that is lovely, Finn, I am so happy for you, I know Mammy and Daddy would be glad too. You deserve some happiness, we all do. I can't wait to meet him, why don't you bring him over for Sunday lunch tomorrow? I'm sure that I haven't packed the roasting tin yet; if I have Steve can barbeque.'

'That would be great. I'm sorry, my darling, I must get on, I have a lame horse and the vet has just arrived. Stay as long as Romany wants to, and I will see you tomorrow with Jack. About 1 p.m. ok?'

Meg nodded and then watched her younger brother walk away, his strong shoulders straight and broad. 'When did my baby brother grow up so fast? Our parents would have loved to see the man he has become.' They would never meet Steve or Jack or anyone else new to the family, all because of Bree. It was so hard not to be upset and angry still. She wiped a tear from her eye and turning she smiled as she saw Steve encouraging Romany, who was now flying around the ménage, her black hair streaming out behind her. She was laughing with the pure joy of it and Meg's heart overflowed with love for her daughter and the man who had breathed life into her.

Romany was chattering all the way home, keeping Meg and Steve occupied. Meg, excited too, told them both about Finn's new love, Jack. 'We will have to pop into the supermarket on the way home,' she told Steve. 'They are coming for lunch tomorrow and I want to impress him. After all, by the sound of it he is going to be a big part of the family.'

'Ooh maybe we should ask Becky and the boys over too, I'm sure that she could do with a break from the packing … oh perhaps we had better do a barbeque after all.'

Steve and Romany laughed at Meg; he picked up her hand and kissed it.

'Anything you say, boss.'

'Oh sorry, Steve, do you mind?'

'I am just glad to see you so happy and excited, love; it will be fun, that's what we all need, a bit of fun.'

The excitement and chatter continued all the way around the supermarket and all the way home too. Which is why Steve didn't notice that they were being followed by a car, the same one that had watched them leave for the stables earlier in the day. The dark blue

Audi was an ordinary car like so many others on the road. The detective was distracted by a lot of things lately; a few months ago, no-one would have been able to follow him and get away with it.

'See what she has done to you? Made you oblivious to everything; that bitch has ruined you, Steve Ryan. Maybe it's time to do something about it and turn your eyes back in my direction.' The person in the car thought before turning off at the next junction. She knew where he was going to be for the next few hours. No point in wasting her weekend; she had plans to make. It was obvious that she was going to have to catch him at work and she needed to plan how to do that. She had hidden the clothes that she had worn the night that they had almost made love in an evidence bag at the back of her wardrobe; it would definitely have his D.N.A. on it, but she hoped that she wouldn't have to use it and that he would see sense, see that he should be with her, not Meghan bloody Callahan.

The weekend flew by, and they had a great time with Finn and Jack was as nice as they thought he would be. Becky and the boys were excited, running around the house choosing bedrooms for when they moved in. For the first time in what seemed like forever Steve felt that he had a chance of a normal life, a family where he belonged and all of the comfort that would bring. He had decided to stay at his flat during the week and with Meg at the weekends, until she had moved into the home that she had swapped with Becky. They had discussed it all over the weekend and he smiled as he thought about the days that had just passed and his time with Romany and Meg. He also looked forward to the time that they could all be together permanently.

Work was mundane at best at the moment with just routine cases crossing his desk. He thought probably for the best, to give himself time to get on top of everything, and to recover. DS Dyson was beginning to worry him a bit. She seemed to linger in his presence more and he had noted that she had pressed herself against him on a few occasions lately and allowed her fingers to linger a little bit too long as she passed him a coffee or a file. He had hoped that the conversation that they had after the pizza night incident had been enough to make clear to Sara that his feelings lay elsewhere. He hoped that she wasn't still under any illusion that anything could happen between them, and he hoped that Meg didn't find out about that night. He tried to think back … had he done anything over the last two years to make Sara think that she had a chance with him or any opportunity to mean anything other than the colleagues that they were? His answer was no, he couldn't think of anything … oh except that drunken snog at the Christmas do over a year ago … surely not! Oh Mary mother and Jesus, was that it! He needed to sort this quick and pinch it in the bud now.

He headed out to the toilet to think; he always shut himself in the cubicle at the end when he needed not to be disturbed. He had just put the lid down on the toilet seat and sat down when he heard the door open and footsteps come into the room. A tap on the door startled him and opening it tentatively he was suddenly pushed back into the cubicle and Sara pushed herself up against him. Startled, he tried to speak but she covered his mouth with her own. Pushing her away from him forcibly he opened the door and stormed out, just as she emerged from the cubicle behind him the door opened and DC Short entered.

'Sorry Gov … Sara; am I interrupting something?' He turned on his heel and Steve watched open mouthed as he disappeared back through the doorway. Sara stood behind him with a smirk on her face; she pushed past him, her fingers lingering on his cheek as she went. Steve had turned to stone, barely breathing, unable to comprehend what had just happened 'Fuck! What the … oh fuck!' Head in his hands he realised that the whole room would know that he had been caught in a compromising position with his DS in the bathroom. How the hell was he going to explain this, he would never be believed if he tried to deny anything had happened.

There was nothing for it, he would have to front it out, and making his way to his office he watched as the whole room quieted and all eyes followed him. 'DS Dyson my office please … now!' Once Sara had entered the room, Steve could barely contain his anger. Sitting down and crossing her legs she deliberately looked up at him. 'What the fuck was that about and who the hell told you to sit down? I want an explanation and I want it bloody now.'

Smirking, she said, 'But you know, Steve, I am so glad that we are back together. I have waited almost two years for you to notice me. You thought that you could kiss me, fuck me, and walk away; well that is not how it works. I suggest that you meet me tonight for a drink and we discuss our relationship and why you insist on denying it. Or I will tell everyone out there,' she said, pointing to the room outside, 'that you raped me. They all think we have been at it anyway and I might just have to tell precious Meg Callahan a few truths about her boyfriend.'

Steve visibly paled. 'What the fuck are you talking about? I never even so much as went out with you let alone sleep with you.'

'Oh but you did, Steve, we made love only the other evening, how can you say we didn't? Who do you think they will believe when I leave this room in tears?' She looked him in the face and standing up her eyes suddenly filled with tears that overflowed down her cheeks. 'Oh, you are so cruel.' She laughed, throwing her head back, then suddenly looking solemn as she turned to leave, she said as she opened the door, 'I'm sorry, darling, I will be more careful next time … I was just so excited to see you.' She said it just loud enough for the person on the nearest desk to hear her; along with a small sob, as she rushed off towards her desk. Turning her chair from the room she made a big thing of retrieving a tissue and dabbing at her eyes.

When Steve looked down a note was sitting on the chair that Sara had just vacated and written on it was *6-30 @ the George.*

'Now I know I am going mad,' he said. What the hell was wrong with him? How did he attract these crazy women into his life and what was he going to do? He picked up his jacket and speedily left the station. Heading for home he quickly changed into joggers and headed to the lake, he needed somewhere to think in peace; what a fucking mess. He needed to decide what he was going to do; the decision to go and meet Sara at the pub would to him be an admission that he was having some kind of a relationship with her. Luckily, he wasn't seeing Meg tonight so he was free to go if he wanted to. He felt torn between doing the right thing and telling his boss and the professional standards, or meeting her at the pub and trying to sort it out on his own before it became a bigger problem than it already was. What did she want with an old and jaded detective that had so many issues that he could barely function? All he knew was at this moment in time he didn't want Meg to find out; they were just getting back on track; this would probably be the end for his relationship with Meg. That would be the end for him too. Perhaps he could talk to her and make her see sense, maybe if he went along to the pub, he might be able to reason with her. After all, she was a sensible girl, he couldn't understand it. Why him for god's sake? She was pretty and she used to be kind of nice, or so he once thought. She was in her late twenties or early thirties with all of her life in front of her. She was certainly very intelligent, not many women made it to detective sergeant at such an early age. Even today the force was biased towards the men. She could have any of the men in the nick, why him?

He felt that he owed her one last chance to stop harassing him, out of respect for her as a person and colleague, but he would make damn sure that she understood the consequences of threatening him with inappropriate sexual behaviour. The word rape rang in his ears. Jesus, he was still in shock from her accusation. He looked skywards.

'Why me? Jesus, Mary, and Joseph, why me? An Diabhul is still coming after me; we still have unfinished business.' His thoughts turned to Bree. 'Could she have anything to do with this ... how? NO!' he almost shouted, she was safely locked up at the Lawn's. This was between him and An Diabhul and no-one else.

CHAPTER 15

"I am really starting to lose faith in the human race."
Unknown

He quickly dressed and headed out the door. Keys jangling in his pocket, he had decided to walk as it wasn't very far, that way he could say his piece and leave quickly and disappear down side streets if she decided to follow him. At least he was meeting her in a public place, and he knew the landlord; he would get there early and ask him to keep an eye on them, so that he had a witness if he needed it. He tried to see through the window, and he was shocked to see her already inside with several others from work. She was sat next to DC Jason Short; the one who had walked in on the little scenario in the toilet. Could he be part of this? Was it a conspiracy against him? Was he going mad? He felt at this moment in time as if he was in a bloody nightmare that he so desperately wanted to wake up from.

Entering the room, he saw DC Short stand up and move away from DS Dyson, looking at Steve the whole time with an inscrutable look on his face. Steve was beginning to wonder what the agenda was here. Did DC Jason Short have feelings for Sara? He was beginning to think so!

He sat down, careful to keep his distance. 'What's going on, Sara, why are all the squad in here watching this little scene play out and what the fuck is going on? Is it some kind of a joke that you all have got going? If so, it's not bloody funny; or maybe you all got bets on who can wind up the Gov quickest, eh?'

She looked up at him, smiling, and reached across and kissed him right there in front of them all. Steve was far beyond anger now and shoved her roughly away. Gripping her arms tightly he leant into her face and snarled. 'I'm not sure what your little game is, you bitch, but it stops right now; do you hear me? NOW!'

He ground his teeth in anger, and he had not realised that he was still gripping her arms tightly. 'I'm sorry, Steve, I won't do that again, please darling you are hurting me, let me go please.'

Unknown to Steve, DC Short had approached quietly from behind. 'I suggest that you let her go, Gov.'

He seemed to come back to his senses and dropped her arms quickly. Horrified at what had just happened, he turned and ran from the pub. He looked back as he passed through the entranceway to see Sara, her face turned towards him smiling, and DC Short with his arm comfortingly around her shoulders. He watched as she gave him one last look then turned back into DC Short's arms, weeping. He felt rather than saw all of the horrified eyes upon him as he left. 'Oh God, what a fucking mess.' He ran and ran, not really taking any notice of where he was going and found himself one street away from home. Thoughts were running through his head; 'I really must be going crazy, what just happened? Did I really hurt Sara? In front of at least ten witnesses too, how the hell could I have been so stupid. I have never hurt a woman in my life, what is happening to me?'

Actually you tried to strangle Meg a few weeks ago, a small voice at the back of his mind reminded him. The panic attack hit him full force in the chest; it was much stronger and faster than anything that he had experienced so far. Falling to his knees he keeled over, his vision blurred as if he was about to pass out, but instead he felt a strong grip pull him up and help him along the street to his door. As if from a distance he heard someone mention his key and the next thing he knew he was being laid on the bed by two people. 'Thanks Jason, I can manage him now, he will be fine in the morning. It's just the trauma he has been suffering so much lately.'

'Are you sure you will be alright with him, Sara? He hurt you earlier on. I don't like leaving you here with him like that.'

'No, really, just go; I will see you tomorrow, it's fine.'

Steve felt like he was drugged. He could hear voices talking far away as if from a distance, but all he wanted to do was close his eyes and sleep. He closed his eyes and was oblivious to the person climbing into bed next to him as his mind took him to a very dark place.

He woke shouting and clawing at the covers. Dawn's light was just beginning to crawl along the window blind, and he felt someone stir next to him. Meg? But where was he? He felt confused and his thoughts were jumbled as he turned over; he looked straight into the eyes of Sara.

'Good morning, darling, I hope you slept well? I have got the coffee on; but I have got to rush. I need a shower and a change of clothes before work, especially underwear. God you were sexy as hell last night … an animal. I think you tore my pants as they came off you couldn't wait. See you later, darling.' She stood, wriggled her fingers in a wave of her hand and disappeared. Steve rolled onto his back, his mouth open in a half scream of horror.

Groaning, Steve swung his legs around to the side of the bed and with his feet firmly placed on the floor he ran to the bathroom and vomited. After a hot shower he returned to dress in the bedroom. Suddenly he started to tear the covers off of his bed, ripping and pulling he didn't care if they tore, he just wanted to clean away any trace of Sara. Throwing the sheets into the washing machine he put it on the hottest wash that he could and returned to dress. Opening up his wardrobe his nostrils were assaulted by a strong overpowering perfume; he recognised it at once as a favourite of Sara's. It definitely wasn't Meg's; she didn't wear perfume often and tended to stick to the little sprays of organic oils from her herbal shop. Lifting his suit from the hanger he smelled it, everything was covered in the cloying scent; all of his jackets and trousers stank. He pulled them all out angrily. He would have to drop all of his suits into the cleaners; his jeans and underwear, shirts and socks, he could wash himself. That would mean that he would have to wear the same clothes that he wore yesterday or fish out a nearly clean shirt and pants from the laundry basket. He was beginning to get really angry again and he didn't want to let what happened last night happen again. How the hell did he get so out of it that he didn't know how he got home or remember sleeping with Sara? As soon as was reasonably possible he rang Dr Watson's office and said that he needed to see her urgently. Thankfully she was able to squeeze him in before her day began and at eight thirty promptly he found himself outside of her office door waiting to be let in after he had rung the bell.

Looking at a rather dishevelled detective in front of her, the doctor wondered what had happened to him and soon she was to hear the whole sorry tale. Steve spoke in a monotone, reeling out everything that had happened to him since Sara had barged into the toilet stall in the bathroom at work till he had awoken that morning to her lying in his bed next to him. 'I just don't know how she got there, Doc, I don't remember anything after I confronted her at the pub. What is happening to me? Please, help me, Doc, am I going mad?'

'No, I don't think that you are going mad, Steve, but I can easily see why you would think that you were. I think that you had some sort of shut down because of the shock of Sara's revelations on top of what you have already been through. What is concerning me the most is the amnesia. There are two scenarios here, Steve; one is that you were having a relationship with Sara and you have forced yourself to forget because of the trauma surrounding Bree and your mind was unable to process your feelings for both Meg and Sara. Or she is telling lies for some unknown reason and is setting you up whilst you are vulnerable as pay back for what she perceives as a rejection by you, to her. You say that you do remember eighteen months ago kissing her at a Christmas party? Are you positive that you didn't follow up on that kiss and enter into any kind of relationship with Sara?'

'No, I don't think so ... I only remember the kiss; it was a drunken fumble with a colleague ... I was lonely for Christ sake ... doesn't that happen all the time?'

'And of course the night that you described as the pizza delivery; I believe that you told me that you kissed her then and almost had sex with her and would have if the pizza delivery had not interrupted you. I have to ask this next question, Steve, and I know that you are not going to like me for asking it ... but did you at any time have sex with DS Dyson at the Christmas party or anytime afterwards? And did you enter into any kind of a relationship with her at any point since? You have been working together over the last two years. By relationship, I don't just mean a sexual relationship.'

'No, I swear, Dr Watson, I have never to my knowledge had sex with or a relationship with DS Dyson except as a colleague and friend at work.'

'There lies the problem, Steve, "to your knowledge", but last night you don't remember how she came to be in your bed.'

Steve put his head in his hands. The impact of what the doctor had just said hit him like a ton of bricks. Of course, from a copper's point of view, it was his word against hers and in the state of mind that he was in, he couldn't prove it either.

'She told me that she kept the clothes from that night and would accuse me of rape if I didn't have a relationship with her. Honest, Doc, she is just a lying bitch, why would she do this to me?'

'The old saying "hell hath no fury like a woman scorned" springs to mind, I can't tell you what to do but I seriously suggest that you go from here straight to your boss and tell him everything that you have told me here today. I think that you need to do that to protect yourself from what inevitably will come. I will also give you some stronger pills to help with the extra stress that you are under, and my advice is to be very careful not to be left alone with Sara for her sake as well as your own.'

'You think I'm lying, don't you, Doc? You think I had sex with her, don't you?' he sneered. 'Well, I am not that kind of man and I love Meg and wouldn't do anything to hurt her.'

'I don't think that you are lying, Steve, but you may not be remembering things accurately at the moment.'

CHAPTER 16

"Life is not fair, get used to it."

Bill Gates

Steve slunk into the office trying to avoid Sara and of course everyone else, who all now thought that he was a woman beater, cheat, and a rapist. As he was nearly at the door to his office, the chief popped his head out of his own door. 'Got a minute, Steve, I have something important to discuss with you?' He looked towards him, he was giving nothing away with his facial expression. Oh well, this is it, he thought, she has already accused me of all sorts of shit and I am about to lose it all. He turned and walked towards the chief, nodding his head in acknowledgement. He passed into the room expecting to be asked to hand over his badge and be told that the professional standards would be contacting him. He started to try and explain but before he could open his mouth the chief asked him to take a seat and went on quickly to explain that Sean O'Dowd had contacted him and requested that Steve come over to Ireland as a liaison officer; apparently the Garda had unearthed some more information concerning the case in Bally-Bay. 'As you are already familiar with the case and the area, he suggested that you go over to help him set up a small task force to investigate. How do you feel, Steve? Is it too close to home for you, and do you feel up to a full investigation of this sort? We can spare you if you wish to go out and help. It seems to me that you are the perfect choice for the job.'

Steve was dumbstruck, he was expecting anything but that and he quickly said yes. This could be a chance to escape from Sara and give himself time to think. Good old Sean, always there when he needed him but this time he didn't even know that he had saved him. He quickly stood and asked, 'When is he expecting me? I can have my desk cleared by the end of day and over there by tomorrow evening, sir.'

'Great, no rush; it is a cold case after all, just make sure that everyone here is up to date on what is going on and then you are free to leave when you wish. Perhaps you will have time to catch up with your mother, I am sure she would welcome a visit.'

The chief nodded at Steve in dismissal. 'Oh, by the way, keep me informed of how things are going out there, DCI Ryan. I expect a weekly telephone call at the least.'

Steve asked everyone to join him in the meeting room and briefly explained that he was going to be away working with the Dublin City Garda as a liaison for an indefinite period of time and that he knew they were all capable of managing without him and to talk to the chief if there were any problems, who would be arranging for a temporary DCI to take over whilst he was gone. The best bit for Steve was watching Sara's face as he gave out the information. Everything had worked out great, he would be away from her, and everything would be ok. No need to talk to the boss and hopefully it would just disappear on its own while he was gone. He was going to ask Meg to join him, they could stay at Mammy's, and she could see her aunt Sian too. Yes, he was happy, but the look on Sara's face said that she was not, and he was glad that he was leaving quickly so that she couldn't spread her lies to his colleagues anymore, or more to the point tell Meg.

He spent most of the afternoon on the phone to Sean and his Mammy making arrangements with them both. He wanted to talk to Meg tonight first, before he booked the flights, as he hoped that she would be as excited as him about going home. Yes, that is what he felt! He was going home, he had run away to try and escape the horror of that night in the church and now he had been away too long. It was way past time that he laid that Diabhul to rest and got on with his life. He cleared his paperwork and his desk ready for the temporary DCI and grabbing his jacket from the back of the chair he practically ran out of the building. Rather than wait for the lift he decided to race down the stairs to the car park. Just as he was within sight of his car, he felt his arm being pulled. Turning he looked at Sara's face, she practically spat her words at him. 'You think this is over, Steve, then think again. I will always be there, so you had better keep looking over your shoulder; you think you are so clever, don't you?'

Steve pulled his arm away from her grip. 'I suggest that you go and visit a doctor to help you with these delusions that you are having about me, Sara. I am glad I haven't got to look at your snivelling face for a while because it makes me want to puke.'

He knew that he shouldn't have said what he did but she didn't get to make his life hell without some consequences, the bitch. He climbed into his car and without a glance back at her he drove away. Thoughts of Meg filled his mind as he drove; he would need to persuade her to come with him, or he would probably lose her for good. This way nobody need know about what Sara had been doing, he may even ask for a transfer to Ireland if Meg was agreeable and then he need never see her again. He smiled as he drove home, calling Meg on the way to ask if she would care to join him for dinner tonight at his flat.

He wasn't great at cooking, but he had managed to cobble together a spaghetti Bolognese that any bachelor would be proud to present to his lady and he had a bottle of red breathing nicely of the kitchen side. He was just pulling on a t-shirt as the doorbell rang. Meg stood on the step looking as beautiful as ever in a summer dress, her bare arms were now brown, her shoulders and face sun-kissed and he knew exactly where her tan lines were. He hoped that he would have time to trace his fingers over them later and that she wouldn't have to hurry home.

'A mhuirni'n you are so beautiful.' He scooped her up into his arms and his mouth found hers as willing and eager to meet his own. After they had eaten, he broached the subject of Ireland with Meg.

'It would be great if you could come too, we could stay with Mammy, and you could visit your aunt Sian. What do you say? It will give us all a break; although I must admit I am not looking forward to what Sean has found out, or what the investigative team will be looking at. I wanted to talk to you first. I would rather not go if you don't want to come.'

Meg smiled up at him; it lit up her green eyes and his heart hurt with a physical pain as he looked at her. Oh mother Mary and Jesus please make this thing with Sara go away. He couldn't bear it if Meg got hurt again and he was the cause of it.

'What a fantastic idea; I was only talking to Romany about visiting aunt Sian and the cousins the other night. School finishes for me next week and Romany has finished all of her exams. I will run it by her but yes! Oh yes that would be lovely. I can get to know your mammy too.' Meg flung her arms around his neck, and he couldn't help smiling to himself. Maybe there is a God after all, he thought. He saw Meg to the door of her car and watched her drive away, the night was clear, and a thousand stars lit the sky. He took a deep breath and let it out slowly, hopefully he could hold back a couple of days and they could all fly out together on the following weekend. He had a few things to arrange anyway, and he promised Meg that he would arrange for all of her furniture to be moved into storage so that Becky and the boys could move into her house whenever she was ready.

The school holiday was what they had agreed on and it would leave it empty for when they were ready. He also needed to ring Sean in the morning to confirm that he was coming over, bringing Meg and Romany would be a surprise for him. He turned to walk back into the door and a sound across the road, at the entrance to an alleyway, caught his attention; he turned quickly just in time to see a figure running down the street. It was hard to make out if it was male or female, but he had a clear idea of who it was. He needed to be more careful, she was obviously following and watching him. Maybe he should give his boss a call and have a chat anyway; at least he would cover himself if there was an enquiry.

The next morning, he indulged himself in a lie in. After getting dressed in an old jogging suit he tackled his list of jobs. First on the list was to get his clothes laundered and his suits off to the dry cleaners as he needed them back in a few days' time. He had wrapped them all in black bin liners to hide the stench and he was ready to explain if Meg had asked about the new fresh air spray that broke and squirted everywhere, but she was too busy getting excited about the trip to Bally-Bay to even notice. He bundled the suits into the car and after dropping them off he got himself a bacon roll and a coffee from the little stall in the park entrance and sitting in a quiet corner on a bench he rang Sean. It was so good to hear his friend's voice that he almost choked up with emotion as Sean's deep baritone voice answered, 'Detective Chief Inspector O'Dowd speaking, how can I help yer?'

'Sean, it's Steve. I am so happy to hear your voice, man; how on earth did you manage to wriggle this one to get me back to Ireland? I reckon it's a conspiracy with Meg, she is over excited at coming over to see her family.'

'Ah Steve I had no qualms about asking for your help on this one. I need a good detective, but I also need someone that I can rely on to have my back, and is familiar with the case; to be sure it's a nasty one. I am already being pressured to sweep it under the rug and not make waves. That's why I need your integrity. It's to do with some information that has come to light that we have found in the records from St Theresa's. There are a lot of inconsistencies of mother's records and babies' births and … deaths.'

'Well that doesn't surprise me, look at how hard it was to find any kind of records in Bree's case. They probably didn't keep any; they didn't want anyone to know what was really going on there.'

'That is just the problem, the inconsistencies are documented well and it relates to the deaths of mothers and babies over a twenty-year period and if you take into account the rates of mother and infant mortality in general over that time, it seems extremely high. At the moment I am getting the team to contact each and every family on the records in the hope of finding them alive and well. There are hundreds, I warn you, but it isn't looking good, and we have only got through a few years so far. That's why I need your help; how soon can you get here?'

'I will be flying out at the weekend, give me chance to settle Meg and Romany at Mammy's and we can start fresh on Monday morning if that is ok with you?'

'Great I can't wait to see you.' Steve hung up the phone and after ringing his mammy he felt happy; she was so pleased that they were coming to stay and couldn't wait to see them all. He breathed in the fresh air deeply. He hadn't felt so good in a long time and, as he had nothing else to do for the rest of the day, he leaned back on the bench and closed his eyes. He felt the sun warming his face and he felt his shoulders relaxing. He hadn't realised how tense he had become, alert to every shadow and sound. Now he could feel himself relax back into the bench. He hoped, and yes even prayed, that at last he could enjoy his life. He had found someone to share it with and he no longer felt the need to just survive and function. He wanted to have everything that he had missed with his new family and the woman that he loved.

He felt rather than saw a shadow fall over his face. 'Damn the sun's gone in,' he mumbled; but on opening his eyes he saw Sara stood over him. The hatred in her eyes almost equalled Bree's in intensity. Why oh why did he seem to collect these bloody women?

They were like a burr stuck in his clothing, a splinter in his finger. What he had been through had taught him one thing, that although they were irritating, they were also bloody dangerous and to never ever underestimate them.

'What do you want, Sara? I am going away, isn't that enough? I am getting out of your hair, as obviously I annoy you as much as you do me. So just what is it that you want from me?'

"What do I want? Now let me see, how about an apology? Or even some respect for the way that I have watched you fawn all over another woman or taken shit from you for months. Maybe I want to understand why you are denying that we had a relationship; or maybe it's because I hate your fucking guts, Steve Ryan, and that you have treated me like shit and now it's payback time.'

She stepped back, her hands on her hips, glaring at him.

'I don't have a fucking clue where you are coming from; you are obviously very sick, and you need help. Sara, for the last time, I have never slept with you. I have never even thought about you as anything other than a colleague. I admit that I was stupid the other night when I kissed you, but I was in a very vulnerable place. For that I apologise, but the rest is all in your head. Can't you see that? Please just piss off and leave me alone.'

'Leave you alone … oh no, Steve, you don't get to walk away from me that easily. You will find out just how persistent I can be, run as far away as you like, and I will find a way to follow until you admit that you are mine.'

Sara stalked off and Steve hung his head in his hands, a feeling of dread in his stomach; he didn't think that she would ever give up. 'What the hell am I going to do now? What if Meg finds out? Oh god, what have I ever done to deserve this?'

CHAPTER 17

"The best way to find yourself, is to lose yourself in the service of others."
Mahatma Gandhi

Meg hurried around the house grabbing bits of clothing and throwing them either at Romany or into a suitcase that already seemed over-full. 'Mum, I can't shut the lid of my suitcase,' Romany called out.

'I seem to be having the same problem,' Meg laughed. 'We are only staying for a few weeks, and we can always buy more out there. It will be fun to go shopping with Aunt Sian and Cass. We can make a day of it, maybe even stop the night in Dublin, just us girls. Oh I am so looking forward to seeing everyone.' Romany just grunted and groaned as Meg slid the zip up on her own case, she then went next door to help Romany do the same. 'Don't overload it, darling, you may have to put your art stuff and sketch books into your carry-on bag. Do you really need all of this stuff? You have more than me and that's saying something.' They giggled as Romany fell onto the bed as she gave one last heave on the case zip, not expecting it to suddenly move.

Steve arrived and carrying the girl's cases down the stairs he gasped as he lifted them. 'Mary mother and Joseph what have you got it here for god's sake ... a body? I will do me back in and be no use to anyone.'

This made them all laugh together and with the help of the taxi driver they eventually set off for the airport. Saturdays were always busy but soon they were settled in their seats about to take off. Steve looked at the two girls sat next to him and sighed with relief that they were all safe, well, and hopefully starting a new adventure together. But best of all he was leaving Sara Dyson behind him. The flight was short and definitely worth it; much better than struggling with the ferry and then a long drive. Steve had decided that he could use his mammy's car and hire one for Meg for the duration. Most of the costs would be covered under the liaison so it made more sense to just fly out. Before they knew it, they were landing in Knock airport and in the hire car driving on the motorway towards the coast and Bally-Bay.

Romany looked out of the window, keeping up a stream of chatter as they went. Her artist eye caught the stunning scenery, and she couldn't wait to draw and paint the landscape. She visibly gasped and so did Meg as the sight of Bally-Bay came into view; it was laid out before them in a blue arc. 'I had forgotten how beautiful this part of the country is, it takes your breath away.' The pretty coloured cottages seemed to tumble down the hill into the sea and the sun sparkled off of the water. The fishing boats bobbed up and down in the breeze, enclosing it all was the grey stone wall of the harbour. Without realising how tense he had been, Steve let out a deep sigh as the turning into the lane that led to the farmhouse came into sight. Home at last. He looked up as he pulled the car around in front of the house to see a small figure waving at them from the doorway. He climbed out and drawing her into his arms he whispered, 'Mammy, I'm home,' as he sunk into her arms. She was dwarfed by her tall handsome son.

Bustling around, Bridget Ryan soon had them all settled and Romany, excited at the view from her bedroom window, decided to go for a walk whilst the adults made tea.

'Don't be long, dusk is settling and the Sidhe' will be out dancing before long,' Bridget called after her.

'Mammy, don't scare the girl with silly folktales.' Steve hugged her tight.

'I don't know what you mean, Steven, the little folk are very active after dark; that's why I never go out at night.' He laughed even harder as his mammy pulled away from his arms with a huff and a stern look on her face. 'It seems that you have been away far too long,' she replied.

Romany and Meg turned and smiled at each other, suppressing a giggle or two. 'I might just come with you, it's a little late to visit Aunt Sian, we can do that tomorrow. In the meantime, I would like to stretch my legs and I am sure that Steve and Bridget have a lot to catch up on.' The girls left and after the door had closed Steve watched as his mammy made the tea. He sat at the old wooden table in the kitchen, its surface bleached from many years of scrubbing and cleaning. He relaxed as the old familiar smells assaulted his nostrils; of freshly baked bread, roasted meats, and the sweet smell of beeswax polish coming from the gleaming furniture. 'Oh, it's so good to be home.'

He stretched his legs and placing a large pot of tea on the table his mammy said, 'Not soon enough by the look of your face, you have lost a lot of weight, by the look of yer I need to feed yer up.' She confirmed her thoughts on the matter by shoving a large plate of freshly baked biscuits towards him. He laughed again and grabbed one from the plate.

'Well I won't have lost it for very long if these are anything to go by. Thank you, Mammy I needed to come home.'

'I can see that in your face, Steven; you look worse than the last time I saw yer and don't speak with yer mouth full.'

'Well thanks Mammy, I am forty-five now!' He smiled to himself. 'And I have to admit I have been having some problems, but nothing that your home cooking and some fresh sea air can't mend.'

As they settled into the old familiar feeling of comfort at being together again, Steve broached the reason for him being home here in Ireland, especially being here in Bally-Bay.

'I am afraid it's not good news, Mammy, I will be stirring up old ghosts that I am sure a lot of people would wish to remain buried, but things have come to light concerning St Theresa's and I am going to be working with Sean to uncover some more truths.'

His mother looked at him with concern in her eyes. 'Are you sure that you want to be doing that, Steven, after what has just happened? Do you think that you will cope as everything is still so raw for you?'

'That's why I need to do this, Mammy, I have to see it through to the end. Wherever that might take me, I have to follow … I have to go there for the sake of all the other girls like you.'

'You're a good man, Steven, but that is what you are; only a man. Please I beg of you, son, be careful not to break your heart or Meg's, nobody ever really escapes from an Diabhul once he has touched your coat tails; no matter how fast yer run.'

Just then the girls bustled back through the door. 'That was timely,' he thought, 'I really didn't want to tell Mammy too much, she is still in shock about Bree; also she can see right through me as if I was naked and I don't want her worrying about me.' He kissed Meg's cheek and, as if nothing had happened, he picked up the tea pot. 'I will warm up the tea. Did the faeries chase yer home, I can see the sun has set?' They all laughed then, including Bridget.

After dinner they all settled into an early night, surprised at how exhausted they felt. 'That's the good sea air for yer. You wait till the wind turns and the tide is out, that harbour stinks. Daddy would make me come with him on the cart to gather the seaweed when the tide was out to put on the fields as manure. God I used to heave with the stench of it … he used to give me a mint from his pocket to help.'

Steve smiled wistfully as he thought about his daddy and then, as if struck, he remembered that he wasn't really his daddy. He had found out when he had been involved in Bree's investigation. The circumstances of his birth weighed heavy on his mind quite often lately, and he wondered if Bree had, had the same chances as he how very different things might have been. He still couldn't understand how his adoptive father could have refused to take both of the babies and leave Bree behind to suffer … Yes he was the lucky one and he had loved his father very much … he just didn't know him as well as he thought he did.

Climbing into bed he turned to take Meg into his arms. 'Are you ok. a mhuirni'n? At least we have tomorrow together before I have to go to work. I am just worried that you will both be bored to tears, there isn't a lot to do in Bally-Bay.'

'I am excited, Steve, I can't wait to see Aunty Sian and I have to visit William in County Mayo and Cassandra in Dublin. We have already planned a huge shopping trip.'

'Oh no I don't think my back will take it if there is more luggage to carry.'

The next day rushed by, they walked into the village and called on Aunty Sian and Uncle John. After the tea was brewed, they settled under a tree in the garden and Romany, enchanted with the amazing floral display, got out her sketch book. Watching her wistfully Sian murmured, 'Just like her grandma, Magda was always drawing, she was so artistic and I can see that Romany has inherited her talent.'

'I can see your talent for gardening. I remember how lovely the garden looked when I was last here, I am sorry that it was under such awful circumstances.' Steve held onto Sian's hand a little longer. Remembering the guilt he felt at asking her the most personal questions about her sister Magda and why he was here again in Bally-Bay.

'Why are you all over here anyway? Not that it's not a lovely surprise for us all,' John asked.

'Well, the girls are here for fun and shopping, and I am here for work. I have been asked to form a task force with my friend Sean from Dublin when more records concerning St. Theresa's turned up. Apparently, there are some quite significant anomalies concerning records of the girl's births and deaths. I am sorry to be still delving into the past, but the girls deserve respect and justice for what happened here and all over this bloody country. Sorry about that, let's change the subject.'

Sian turned, fussing with the tea and cakes, but Steve could see that she visibly paled as he talked about St Theresa's. 'I am not surprised,' he thought, this must be hard for all the people who live here, knowing now what went on behind those grey stone walls.

The afternoon was pleasant and reluctantly they all stood up to leave. Romany, packing away her paints and sketches, stood and sighed. She too was enjoying the outside and the fresh sea air. Meg looked at her and hoped that this time together would heal them all. Shaking hands with John, Steve heard him whisper, 'Walk with me a while, will yer?' As they left the girls to pack up the tea things and chairs, he looked at John with concern. 'Do yer realise just what a cess pit yer will stir up, Steve? I hope that yer are ready for what yer find. There are a few people who would wish that certain things stay buried; I don't suppose that is possible now?'

'I know, John. I will try and make sure that the greatest respect to everyone concerned is given; but I also will not stop until every stone is turned and everyone involved who is still living is brought to justice, and those now dead named and shamed … that is the least they all deserve.'

Leaving with a wave they climbed the road leading out of the village, at the top of the hill they turned to see the brilliant blue sky starting to turn to orange and pink. 'Come on, we better cut across the fields. It will be dark soon and I don't want Mammy thinking that we have been taken by the Sidhe' en-route.' Steve climbed through the old gap in the hedge, pleased to see it still there. Many a time when he was late, he had squeezed through this same gap and dashed across the fields towards home, knowing his arse would sting from his mammy's slap if he was a minute late. He made a run for the faery thorn on top of the hill where his father's grave now rested and turned, calling encouragement to Romany and Meg. Puffing and panting they tumbled through the back door. Bridget stood with arms folded, a smile playing on her lips.

'Tardy as always, Steven, was an Diabhul on yer heels?'

'Ay Mammy and he almost caught us.' He made a grabbing motion towards Romany and Meg and they jumped and shrieked with laughter.

'Sorry we stayed so long, time just ran away with us, it was so lovely to catch up with Aunt Sian and remind us all of Mammy.'

'Nonsense love; your mammy was a good woman and of course you want time with your family. Come on, Romany, perhaps you can help me lay the table for dinner.'

They all entered the kitchen and the warmth of the place and the smell of something delicious hit their noses. 'Aw! Mammy you haven't ... not my favourite.'

The girls looked at each other and both together uttered, 'Irish stew.'

CHAPTER 18

"The evil that men do lives after them; the good is oft interred with their bones."
William Shakespeare

Steve set off early the next morning for the long drive to Dublin to meet Sean and his team. Arriving at the Garda station it brought back memories of when he had sat and trawled for hours through the musty boxes of records from St. Theresa's. He wondered what poor sod had done the same to find the information that so concerned his friend. He went through and Sean was waiting with coffee in hand and a huge hug. 'Man, it's good to see you, let me take your coat and bring you up to speed on the case so far. Then we will have a meet, and I can introduce you to the team. Not that it's much of one because it's a cold case. I have only been allowed a couple of constables and yourself, as your end are paying. When we are all together, we can see what the latest updates from the weekend bring.'

Settling into a chair behind his desk and Steve ensconced the other side, Sean looked to his friend and asked, 'Well how are yer feeling? Are yer sure you are up to this? It looks so far to be a really nasty case and I know how close you are to all of this. To be honest that is why I wanted you as I have already had a bit of opposition to me looking at the records already. The church is worried and my Gov of course goes to all of the charity functions etc. They certainly do not like me stirring up all the shite from the bottom of the bucket.'

'Well, what did you expect? Anything to do with St Theresa's that turns up, shit seems to follow.'

'Well this time it's really nasty, not that it wasn't a sorry business before; but a young garda was assigned to finish the job of putting all of those records onto a digital format. As you know, Steve, young Collum O'Brian was tasked with the job originally, before his death. And this young fella is a sharp young man, and he noticed some discrepancies among the records for girls entering into St Theresa's and the number of girls leaving. He also noticed that the death rate for the babies was extremely high. He brought it to my attention, and we have been trying discreetly to trace all of the young women involved back over the last twenty years; records stopped in nineteen ninety when the place burned down. That is as far as I am allowed to go at the moment. As you can imagine we have had a lot of stonewalling from the families and of course the women themselves, as they don't want their new lives interrupted. The outcome has been, as you can imagine, exhausting and we are being put under pressure to sweep it back under the carpet. What it has shown so far is that a lot of these girls never returned home again, and we are barely scratching the surface.' Sean rested to catch his breath.

'So what you are saying is that some of the girls died in suspicious circumstances, as did the babies? Are we talking murder, neglect, or what?' Steve looked at his friend anxiously.

'What I am thinking is that they might not all of died giving birth … some of the records record deaths before the pregnancy due dates. They kept records as the girls were not part of the orphanage, but they were sent there until they had given birth and then were returned home, leaving their babies behind to be adopted.' Sean sighed. 'The worst part is the amount of babies' deaths recorded before adoption could take place. If you are ready, we will go and see the other part of the team and I will introduce you and see what the weekend turned up.'

They both stood and walked to the incident room that they were using. Steve gasped as his eye travelled along one wall that was being used to place information on. It was covered in pictures of girls from one end to the other. Even Sean looked a bit taken aback as he addressed the room.

'Ladies, gentlemen, this is Detective Chief Inspector Steve Ryan, a dear friend and colleague on loan to us from England. Steve, this is Garda Siobhan Thomas and Garda Connor O'Brian … Collum's brother. He was the sharp young man that I told you about, that discovered this.' He waved his arm and gestured around the room. Steve nodded in acknowledgment. 'What have we found that's new? I can see yer have been busy.' He directed the question to Connor.

'Sir, since Friday we have uncovered at least one hundred and fifty unaccounted for girls and we have barely covered halfway. We are waiting for five more to return calls and we are just about to start on the next five hundred names on the list; but we have identified the names and have pictures for all one hundred and fifty girls up to date.'

Sean and Steve scanned the wall, the faces of the girls staring back at them young and fresh, but their innocence lost. 'I had no idea that it would be on this scale, I think I will have to try and squeeze some more help from my boss. Oh my God, are you sure that you want to deal with this, Steve? I will totally understand if you want to drop out.'

Steve looked at the faces one by one, their eyes stared back at him from their photographs; he could imagine their suffering and he thought of Bree. 'No, they all deserve justice, and we will bloody well make sure that they get it.'

'Well, I think that we need to move the whole team down to Bally-Bay and I have a feeling that forensics are going to be very busy. In the meantime, I will go talk to the boss and see if I can drum up some more help. Good work, Connor and Siobhan; keep going with what you are doing and, Steve, I wonder if you could start to sort what we have on each girl into individual files. We will need family contact details possibly for D.N.A identification. God I can't believe how they got away with it for so long if these numbers are correct. In a way it's a good job that we are only looking at records back to nineteen seventy.' Sean picked up his coffee cup and taking a large swig he raised his mug. 'I had better stick another pot on, I have a feeling it is going to be a very long day and we will need plenty of this.'

Steve smiled at his friend and sighed, oh it felt good to be doing what he did best, especially working with Sean, it brought back memories of years gone by. Walking towards Connor he placed a hand on the young constable's shoulder. He thought about the young Garda that Bree had killed after she had no use for him anymore; and also how she had made his death look like suicide. He was relieved to be able to tell the parents that wasn't the case. Even if he couldn't give them their son back, at least they would know that he died at the hands of someone else. 'Sorry about your brother, he was a good police officer and I hope that your family have found some kind of closure if not comfort in the new information found.'

'Thank you, sir, if it hadn't been for you, my parents would be living in hell. At least you brought them some peace.'

He turned and headed towards the desk that would be his for the next few months. As he turned his back on the room, he felt the weight of a hundred and fifty pairs of eyes reaching out from the photos pinned on the wall and he hoped to God that there were not anymore added to that list but in his heart he knew that would not be the case. A few hours later and he had a large pile of folders teetering on the corner of his desk and Siobhan had added five more photographs to the wall.

Sighing softly, Steve offered to go and fetch sandwiches and coffees for everyone and passed Sean's office. He still wasn't back from his meeting with his superior and Steve thought to himself if they did not allow them extra help they could become overwhelmed with the workload. He knew how they were all tied by budget cuts and of course this was a cold case, what the hell did people care about a few girls who got into trouble years ago? They were still trying to plough their way through all of the names on the list. Which although a very long one already, he didn't want anyone missed. Each and every one of those girls deserved to have some dignity and respect in death ... even if they didn't get it in life.

Once outside he took a deep breath of Irish air, it had been ages since he had walked these streets with Sean, turning the corner he headed for the best little coffee shop in the whole of Dublin, well he thought so. The small bell rang as he opened the door; it was as quaint and old as the shop itself. The smell of delicious things cooking hit his nostrils and he was transported back to 1990 when he worked alongside Sean as his Sergeant long before either made detective and life seemed somehow simpler then. The cases they worked on seemed less serious, a drunken brawl here and there and the odd stabbing but very rarely a murder. He chuckled to himself, not like Father Brown on the TV. Mammy loved that programme and he seemed to be tripping over dead bodies wherever he went on his old black bicycle, his soutane flapping out behind him.

Looking up, the girl behind the counter smiled at him and he looked down. 'Sorry, just reminiscing about the last time that I came in here. Sadly, it was a long time ago, I am happy to see that nothing has changed. These look so good, I don't know what to choose.' He pointed to all of the cakes and pastries behind the glass counter. After making his choices from the array of cakes he added a few sandwiches and the requested coffee. They would need to keep their strength up if this was going to be as bad as he thought. His gut told him that they had barely scratched the surface. Grabbing the paper bag and tray of drinks he made his way quickly back to the station. Meeting Sean at the doorway, grabbing a crafty fag, he said, 'I thought yer gave them up with the drink, they will kill yer just as well.'

'Well I did once but after what the super just told me I bloody needed one. Come on, I will fill yer all in; thank god yer got something to eat, I think we are gonna have a long one; perhaps yer had better ring Meg to tell her you'll be late.'

Steve glanced at his friend as they made their way into the station, taking the stairs two at a time Sean started to wheeze. 'See I told yer they will kill yer.' And he smiled as Sean coughed again. 'I'd pat yer on the back but me hands are a bit full,' he said, brushing past him and through the doorway first. Just like old times, the rivalry between them and the friendship fell easily to them as if they had never been apart.

Once back and the coffee and sandwiches consumed, Sean turned his attention to the board. 'Well, my friends, after a lot of wrangling, bowing. and scraping to the chief. he has kindly agreed for us to have some help, another constable will be joining us temporarily tomorrow. Just till the end of the week when he hopes that we may be more clear on what exactly we are dealing with. So, what has been happening since I seem to have wasted a whole morning? The chief, as you can gather, wishes that the whole bloody thing would just go away so he is not allowing any wasted resources, or over time on this … so I expect you all to give it the best shot we can. We can look at what other resources will be needed, such as forensics etc., after we know what we are up against. Right let's get cracking!'

Sean looked at the pile of folders mounting on Steve's desk and picking one up he looked at the picture of the young, fresh-faced girl staring back at him. 'We need to do this, don't we, Steve? We need to go back and sort it once and for all? So everyone can get some peace.'

'Yes, we do, I shouldn't have left it last time and I am forever sorry for that, maybe I could have saved everyone a lot of grief and hurt.'

'Yer couldn't have done anything, man, you were just a kid, don't blame yerself now. Let's do this together as friends and bloody good detectives I might add.'

Sean laughed at his own joke, but Steve was lost in thought, still in the past, in a church in Bally-Bay.

'I don't think we will get any help from above, but perhaps a higher being will lend a hand, yer never know.'

Sean made the sign of the cross on his body and Steve laughed.

'I think yer will be outa luck if yer are relying on that kinda help now.'

The day was long and before they all left to get some sleep, sadly ten other faces had been added to the wall. Ten more beautiful girls with smiling faces, with all of their lives ahead of them, stared back out at the team as they turned off the lights and left the building. One hundred and sixty-two beautiful young girls on the cusp of womanhood, sadly to be joined by others tomorrow and probably more the next day too.

CHAPTER 19

"Justice is truth in action."

Benjamin Disraeli

Sean and Steve, along with their small team made up of Connor, Siobhan, and the constable on loan for the week, ploughed through the names on the original list of records. It was mind-numbing work and each and every day they all left exhausted and drained. Each day Sean and Steve reminded the team that each and every one of those names belonged to a person, a girl who had a family, someone's daughter or sister lost forever. Steve was very quiet when he got home, and his mammy noticed before Meg, who, with Romany, was enjoying the time relaxing with her family. Catching him at a quiet moment she asked, 'Are you alright, son? I know this business with St Theresa's is like opening a door that you thought that you had closed a long time ago.'

'Ah mammy I wish I could slam it shut again but those girls' faces haunt me every night; I know that it will remain open till every last one of them have been laid to rest and justice is seen to be done for them. I also know that is not going to be an easy thing to find for them, but I promise you I will do it or die trying.'

The weekend whizzed by and although he seemed a bit distant, Meg hardly noticed. She was so excited to be going to Dublin shopping next week with Cassandra and Aunt Sian that they had talked about nothing else all weekend. 'We plan on doing some sight-seeing while we are there, and Cassie has managed to get us some overnight room's right in the thick of it. Romany has a list of places to visit as long as your arm. I am sorry that you are working, darling; I so wish that you could join us.'

'You go ahead and enjoy yerselves up there with the Jackeen, just bring me back some of the black stuff. I pass the brewery every time I come in to work and never have been for a look-see.'

'I swear that your lovely Irish lilt is growing stronger by the day; I think it is very sexy,' Meg whispered in his ear. At least he left her with a smile on his face; she was worried about him. He hadn't wanted to talk to her about the case, or anything else for that matter. As usual he was holding it all in. After these few days away with the girls she would try to get a couple of hours on their own and talk to him. They had been rushing about here there and everywhere ever since they had touched Irish soil.

Steve arrived just as Sean entered the carpark and they walked in together. 'What do you think; will we be setting up in Bally-Bay by the end of the week?' Steve asked.

'Possibly. I want to get through these names before I go to the boss and start asking for geo equipment and full on forensics. Do you think you could take a few of the names from the top of the list and go to St Theresa's and just have a look at any names on headstones that might be any of our girls? It might help to see if they are in a different area. At least if they are, we will know where to start looking for remains.'

'I will go in the morning before I come in, because Meg is away having a bit of craic with the girls here in Dublin for a few nights. That way she will not know what I am up to. I am trying to keep the worst of what we suspect away from them all, especially Mammy, although she knows exactly what is going on. It is as much about justice for her as it is for the other girls.'

They settled in for the rest of the day, working their way through the list of girls whilst Sean checked with relatives whether the name on the list was alive or dead, or even worse, never heard of again. At four thirty Sean stretched and called out, 'Right, catch up time people; let's see where we all stand now at the end of day.'

Steve placed the latest file on his desk. He had made three distinct piles, one consisted of alive and well. He liked that pile best. The second were dead but known cause of death after the years at St Theresa's. The third, the largest of them all, were girls unaccounted for only in the records of St Theresa's listed as death due to childbirth. And every single one of them had no records from before; no relatives or addresses; just names on a list. He began to wonder if they even existed at all. Turning his attention to the room, he grabbed the pile of missing and unaccounted for girls. Plonking the pile down in front of him he looked to Sean and the others, each seemed to bring to the table a pile of folders as large as or even bigger than his own pile.

'Well let's start with Connor.' Sean waved his arm in the direction of the young constable.

'Sir, as you know, I was continuing to look through the original files, trying to identify any of the girls that seemed to have died before giving birth that didn't cross reference with any birth records from the babies. So far we have identified sixty-seven more names, they have been added to the board.'

'Thank you, Connor. Siobhan what have you got for us?' Sean asked the pretty police constable that had quietly worked away in the corner all day. 'At least your pile of folders seems smaller than the others.' He winked at her. 'Please give us some good news.'

Siobhan stood. 'Sorry sir, in a way my pile is the worst as these are the girls that actually gave birth and their babies were found and accounted for in the adoption files, but they disappear from any records after the birth. There are twenty-seven so far; the worst of it is their relatives never heard from them again. They all presumed that they had run away because of the shame of the pregnancy, and I can find no trace of them on any records or data bases in the following years, after their initial entry into St Theresa's.

Sean and Steve both looked shocked. '"Twenty-seven you say? And are they all accounted for on the board?'

'No sir I was going to put them up on a separate board as we know these ones actually existed and gave birth to healthy babies that were then adopted.' Siobhan pointed to a new board set up at the end of the room. Steve took his turn and stood pointing to the largest pile of all as he spoke.

'Added to this pile I have managed to whittle mine down to the original one hundred and fifty-five unaccounted girls from the board. I have seven deaths from natural causes that have happened over the ensuing years and best of all sixty lovely ladies alive and well,' he said, pointing to the middle-sized pile on his desk.

The shock on Sean's face was clear as all of them reacted to the news that they may be dealing with almost two hundred girls.

Steve turned his chair to look at the faces staring back at him. 'At first, I thought maybe it was a scam … a way of them making money; if they were paid per girl, had these been made up names to fleece the parish of some money? But all of those faces have a name and a story to tell; we are just going to have to listen to them all and find out the truth of the matter.'

'I just don't know how I am going to explain the enormity of what we have uncovered to the boss. All I know is that he is not gonna like it. Right, well done everyone, some good work done; I suggest we have a good night's sleep and see you all in the morning.'

Steve stood, he stretched his long legs. If he got moving, he could be back home before nightfall; he could go checkout the small graveyard at the back of St Theresa's tonight if he hurried.

Detective Sergeant Sara Dyson placed the receiver back on the telephone on her desk. The conversation she had just had with the Detective in charge of the murder case in Bristol had received all of the documents from Steve concerning Magda's part played in the murder of the drug addict in the alley way. They had her confession to being in the place at the right time, it fit perfectly. They had not managed to retrieve the sweatshirt from the bin that she had been wearing as it had long gone. The only discrepancy was that she had not been charged with the murder. He was wondering if Steve could visit Magda and if he thought that she was able to understand then charge her with the murder. He would send over the file with the victim's name in and all autopsy photos etc. Sarah didn't tell him that Steve was no longer here but seconded to another case. Her curiosity had got the better of her and she was going to ask the boss in the morning if she could do the visit. After all, her and Magda had something in common: they both hated Steve bloody Ryan.

She had loved him at one point but now her desire for the man had waned. He had treated her with contempt for the last time. Leaving her before they could resolve the issues she had over his mistreatment of her. He thought he was being so clever when he took the job in Ireland, to be honest she thought he had escaped her reaches for the time being and was biding her time, knowing that he would have to come back one day.

The next morning, after overhearing a bit of the chief's conversation, she had gathered that it was Steve that he was talking to when she heard the word Dublin and Detective O'Dowd and by the sound of it things were bigger over there than first thought so he would probably be longer than first expected. She tried to find out from the chief when the new DCI was expected as stand in for Steve. Catching sight of her standing by the door he called her in.

'Ah Sara, things are not quite turning out as expected over in Ireland and it looks like DCI Ryan will be staying a little longer than we at first thought, the case is becoming more and more complicated and from what he was saying the extent of it is still an unknown. We may even need to draft in a little more help.'

After the news she had not expected sunk in, she stuttered out to the chief super what she had been on the way to tell him. 'The Bristol team just want confirmation that she has been charged, sir. I am quite happy to pop over to the Lawns and see if that is a possibility. Thank goodness that Steve is not here as I know he would take it on himself to do the visit ... Oh and by the way, sir, if help is needed over in Ireland, I am happy to go; I have no family ties to worry about unlike the rest of the team, sir.'

He eyed Sara Dyson up. 'Thank you, Sergeant, well done on the Magda case; go and visit and tie up the loose ends for good. I will let you know if you are needed in Ireland.' He dismissed her and as she turned to leave, he spoke. 'You are on the way to becoming a good DCI, Detective Sergeant Dyson, well done.'

She had wracked her brains for an excuse to get back into his life, but she would need to be patient a little longer. This could be the perfect way to get back with Steve. She had told him that he couldn't get away from her that easily.

She got through to the Doctor at the Lawns in charge of Magda's treatment quite easily from Steve's file notes and although he was reluctant at first to have his patient questioned again, a firm nod to the importance of the police procedures left him in no doubt that she would not be fobbed off, and was enough for him to agree a small concessionary few minute interview. She smiled and walked out to inform her colleagues that she would be out for the rest of the day looking at a cold case. Leaving the carpark, she practically whooped with joy at the thought of seeing Steve again; she could always nudge the chief in the right direction, with an innocent enquiry, if she hadn't heard anything by next week.

Heading through the double barriers of the Psychiatric facility and pulling around the curved driveway, she stepped out of the car. Taking a deep breath, she headed up the front steps to the large door and rang the bell. Magda had been quite formidable the last time she had seen her, and she wondered if she was any calmer now or if she was still being sedated. She was greeted inside the large reception area by a man in a white coat, his name label hanging from his coat pocket proclaimed him to be Dr Phillip Jones. After the introductions he looked at Sara and asked, 'Were you part of the original team that arrested Magda?'

'Yes, Dr er … Jones.' She leant forward, reading his name tag. 'I only really saw her in the police cell after her initial arrest; her hysteria was something to remember. I can assure you that I will be as brief as possible, it is really just a formality. Can I ask, Doctor, is she able to understand what I will be saying to her as I will be making a formal charge; and I will admit I am a little daunted as she was quite terrifying?'

'Yes, she understands, but she may not reply; I will just request that you keep it brief and all conversation is to stay within the remit please. She got very distressed when her brother visited … Detective Ryan, and it took days to settle her again.'

Sara smiled. 'Well let's get it over with.' She followed Dr Jones through the building, passing rooms with doors facing on to the long corridor, cell like in appearance and each with one person inside, sometimes sat in a chair, or in a bed, or at others banging on the walls or doors. Crying and screaming drifted on the air from all directions, assaulting her ears, so it was of great surprise when they arrived at a door to a room with a woman with bright red-gold curls, sat sedately looking out of the window at the end of the room. The bed was made neatly but no personal belongings were in sight. No books or pictures adorned the walls and it once again reminded Sara of a cell back at the nick. Except for the fact it was a lot cleaner and smelled a lot sweeter. She looked at Magda, she seemed calm and hopefully she could get this done and over with quickly.

'Please don't be fooled by her apparent docility, she can attack at any moment. I will leave a nurse with you, please respect what I have asked of you and only a few minutes.' He turned and left Sara standing in the doorway with a rather muscular man dressed in whites stood behind. He gestured for her to enter. Sara approached the figure tentatively, pulling up a chair, so far there had been no reaction from Magda to her presence.

'Hi Magda, I am Detective Sergeant Dyson, I wondered if I could have a few words with you concerning a male body that was later found to be that of a well-known drug addict, Peter Chapman, found in Bristol on October 10th 2015. You have already admitted in your statement to my colleague DCI Steve Ryan that you were in the vicinity on this date and DNA results from the crime scene have matched to your profile. So, this is really just a formality. Do you understand what I am saying?' Sara looked to the nurse who shrugged his over-large shoulders. She decided to plough ahead anyway. 'Magda Reilly, you are charged with the murder of Peter Chapman on the 10th of October 2015, you do not have to say anything, but it may harm your defence if you do not mention, when questioned, something which you later rely on in court. Anything that you do say may be given in evidence in a court of law—'

'My dear brother Steve, how is he? Dead I hope?' Magda interrupting; turned her face towards Sara, her green eyes alight, the smile on her face almost a grimace. Sara was struck with the likeness to Meg, just as Steve had been; the shock obvious on her face. 'Ah of course … so you are another one in love with my brother. Don't try to deny it. I can see it plain as day. Ah, but you hate him too … don't you? Hate him just as much as I do, ha ha … Tell me something, will you hate him enough to finish the job I started? Yes, I think you might. I see an Diabhul in your heart too, he has touched your soul.'

She reached out unexpectedly and grabbed Sara by the arm, she gripped her fiercely and where she touched her, her skin burned. She spit in Sara's face, laughing; she was suddenly pulled away and Sara, shocked and trying desperately to finish reading her rights to Magda, looked deep into the green eyes and she could swear that she saw the Devil staring back. She stumbled from the room and echoing behind her she heard Magda say, 'He will kill you in the end, your blood will run through his fingers; you know that you can't have him. Blood follows blood and he belongs to an Diabhul ... that's why he is mine.'

Sara felt a chill to her bones as she drove away from the building, she couldn't get the words that Magda had spoken out of her mind. It was as if she had looked inside of her soul and knew her thoughts, but that was impossible ... wasn't it? She shivered as the country lanes hurtled past and soon gave way to motorway. She was glad to be coming back to civilisation and home, her hatred for Steve burned even brighter, as if lit from the inside. Maybe Magda had lit that fire, or kindled the flame? But it burned brighter now, more than ever.

CHAPTER 20

"The human dilemma is not whether to do right or wrong, but rather to do right when it matters the most, and wrong when it matters the least."

Unknown

Steve, Sean, and the team battled on throughout the rest of the week, adding more names to the board, or crossing them off as and when they were found to be alive and well. Unfortunately, the latter were fewer than the former and the numbers grew. Wednesday morning arrived and Sean had been giving regular updates to the chief superintendent; he came out of his office smiling. He looked at his exhausted team and said, 'Hopefully we will have some more help by next week, but I would really like to get through the list over the next day or two. On Monday, we will organise what we will need when we transfer to the site. Thanks everyone for your efforts, now crack on.' He stood smiling as his phone pinged, he made his way outside to answer it.

'Sara, great to hear from you. I hear you are going to be coming over to join us and show us poor dumb Irishmen how it's done. While you are here, I would love to show you the sights of Dublin. You haven't seen anything till you have had some craic at Murphy's bar and the music is great.'

'I will look forward to that and to seeing you again. The boss has agreed that I can come over on Friday night after the new DCI is in place here; so perhaps you could show me around over the weekend? I would appreciate a suggestion for a place to stay too, seeing as it's your home turf. I have just a small request, don't tell Steve that I am coming over; I really want to surprise him. I am sure he has missed his old colleagues already.' Sara laughed. 'I can't wait to see you on Friday or Saturday?' she said in her best flirty voice.

'I can meet you from the airport if yer like?' After making arrangements and giving advice on places to stay, anywhere in or near the pale (Dublin). 'Although we will probably all be shifting down to Bally-Bay within a week.' He smiled to himself as he cut off the call. Sara Dyson was a good copper and quite a looker too. He was ready now for a relationship, nothing heavy, just a mot (girlfriend) would be good, and she didn't sound too unhappy to be seeing him again either. He had hope again and he knew that his old mate Steve would put a word in for him with the beautiful Miss Dyson. Turning back into the building he found it hard to hide his smile.

Back in Cambridge, Sara's smile disappeared from her face as if turned off like a tap; the pleasant girl on the phone had gone. In her place she practically snarled as she snatched a paper from DC Short as she entered back into the room. She would show Steve Ryan how to play games. He would sit up and notice her then, and his best mate Sean was just the man to help her to do it. After tidying up a few loose ends she was off out of the door on Friday afternoon without a word to any of her colleagues.

DC Jason Short watched as she disappeared out of the door. He had hopes that some kind of romance might have been possible between them, especially as he had supported her after Steve had treated her so badly. But the way that she had been behaving since he had gone over to Ireland left him in no doubt that he didn't stand a chance. In fact, he was glad that she didn't turn to him again as he was beginning to be suspicious of some of her behaviours over the last months. Maybe Steve had been telling the truth all along and there was nothing between them and never had been, and that she was a complete nutter! He shivered, the last thing he needed was some bunny boiler as a girlfriend. The one-night stand he had with her was enough for him. He hoped that Steve was prepared as she had managed to wangle her way over to Ireland behind him; and Steve thought he had escaped her for a while. After all, the poor bugger had been through hell, he deserved a break. He couldn't see what all these women saw in him anyway.

Sean and Steve worked late throughout the week and the last name was added to the board on Thursday evening. 'Come on everyone, go and get some rest, we will have a team briefing first thing at nine a.m. and then we can decide our next step.'

Gathering up the files that he wished to take with him, Steve noted some of the girls' names into his notebook; he had not had time to check out St Theresa's the other night and he was determined to get home and do it tonight. At least he could bring the last piece of information to the table in the morning.

Sean hesitated at the doorway and watched his friend making notes. He had noted that his friend's anxiety had been better and although they had all been very pressured and stressed, he had not suffered any of the horrid attacks that he had heard about and witnessed himself in the carpark in Cambridge since Steve had been in Ireland to Sean's knowledge. The good sea air in Bally-Bay was obviously doing him good. He sighed, at least having Sara turn up should cheer him even more. What a great surprise for him to have his right-hand man (so to speak) over here helping out; it should make him feel more comfortable. And he himself was looking forward to maybe some double dates with Steve and Meghan. He called goodnight to Steve and acknowledging his friend Steve rushed off behind him. On the long drive home, Steve was hoping that they were wrong about the amount of girls and that maybe it was a scam, a way of the nuns making more money for their home and orphanage. He wasn't expecting to find much anyway in the small cemetery behind the ruin of St Theresa's, they probably would never know what really went on as most of the evidence would have been destroyed and buried long ago.

Turning into the lane that passed his family farmhouse he continued on further into the village, the sea and harbour always caught his breath. The seagulls screamed overhead and wheeled in their dance, swooping and diving into the sea, to then sit bobbing on the surface, like the ducks in a fairground game. He stopped at the rusty gates chained together; he knew of old the sharp embedded pieces of glass on top of the wall from his childhood. He rubbed his arse cheek, remembering the times that he received a 'clither' from his mammy, especially the day he came home with a deep cut to his hand after trying to climb the stone wall that surrounded St Theresa's, because she knew where he had been.

He walked around to the boot of his car and pulling free a pair of large bolt cutters he made short work of the chain. Pulling the rusty gate open he made his way up the driveway. It was mostly covered in weeds and brambles, and he could see how long and unkempt the graveyard was. He stepped with caution around the side of the building; glass and debris lay everywhere. He stepped away from the building wall as some glass remained in what was left of the windows and the wall itself, or what was left of it bowed alarmingly. The last thing that he needed was it to collapse on him. From what he could see through the glassless windows, the building had been well used by local kids and drug addicts. Old drug paraphernalia was strewn amongst the rubble with the takeaway wrappings of the local food outlet and bottles, some smashed, others full of God knows what. Something else for the team to be watchful of, he thought. He also noted that some of the nearest graves had been vandalised, their stones toppling here and there like a ragged rows of teeth. He made his way further in and scanned the names on the gravestones. He cleared the moss and lichen away to read the names engraved on the stones from the past. Some of the names seemed familiar to him from when he attended the school. The sisters taught the local children, and he could put faces to a couple of the names that he recognised. Chuckling to himself as he remembered what a scallywag he had been for the aging nuns and he could still feel the sting of the strap on his hand. Folding in his fingers, he thought that he could feel it now. He made his way deeper into the cemetery, stepping over fallen stones and looking around him in despair. He thought that he would never find anything amongst the overgrown mess. Standing upright after clearing yet another stone of moss to find yet another sister Dominica Joan, he thought he would have to give up. So far, he had not found one grave to mark any of the girls reported as having died in the records, only Nuns.

Scanning the area, his eye alighted on a small area in the far corner of the cemetery, a small space had been cleared and he could see some colour poking out of the grass. He made his way over to the area where he thought that he had seen some colour. He stopped and scanned again, maybe he had imagined it? He couldn't see anything now. It was probably just a chocolate bar wrapper blown over into the corner from the rest of the detritus that blew about his feet. Stooping to move a fallen stone he turned his head sideways and yes there it was again, a bright spark of yellow that showed amongst the tall grasses. Keeping his eye on the speck of colour, he made his way across towards it, almost twisting his ankle as he was so keen to not lose it or take his eye off of it even for a moment. It was as if he knew of its importance.

He approached slowly and, as he neared, the object came into view. It was a duck! A bright yellow duck: very faded and dirty, the kind of rubber toy that you would put into a baby's bath. He could see that someone came often to the space and a small area had been cleared. On reaching the toy he picked it up, he could see by the condition that it had been there for a long time. The rubber was old and beginning to perish, it was soft and pliable, not like the plastic of today he thought. It was grubby and green from the plant debris; brushing the dirt from it and wetting his finger he rubbed at the duck until the yellow colour showed more clearly. Turning it around in his palm he found something written underneath, in very small writing. 'Your name was Christopher, and I will never forget you. All of my love till we meet again. Your loving mammy.'

Looking around, he could see that the small space had been encircled with pebbles to make a small ring and the duck had been placed within it. He carefully placed the toy back down in the circle before taking a picture on his phone, and he began to search along the wall a little further. He could make out what had once been wooden crosses with names marked on them underneath a large Hawthorn tree; its branches twisted towards the ground making a dense and thorny barrier. He cleared away the thorns from one cross that he thought looked more intact. As the thorns dug into his hands, he felt the blood run down his shirt sleeve; unable to let go of the twisted branch he stood stunned as he recognised one of the names from his list. Tearing the undergrowth away with his bare hands he discovered more and more markers, the names tumbled around his tongue as he read them; each one almost choking him as he recognised them from his list. He looked up and stood, he had only cleared a very tiny area alongside the wall but already he could see the small wooden crosses, or what was left of some of them, stretched as far as he could see. 'Dear god; if each one of these is a grave then there are more than we thought,' he spoke out loud and turning he retched at the thought of all of those faces on the board and all of the babies underneath the earth where he stood. He had seen enough! He stumbled his way back to the car and securing the site with a new padlock he would have to ensure it was properly secured tomorrow but at least he would have something to tell Sean in the morning. Sitting in his car, his head fell into his hands and the eyes that had been watching him turned away and a slim figure crept from the cemetery and across the lane to the field and hedgerow beyond; a small yellow duck clutched in their hand.

He turned on the ignition and pointed the car in the direction of home. He knew this information that tore at his heart would bring nothing but grief to his mammy and all of the girls just like her. In a way he had been the lucky one; his mammy had been able to keep him, and neither of them had died, although he thought perhaps it might have been better for his sister if she had. His thoughts turned once again to the circumstances of his birth and how he had been the lucky twin.

Turning into the lane, he could see that Meg and Romany were back from their jaunt to the pale and slapping a smile on his face he climbed out of the car to be greeted by three beautiful women; what a lucky guy he was. He scanned their smiling faces and swallowed the lump that was building in his throat and blinked quickly away the tears forming at the corner of his eyes. 'Well now this is a reception that any man could be happy with every night.' And kissing his mammy and Romany on the cheek, he thoroughly kissed Meg on the lips and asked, 'Well did yer miss me?' Pulling them all to him they made their way indoors, Romany and Meg trying to outdo each other with the telling of what they had done in Dublin. His mammy smiled and he enveloped her in a hug and practically carried her into the house.

Steve was quite subdued at dinner, but the girls didn't notice as they told with excitement of their visits to the museum and learnt the history of Ireland and about the terrible famine. How they danced to music in Murphy's bar in the Temple district and how they strolled around the grounds of Trinity College in the sunshine and visited the Kells Library. 'Now that was a sight to see,' Meg sighed. Romany pulled out her sketchbook and showed Steve the most beautiful drawing of the Ha'penny bridge that spanned the Liffey.

'Well that's all well and good but did yer bring us a drop of the black stuff home with yer?' Steve laughed as they all slapped at him together. Laughing, they realised how late it had become. Steve offered to make a cup of tea or chocolate before bed. Romany, stretching, refused and retired; Meg decided that a bath would be good and that left Steve and Bridget. Steve stirred the tea in the tea pot, he loved how his mammy insisted on real tea leaves. 'Ach away with yer that's not proper tea,' she would say about teabags, and wouldn't have a bite of them in the house. Pouring her a cup she watched her strong son add some milk, the smiles from earlier had disappeared and she looked down at the blood on his shirt cuff and the scratches on his hands. 'What's going on, son, are you ok? I can see that your thoughts are not really with us tonight; is it work, is it St Theresa's? Because I would rather yer leave it be than torture yerself.'

'Ah Mammy if only I could leave it be, that would be the simplest thing to do; but yer know that they say life is never easy and I am so grateful to you for giving me a life to live when others didn't have that opportunity. The least I can do is recognise their sacrifice.' Steve reached over and, squeezing his mammy's hand, he asked, 'Now, is there any more tea in that pot?' After rinsing the cups out and leaving them on the sink to drain, he kissed his mammy's cheek and held her just a little bit longer and a little bit harder than usual. 'I'm so sorry, Mammy, I hope by the end of this investigation that you can forgive me,' he whispered in her ear before turning towards the stairs and bed. He was sure that he wouldn't get much sleep but at least he could pass the guilt he was feeling onto God as he knew that they would need to find some faith to deal with the tribulations ahead.

CHAPTER 21

"It is sometimes an appropriate response to reality to go insane."
Phillip K. Dick-Vallis, author

The morning mist rolled across the fields as Steve made his way to work, driving along the lanes that would then lead on to more major roads and eventually to Dublin. 'The pale', he often wondered why it was called this by any Dubliner worth his salt. He would be classed as living beyond the pale; to be classed as in 'the pale' would incorporate all of the areas in and around Dublin itself.

He thought then of his colleagues back in Cambridge. At first, when he had arrived in England, he had found his strong accent to be the butt of many jokes and all of his Irish colloquialisms made them laugh even more. He was a good-natured man and would join in the laughter; it helped to ease him into the team and his unassuming manner did the rest. He realised now that he hadn't been happy and had been living a lie for a very long time. He had buried himself in his work, never allowing himself to stop and breathe, just in case he allowed himself to think. If he did, he knew that he would be transported back to a church in Bally-Bay with hysterical laughter ringing in his ears as his eyes fell upon the sight before him. That was until his Meg had come along. She had opened his eyes to what life could be like. How he could be loved and have someone that he loved too. For too long he had lived in the shadows, running away from Bally-Bay and life itself. He took in a deep breath of fresh air before he hit the city and smiled to himself, it was good to be back at the Met, even if the reason that he was here was an awful one. He pulled into the carpark and found a space just as Sean arrived too. He could see someone in the passenger seat next to him, a woman He smiled to himself, crafty ole Sean has got himself a mot (girlfriend), was he dropping her off?

He climbed out of the car and leaning in to grab his briefcase he froze as a voice that he recognised greeted him from behind.

'Morning Gov, aren't you the lucky one? I have come to join you and help with the investigation. Lovely Sean here has been helping me to settle in and we had fun whilst he showed me the sights, didn't we, Sean? Or I suppose I should call you sir now that we are working.' Sara Dyson smiled widely at Sean and Steve, unable to comprehend, turned around to see the glee in her eyes as he took in her words.

Steve's breathing began to change, he couldn't believe what he was seeing.

'What is she doing here?' he pointed a finger at DS Dyson, his hand shaking.

Sean misunderstood Steve's reaction, thinking how pleased he would be to see his old friend. He knew they had become close friends and colleagues. 'Sara ... err DS Dyson has transferred over temporarily to help us to organise the case information. I thought another pair of hands would be helpful. I picked her up from the airport on Friday, we had a great weekend seeing the sights and now she is ready to knuckle down to some work and give her old mate a surprise. I will leave you to say hello and meet you in the investigation room in ten.'

Sean had not noticed Steve getting angrier by the minute, or his pallor and breathing, he brushed past him and made his way to the door. Sara stepped forward. 'Hi Steve, I bet you have missed me? Thought you had got rid of me for a while. Luckily the lovely Sean is just panting to see me again and invited me over to help. Now who would of thought it?' She smiled into his face smugly.

'I don't know how you managed it, but you keep away from me and Sean, or else—'

'Or what, Steve, you will make a complaint, you will tell the boss? I don't think so somehow, do you? By the way, Magda sends her love and regards.' She turned her back on him and headed towards the door, safe in the knowledge that he wouldn't touch her here. Steve buckled, his breathing spiralling out of control, his heartbeat pounding in his head. What did she mean about Bree? Surely she hadn't had contact with his sister … had she? God almighty his nightmare had returned. His thoughts whirled around his head; how could she have seen Bree or had contact? He wished now that he had confided in his friend, he had been so relieved and yes, just a little smug at the thought that he had escaped Sara's clutches, and he was beginning to get his anxiety under control too. The new tablets from the doctor had helped a lot; that is until today, the shock of Sara turning up had thrown him back under that particular bus and at this moment in time he was trying desperately to pull himself free.

Gaining control of his breathing using all of the techniques the doctor had given him to cope with his anxiety, he made his way inside. For the moment he would be as professional as possible and try to think of a plan to get rid of Sara. He came into the room and looked across at his friend; Sean was standing in front of the board with the girls' pictures on and Sara was stood next to him, smiling and touching his arm. So that was her game, to try and make him jealous. Well he didn't care what she did; but she knew bloody well that he would hate to see his friend hurt. She turned towards him, smiling.

'Ah here he is. Come on, boss, we are all waiting for you; coffee is made … just how you like it.' Sean smiled at him and moved to take his place at the front of the room, so he missed the smile as it dropped from her face and the glare towards Steve as she sat at the large table covered in files.

'Right everyone, let me introduce DS Sara Dyson, a colleague of Steve's who has joined our investigation. Perhaps after the briefing you could catch Sara up to date, Steve. Now what more have we dug up on the girls; Siobhan have we finished going through the list at last?'

'Yes sir, I finished the last name on Friday and passed any unaccounted for names to Connor ... err Garda O'Brian to try and contact.' Siobhan sat abruptly and Sean smiled reassuringly at her; he remembered how daunting it was the first few times having to stand and address the team. He also liked to keep it informal on a first-name basis; he had learned over the years that a team gelled better when more relaxed.

'Thank you, Siobhan, good job, thank god that list is finished with for now. Connor what have you discovered for us? No more names to add to the board I hope?'

Conner stood almost as abruptly as Siobhan had sat down. 'Well sir I am sorry to say that I do have to add thirty-one more names and I have just two more to catch up on that I need to confirm if they are living. I have added the names to the board, sir, but I have been unable to find photos for all of them; we have three missing faces, but all together we now have two hundred and thirteen identified girls; plus twenty seven on the other board that we positively know that the babies survived, and were adopted; the mothers were not so lucky apparently. So, to sum up, if each girl has a baby unaccounted for then we have nearly five hundred bodies, sir.' Connors eyes fell and he sat, almost fell into his chair as the enormity of what he had just said sunk in.

Sara gasped, 'Jesus, no wonder you needed help with this case ... oh god those poor babies and girls.'

Steve stood, he cleared his throat and looked to Sean as he spoke. 'On Friday I went to St Theresa's before I returned home. At first it was so overgrown in the graveyard that I could only clear a few headstones manually. It is in a bit of a state with fallen stones and hazards everywhere from broken glass to fallen in graves. Each name that I uncovered pertained to a Sister that had died naturally over the years; I even recognised some of the names from my childhood school as my teachers and they were old women back then. But I searched a little further back into the cemetery, and I found a very small, cleared area. It was obvious that someone had cared for this small patch, and I found a child's toy; the sort that a baby would play with.' He described the writing on the duck then pinned a printout picture from his phone up on the board. 'On closer inspection along the north wall were a number, a very large number, of wooden crosses in varying degrees of decay and disrepair. I did manage to find a few names on some of them and I recognised them from our list. The worst part, and I hesitate to hazard a guess, but there seemed to be hundreds of these markers all along the wall. Way more than our estimated amount; but then we have only been dealing with the last twenty or so years, back from the closure of the place in nineteen ninety-five. We still have another list of names, exactly the same to look at, before nineteen seventy. I think records were more hit and miss before then, obviously whoever took over the record keeping in nineteen seventy was a bit more vigilant and organised, which hopefully will make things a little easier for us.'

Steve sat down and scanned the faces in the room, each and every one of them seemed stunned; he of course had, had the weekend to process the enormity of the situation. He looked towards Sara and even she seemed to be taking it all in. One thing he did admire her and respect her for was the fact that she was a bloody good copper. Let's hope getting involved deeply in this case would help to keep her off of his back.

Sean leaned over towards Steve and, dismissing the rest of the team, he asked him to stay behind. When the others had left the room, he turned to his old friend and pushing his hands through his hair he took a deep breath. 'Bloody hell, Steve, what in god's name have I done? Maybe I should have left well alone.'

'No if you walk away from this now, you will never know peace. Knowing you as I do, you couldn't do that. It would go against everything that you believe in, and the whole reason that you – we – do what we do. Those girls and wee ones deserve peace, and we need, no, we have to give that to them; it is the least that they should have. As decent human beings and officers of the law, how could we not give them that? I really don't think that anyone except God alone can give them justice.'

Sean nodded his head. 'I will go to the boss today and hopefully we can have a forensic team and diggers there by the end of next week. At least thanks to you we will know exactly where to look. Perhaps we could ask you to draw us a rough map today marking out the different areas; we don't want to cause trouble with the church … now damn; I forgot, before we can start we will need permissions to disturb the graves, they are on hallowed ground. Not that I mind disturbing the nuns, they don't deserve to rest after what they did to those girls. I bet they are all in purgatory as we speak; I don't even think Hell would have let them in. I know that permissions could be a hurdle as they want everything to stay well and truly buried; Jesus, Mary and Joseph what a bloody mess.'

'Talking of messes, I don't know how to say this but please listen to me; stay away from a relationship with Sara … err she isn't what she seems, and she has got herself over here to follow me.' Steve could barely look Sean in the eye.

'What the feck does that mean? Have yer been shifting her, Steve?'

'No … no, I bloody haven't, but she seems to think I have … Oh god I can't explain to yer. Please can yer just trust me as a friend, who cares about yer. Just stay away from her, she's poison, please mate just listen to me.'

'Why the feck should I, Steve? All I am trying to do is have some happiness in my life and she is certainly fun to be with and seems a decent sort ... what the feck do yer care for? Yer have Meghan and a ready-made family. I can't even see my feckin kids.' Sean stormed off, heading towards the boss's office.

Steve sat for a moment; 'Well that was bloody brutal, he certainly ate me head off,' he thought. 'I know I deserved it but what is more worrying is she has her claws into him already something fierce.'

He stood and as he entered the room he saw Sara smirk, she had obviously overheard or witnessed the friend's argument. Either way she knew it concerned her. He went right past her and strode outside, he needed some fresh air, away from her poison, before he did something he would regret. He had never been an angry man before, but she was testing his sanity as well as his strength of character. He didn't know how he could bear to be in the same room as her; let alone watch her destroy his life and his friendships ... she had to go.

CHAPTER 22

"There may be times when we are powerless to prevent injustice, but there must never be a time when we fail to protest."

Ellie Wiese

Steve tried to concentrate on making a half decent map of the ruins of St Theresa's. He had managed to find online the land registry for the site and from there he had cobbled together a usable site map using technology from different online sources. He had kept his head down all afternoon, not even glancing up at the sea of faces on the board. Garda's Siobhan and Conner were trying to collate the list of names and contacts for each name on the list; in case permissions were needed from next of kin for disinterment of the girl's bodies. Suddenly he felt a presence behind him. Pulling out a chair Sara sat down next to him, he tried to pull away from her nearness, but she had made sure that he had nowhere to go by placing her chair as close as possible to his; the other side of him was just wall.

'Well now aren't you supposed to catch me up with the case? A bit of a shock was it seeing me this morning? Now, what have we got happening here?' She leant over as far as possible towards him, her head almost touching his, to see the computer screen. Just as Sean came out of the boss's office, he saw them together and to his eye they looked very cosy together; perhaps that's why his friend wanted him to keep away from Sara. Well, he wasn't going to give up that easily, they always had a bit of rivalry between them over the girls when they were kids. As far as Sean was concerned nothing had changed. He couldn't see how Steve looked totally panicked and was trying desperately to move away from her. Sara looked up and saw Sean watching them; she gave him a huge smile and waved. Smiling back at her he headed towards them.

'Well as I thought we will need permissions from the church to dig in the cemetery and exhume any bodies. The boss is onto that now and he is making a few telephone calls to a couple of Bishops he knows. So, as we can't do much more today, I suggest that we all have an early night and meet fresh in the morning. Sara, I will give you a lift back to your hotel; there is no point you hiring a car as I can pick you up again in the morning. It's only for a few days as I hope to be moving everything to Bally-Bay by the weekend. Perhaps you might like to go out for dinner again tonight, I know a great little place near your hotel; we all got to eat?'

Sean smiled at her whilst looking at Steve, daring him to say something. Sara looked at them both and could see the muscle in Steve's jaw working as it was clenched, before she smiled and said, 'That would be great, Sean, but to be honest I am pretty tired. I was just going to get something from room service and loll out for the evening; maybe go through some of the case files to catch up a bit; but I will have that lift thanks; maybe another time.' Her smile was so sincere, how on earth could Steve say she was poison? Sean thought as he looked into her lovely, smiling face and back at Steve who seemed to be simmering.

'Come on then, princess, your carriage awaits.'

Sara laughed and grabbing Sean's arm she rose from the chair and turning she called, 'Night Steve, send my love to Meg.' Grabbing her coat and bag she sauntered out of the room. Sean, following behind, turned and gave Steve the finger and swaggered out after her.

Steve's fury knew no bounds; he practically flew out after his friend and begged him not to go with her, but he knew that he wouldn't listen. He had enough on his plate without this, he needed to do some thinking. He either needed to come clean and tell Sean the truth, but that would mean telling Meg too and he was really unsure how she would take it. They were already teetering on the edge, and this could just be the thing that tipped their relationship over. He decided to take his map and head back to St Theresa's on the way home, he hoped that he could see a way of digging the girls and babies graves without disturbing the other sites. He had thought how the work could be relatively hidden from the general public and residents and wanted to see if it was viable to get the equipment and temporary buildings on site that they would need to carry out the exhumations. He also knew that he had a task on his hands as the opposition from the church would be huge. Hopefully the Chief Superintendent was on their side, if not he had some ammunition ready. He had already found that a huge inquiry had been taking place at other sites to do exactly the same. The government commission inquiry – Mother and Baby Homes 2015 – was currently still underway and from what Steve had read so far the findings had been momentous; at one site alone in Cork over nine hundred babies' bodies had been found in a deep pit and hundreds of the poor wee souls had been given up for medical science as anatomical subjects. Either way, just as in their Bally-Bay case, the infant mortality rates were extremely high but the difference at Bally-Bay were the deaths of the poor mothers too. He sighed at the enormity of the task that lay ahead and gathering his map he left. The anger that he felt towards Sara earlier had dissipated as his thoughts turned to the task ahead.

Standing back amongst the long grass in the overgrown cemetery he thought of Bree, how Meg had described meeting her that day in the churchyard next door, and how Bree must have hoped for rescue from her abusers. He still thought of what his sister had to endure but he also thought of his friend Jonathan; Meg's brother who died at her hands for getting in the way and how he had nearly lost both Meg and Romany to her insane and irrational thoughts that Meg was her family and that she needed to make them pay for what she had suffered. His thoughts also turned to Father Benedict, the perpetrator of the abuse and the evil sisters that had helped him to hide his behaviour towards all of the young girls in his parish. It was easier for them to turn a blind eye or, as was beginning to be made clear to him, support and help him to achieve his evil goals.

Breathing deeply, he turned shivering and shrugging, as if he could let the weight of their suffering slip from his shoulders along with his own demons. Instead, he felt them grip their talons into his flesh even harder, and his resolve for justice for them all tightened. He spread his gaze towards the spot that he had found the little duck. Expecting to see a glimpse of yellow he saw a slim figure creeping quietly away over the wall and off to the fields behind. He thought that he recognised something familiar about them; but he shook his head trying to remember why. 'Hopefully it will come back to me,' he thought as he watched the figure move out of sight.

Pulling his copy of his map out, he scanned the area where he had found the most crosses, good, they were all up in the top right-hand corner away from the other graves and the road. By the look of it they could possibly come into the adjoining field and work from there as a small track ran adjacent to the wall that also ran in the opposite direction where it joined the road. That must have been the way that the figure that he had seen earlier had gone. As the field crested the hill, a stand of trees could be seen and a small, wooded area followed around to the right where it followed the edge of the field. This would all help to shield the unit from prying eyes, marking on his map the field, the far tree line, and the track. He then noted the graves of the sisters and the positioning of the crosses against the wall. He felt that he had done a good job and that the geophysical survey guys would have easy access to the site first and foremost, if a small section of wall was removed at the furthest point of the ground.

Satisfied, he turned to walk away and he was surprised to see a small girl watching him from a few yards away; she had bright red curls. He put his hand up to shield his eyes from the setting sun and he blinked in the brightness, as he opened them again, she had disappeared. Strange, he thought to himself, that she seemed to be here on her own, and where had she gone? Perhaps over the wall like the figure from earlier but he knew the consequences of doing just that. He rubbed at the scar across his palm and curiosity got the better of him. He ran as fast as he could across to where he had spotted the child; he found a really old gravestone on its own at the spot. It was much older than the rest, its letters worn and ground away over time. He could see that they had not been formed by a stonemason, the edges of the lettering blurred and rough, the marks showed that they had been scraped into the stone over and over. The moss and lichen had all but covered the whole stone and it had broken across the middle with only a jagged piece remaining above ground. Picking up a small stone, he started to scrape away the debris and just as the letters began to form a readable name, he dropped the stone in horror, staring at the name carved long ago by someone's hand. He sat down abruptly on his haunches. As he said the name aloud, he traced the letters with his finger to ensure that he hadn't made a mistake. 'Magda Reilly'. He read the name but his search for more information gave nothing back. If there had ever been a date on the headstone it was worn away long ago; perhaps forensics could make it out. He stood, his head spinning with questions, and as he did so he felt a pressure on his palm, as if a small hand had been placed in his.

Looking down at his hand, he clenched his fingers, it felt cold; he shook it as if to restart his circulation. Deciding to go he re-traced his steps and made his way down to the huge rusty metal gates that were barely hanging on their hinges at the entrance to the drive where he had earlier left his car. Climbing into the seat, he slumped with exhaustion. He knew that he had a decision to make, the choices either way would be hard. Should he tell Meg everything, including about Sara and that she had followed him here? Or go home now and give up this case, leave it to Sean to sort out? He clenched his fingers again as if he could still feel the small hand in his and closing his eyes he saw the name on the headstone and he knew there and then that no matter what the cost to himself, he had been tasked with finding out the truth and the policeman in him would help him to do that. Turning the car around, he headed home, a decision made in his heart. He would either lose everything that he held dear or he would gain the trust that he longed for from those that he cared about. He turned into the lane that led to the farm and home and he stopped halfway. He got out of the car and making his way across the field and up the grassy hill that looked down on the farmhouse, he felt the dampness of dusk soak into the bottom of his trousers. He reached the Sceach Gheal (Faery thorn) under whose branches his father now lay. He knelt and placing his hand on the earth he sobbed. 'Give me the strength that I need, Daddy, to do what I have to do; I'm afraid, yer see? I am afraid that I won't have the faith needed for such a task. I know that you and Mammy took me from that place, and that I knew nothing but love from yer, but yer shouldn't have left her behind, Daddy. Did yer know what was going on? Cos if yer did I can never forgive yer, Daddy … never!'

Standing, he turned and saw how darkness had fallen. The lights from the farmhouse shone yellow out into the night, calling him home. He didn't want to go because he knew what he had to do; and he didn't know if he was strong enough. Straitening up he glanced up at the sky and took in the wonder of the universe above him, the stars bright and glowing in the sky and the tinge of orange still slightly visible on the horizon. Suddenly he knew that he wasn't alone. The pictures from the board, of the faces of the girls, swam before his eyes. Each one boring into his soul and he felt a warmth creep through his body, and he knew that he could do this. Whether he would survive was another matter. He made his way down the grassy slope and climbing into his car he felt his shoulders relax; you got this, Steven Ryan … you got this.

Upon entering the farmhouse, he felt the warmth hit him first, then the smell of something delicious cooking. He entered the kitchen to be greeted with the three most important things in his life, laughing, their heads together over a pot on the stove. One had hair as black as a raven, one as red as fire, and one as white as the snow on the hills. He smiled at the picture before him, and he was sure then in that moment that everything would be ok. Tomorrow was soon enough to destroy the image before him; tonight, he would savour it and enjoy every moment that he had left.

CHAPTER 23

"The trust of the innocent is the liar's most useful tool."
Stephen King, *author*

Steve moved gently in bed, trying not to disturb Meg, his arm had gone to sleep long ago and it was becoming painful. Sliding it out from under her, he looked at her beautiful face framed by the glorious red curls. Again, it reminded him of his own sister except Meg had no hard lines that ran down each side of her mouth. He knew that Bree's face would never lay supine and as carefree as his lover's did now. Meg had planned a full weekend for them all, with a picnic on the beach and a full on family roast dinner with Sian, John, Cassie, William, and all the grandkids. It was thoughtful of her, he thought, to include his mammy in the gatherings; she had refused the beach picnic thinking that it would be a little too much for her in the heat but said she would join them on Sunday at Sian's. Saturday night he had decided to gather them all after dinner and make his revelations about Sara Dyson. He wanted them to understand above all else just how dangerous she could be. He also thought that having a big family dinner would help to deflect some of Meg's anger. He knew it was cowardly and he would answer all of her questions but some things he needed to keep hidden, the pizza night for a start.

Making his way downstairs, he found his mammy sat at the table already up with a cup of tea in her hand.

'Jesus, Mammy, it's barely dawn and yer are up drinking tea.'

'I could say the same to you, Steven, couldn't you sleep either, love? There is plenty in the pot if you want some.'

He smiled and reaching for a mug he filled it from the large tea pot keeping warm on the stove. Joining his mother at the table, he added some milk from the jug. He looked at the delicate china and it took him back years. How life had changed for everyone. Perhaps secrets are better left buried. All it had done was bring heartache to his family and loved ones. A small voice inside him whispered, 'Ah but uncovering those secrets enabled you to catch a serial killer and save the girl that you love.'

'You seem very thoughtful this morning, Steven; a burden shared is a burden halved as they say.' Picking up his mother's hand he kissed the knuckles that were wrinkled and bent by arthritis and age and the harsh work of the farm.

'Ah but you also know what curiosity did to the cat, Mammy.' He laughed and she smiled with him. 'I'm off for a walk before the others force me to the beach for the day to enjoy meself. Shall I bring back some fish from Murphy's for tea, Mammy?'

'Yes that would be lovely, son, I just fancy a nice piece of haddock.'

'Well, I will see what I can do for yer then.' He headed out of the door just as the sun had risen, he headed across the fields down towards the harbour. He would catch the boats as they came back in and get the fish for mammy. As he approached the old stone wall that encircled the harbour, he looked up as he heard an engine puttering from a boat making its way back in. The sun glinted off of the water and it brought back memories of childhood. His father calling to him not to fall off of the wall as he ran along the top, following the curve of the harbour, whilst he himself stopped to chat to the fisherman. Suddenly a cloud drifted across the sun and another memory filled his mind, of a dark figure with garments flapping in the breeze, walking along the other side of the harbour. How the chatter of the men stopped suddenly and how they doffed their hats or bowed their heads in deference to the priest as he passed by. Black garments and a black soul to go with it ... Father Benedict. He remembered how scared everyone was of the priest and how the girls cried when they came back from his study. He thought that they had a caning … now he knew that it was much, much worse.

One thing his sister had done was stop his evil in its tracks. The image of the priest lying across the altar in the church, his head a bloody pulp, came to his mind and he rubbed his eyes, as if to remove the picture. He turned back towards the harbour and the boat that he had seen earlier was busy unloading his catch onto the cobbled path, the boat now bobbing, tied to the large iron rings that served as a mooring, set deep into the wall held by rusting bolts that clung to the plate that held it in place. The air was sharp with the tang of fish, and he called out.

'Good morning Mr Kelly, it's good to see yer; Mammy says have yer got some haddock enough for four please.' The old man in bright yellow waterproofs peered out from Rheumy eyes, trying to focus on the person speaking to him.

'Well is that young Steven Ryan? I haven't seen yer for a long time, since yer father passed, I believe. How is yer mammy, these days?' Mr Kelly smiled up at Steve, a young man who had been helping to unload the fish leaned over the wall and holding out his arm pulled the older man up onto the top of the harbour.

'My grandson Michael, he helps out on the boat now.' The old man nodded his head towards the youngster. 'And I think you will remember Matthew, my son; I think you went to school together?' A man approximately Steve's age nodded as he continued hauling the crates up onto the side.

'Yes of course I remember Matthew, we used to steal the apples off of old Ma Owens's tree. She caught him once and he got such a blathering, his arse must have stung for a week. I was too quick of course; only the slow eejits got caught.'

Steve winked at Mr Kelly and the men all roared with laughter.

'Why are yer back home with us culchies? Is yer mammy ok? The last I heard yer was a Detective over in England?'

Steve didn't want to reveal the real reason for his visit as he was sure that would be clear enough to the locals once the team moved the equipment into the village. He also knew that things would get out quickly enough when he approached the farmer Aidan Doyle about using the track and field as an entry point into the graveyard. The same could be said when the O'Connells, who owned the guest house on the cliff top that overlooked the bay, were asked for rooms for the team. They could always make room at Mammy's for Sean.

Smiling, he looked out to sea. 'Oh you know, just a quick visit and back to the grindstone. Mammy sent me for some haddock if you have some, it's her favourite. I need enough for four please.' He didn't elaborate about Meg or Romany either; although by the look Mr Kelly gave him, he already knew that Sian's niece was staying at the farm with him. Taking the fish and handing over some money, he thanked Mr Kelly and with his hand raised in a gesture of farewell he made his way home. Trudging across the fields he contemplated what he would say to Meg about Sara, all he knew was that if he wasn't as truthful as possible then she would know, and he could say goodbye to any relationship that he had with her. He began wondering if he should say anything at all? But look where that had got him so far, he thought that he had resolved the problem and instead he had made a bigger one for himself and his friends and family, as Sara had proved by showing up like a bad penny. Perhaps he could give his therapist a call and ask her advice first. Yes! That's what he would do and nodding to himself he knew that he was avoiding the problem for the moment and also knowing that it wasn't just going to go away. He was a coward and apart from trying to wriggle out of the confrontation that he knew must happen at some point, he was like an ostrich hoping that by putting his head in the sand that it would just go away. He had too much to lose and Sara Dyson knew it.

The weekend sped by, and Steve even dared to let himself relax. He got on well with William and Meg's uncle John and whilst the women were gathered, it turned out that Cassandra, Meg's cousin, was pregnant with her third child and the talk was all about grandchildren and babies. He heard his mammy wistfully sigh as Sian asked if she had any grandchildren and replied unfortunately not. Steve knew how much his mammy had yearned for this to happen over the years and had watched the disappointment on her face every time his current relationships disintegrated, and she eventually accepted that she would never know this pleasure, as the time of him being alone stretched from months to years. If I had met Meg earlier in life, I might be a father now, he thought to himself. She is the only person that has been able to find the real Steve Ryan as he had been hiding away for many years. Not wanting to commit or have a real relationship with anyone, he had avoided sharing his life or opening up to the possibilities of family.

That was up until this girl with red curls and green eyes came into his life and swept away all of the defences that he had carefully built around himself over the years. He re-enforced it every now and then, when his single status changed. Just in case anyone penetrated it. Girls soon gave up on him once they hit that barrier a few times. He had certainly built it of strong stuff, that is why it was so vital not to do anything that upset the equilibrium, he knew it was hanging by a thread and Sara Dyson held the scissors in her hand.

Jerking himself out of his reverie, he suddenly sat up as he heard Meg mention the case and why he was really here. He tried to close down the conversation before he was exposed and in trouble, before he could John spoke. 'Well, it was such a long time ago, sometimes these things need to be let be … for the sake of everyone.'

Holding his breath for a few moments he replied, 'I am breaking the rules even discussing it with you but suffice to say that if we just let it go and continue to turn a blind eye and don't stand up to what is wrong with this country, as the power that some wield over the innocent is used to corrupt, abuse, and lie, instead of nurture and protect, then we are as guilty of the crime as they themselves.'

'And I do agree with you, Steve, but what is past can't be mended no. Let sleeping dogs lie, not poke them with a bloody great stick.'

'It's because people have thought like this for too long, John, that the perpetrators of the most terrible crimes have been able to get away with it. Men are what their mammy's make them, but priests are given the power of God to use and abuse as they wish … it's time that we all see that they are just men like us and must be made accountable for their actions too.'

He stood and held his hand out to Bridget. 'Time to go home now, Mammy.' Looking up and placing her hand in his, she smiled.

'Well, I made a bloody good man, and I couldn't be prouder at how he turned out.' Rising, they said their goodbyes and left to walk the lane back to the farmhouse, across the field and past the church and grounds of St Theresa's.

As they left, John gently placed his arm around Sian's shoulders and whispered to her, 'That is why we need to forget the past, but I fear that Steve will not stop till he uncovers everything; he is a principled man and I do believe that an Diabhul drives his conscience.'

Peering through the now darkening sky, Bridget, her arm pulled through her son's, looked across at the gravestones. 'I hope that you leave no stone unturned, bring those girls and babes justice, they don't deserve to be swept away and forgotten about just because it might embarrass the church. Well so what? They turned a blind eye to murder and brutality, it's time that everyone's eyes were opened to what went on here. It is what it is.'

He patted her hand gently. 'I promise you, Mammy, I will do whatever I can to bring it all out into the open and that every single one of those girls and babies are acknowledged and given the respect they deserve.'

CHAPTER 24

"If something is important enough, you do it! Even if the odds are not in your favour."

Elon Musk

The rumble of trucks could be heard from a distance as they entered the village of Bally-Bay; it was still early and the only witnesses to the event were the fisherman on the quay. Stopping just short of the crest of the hill that led down to the harbour-side, they turned into the small lane that ran across the field belonging to Aidan Doyle and drove up the hill following the wall of St Theresa's until they reached a spot just over the brow of the hill, out of view from the road and pulled into a space made for them to park. One after another they pulled in until there were at least half a dozen vehicles. The large lorries carrying the port-a-cabin's that were needed for a short stay circled as if in a wagon train out in the wild west. The village, just awakening and bleary eyed, wondered from behind their curtains, what was happening? It looked like an invasion. They soon realised though that the trucks had driven far out of sight of any gobermouch; the only person who could see anything at all was Aidan Doyle whose land the police vehicles had stopped on. Over the next few days, he would receive many a visitor at the farm and would be brought a few pints at the pub, and although he would accept the beer, Aidan's lips were sealed tightly shut as he had a great respect for his long-time neighbours the Ryan's and the Garda put the wind of god up him after a small drunken incident long ago in his youth. Steve used this as a reminder to ensure that his compliance was assured. Although he knew himself that gossip would abound around the small community and that it wouldn't be long before two and two were put together.

Steve struggled to get out of bed, unable and unwilling to face the struggle between his upbringing in this small community of friends and neighbours and his own conscience. Meg rubbed his back as he sat on the edge of the bed, and he could easily have just turned around and climbed back under the covers. They hadn't had much time together since they arrived in Bally-Bay and certainly had not had any time alone. He promised himself that next weekend he would whisk her away to a quiet restaurant for a special meal, a little wine, and maybe some romance thrown in.

'A mhuirni'n, I'm so sorry, I must go. I would much rather stay and hold you in my arms, but those souls are calling me, and everyone is arriving this morning. I will try and get home early tonight, and we can make some plans for the weekend.'

'It's ok, my love, you go and uncover the truth and give Sean my love. Is he coming back with you to stay here?'

'I have asked him to, but I am unsure what he is up to. He is talking about staying with the others at the B&B only because Sara is there.'

'Oh you didn't say that Sara had come over with you; you must get them both over for dinner. Do you think something might happen between her and Sean? How lovely, we can match make.'

Meg was shocked when he turned and spat out, 'I don't want her near here, or Sean, she is nothing but trouble.' He toyed there and then about spilling out the truth, but he just couldn't bring himself to destroy what he had with Meg … better to hold on for as long as he could. Whereas Meg was feeling totally confused about Steve's reaction and before she could dig any further for answers, he quickly got up and left the room. Before she could pull the covers back up, she heard the water from the shower running in the bathroom. She lay back in the bed pondering his behaviour and shrugged as she put it all down to pressure of the case.

Steve decided to leave his car and walk the distance across the fields to where the crew of the geophysical survey unit were drinking coffee and chatting about the day ahead. Sean and Sara were off to one side, heads bent together focussed on Steve's map, and young Gardas Connor and Siobhan stood excitedly waiting for things to kick off on their first major case. Steve took the scene in as he approached; Sean and Sara looked up and she stepped back from Sean and greeted Steve with an overly affectionate 'oh good morning, boss, I hope you had a good weekend?' before turning on the biggest smile towards him. Sean, pushing forward to greet Steve and stop their interaction, didn't see the smug smile that she gave to Steve behind his back. She had plenty of time to work out the old pal's relationship and found herself in a superior position. She could manipulate Sean's eagerness and jealousy of his friend and at the same time frustrate Steve because he couldn't say anything. She long ago worked out the competitive one-up-man-ship left over from their time as young Garda together. The dynamics of this relationship, as far as she was concerned, had never changed. She had, however, forgotten that Steve had found his true love in Meg and wouldn't play her games, but this made him vulnerable, and she was good at finding the weak spots.

Walking over to the geophysics crew, they marked out a grid over the area at the very top of the graveyard and beyond that covered the piece that ran down adjacent to the wall. The men proceeded to get their equipment ready to start and Sean, pleased to get going, said to everyone, 'Let's crack on and see just what we are dealing with, people. Connor and Siobhan, can you walk down and place a line of tape between where the nun's graveyard finishes and the other starts? Fellas,' he called to the men, 'can you make sure that nothing is disturbed past the tape line? Thank you everyone, let's go!'

Everyone headed out to start the tasks that had been given to them. 'Steve, a word … they will shout when they find anything. Sara, can you supervise?' He turned and heading to a large unit that had now been set up as their incident room, Steve followed, climbing the three steps they entered. A small team of two garda were busy setting out onto the boards all of the information that had been gathered so far, as well as the girls' pictures which now stared back at them as they entered. Leading his way to the very back of the unit to a couple of small desks the friends sat and, turning toward Steve, Sean looked at his old friend with an approving gaze.

'Well, you're the dark horse, aren't yer? I know something has been going on with you and Sara, she has done nothing but talk about yer all weekend. Does Meg know you got a thing with her or is she as in the dark as I was?'

'I promise you there isn't anything going on with me and Sara. It is all in her mind. I have never, or ever, thought about her as anything but a colleague. Look I will be straight with yer as you are my best friend. Before I came over here, she was causing me a bit of trouble; making up fantasies about a relationship that we have never had and threatening to tell Meg. I came here to get away from her and she bloody followed me here. It's all in her mind, she is fucking crazy … I was going to report it but thought if I got out of the way for a bit she would give up. I really don't know what to do, Sean, I really don't.'

Sean looked at his old friend, he had always known him as a reliable and honest man. In fact, he had often teased him when he was the one that wouldn't break the rules when they were training, but he also knew how they would try to steal each other's girls. Steve had told Sean once of a particular time that he had thoroughly kissed his latest girlfriend and more, but stopped one step short from having sex with her. Sean had been hurt as he was becoming quite fond of her, but rather than lose face he dropped her pretty quick, never knowing Steve had lied to him because he was angry about

Sean putting his name on the voluntary list for night duties, which he endured for over a month. Watching the wretchedness on Steve's face, he could clearly see the pain his friend was in. 'Well, what can we do about it? I think you need to tell me the whole story over a beer. I will come back to yours tonight and we can talk about it.'

The relief on Steve's face was clear and just knowing that his friend was on side he relaxed.

'Thank you for believing me, Sean. I am sorry if she has hurt you already. I tried to stop her, but I can't do this on my own and she knows that I have too much to lose.'

'Well, we will sort it out later and make a plan. She shouldn't be allowed to get away with it. In the meantime, let's go be heroes.'

Steve and Sean came out of the portacabin door laughing and joking; from her spot under the trees where she had been watching. She could see an animated conversation between them and sensed it was about her, but she wasn't close enough to hear what was said. She left the shelter of the tree and sidled up to Sean, he abruptly took charge and instructed her to go and sort things inside the unit and organise the paperwork for exhumation in preparation for the results of the geophysics boys' findings. He watched her walk away and he could see her anger in every step at being side-lined. He just wanted her busy, contained, and away from himself and Steve so that they could concentrate on the job for at least a day.

The day was hot and dusty and by the time the team had finished surveying half of the site everyone was happy to call it a night. Calling everyone together, Sean told them all to head to the Kittiwake B&B out on the road where a meal and a bed were waiting for them all. 'I have been told on good authority that the breakfast is great so tuck in as I know tomorrow will be another long hard day. I will see you bright and early at 8.30 a.m. I will be spending the night with Steve and his family, catching up on old times … err Sara you can take my car and could you tell Mrs O'Connell I will not be using my room just yet but to keep one open for me just in case. Right then, goodnight to yer all.'

He turned towards his friend, and they watched as the team piled into cars and headed out down the track across Aiden Doyle's field that led to the road and then on to the village. Before she had left, Steve had watched as Sara's face had changed; firstly, he could see the shock as she found that Sean wasn't coming back to the B&B, then she had glared at him with such hatred in her eyes he had to blink as he swore that he could see Bree in her face. Just as swiftly it disappeared, and he watched as she calmly took the keys to the car from Sean, and smiling at him, bid him good night. Turning to the others he saw her call them over for a lift and she headed away as if nothing had passed. The look of hatred merely a blink of an eye, or his own imagination. He often questioned himself and sometimes his own sanity.

Sean and Steve walked across the fields towards home; as the sun went down, they lingered at the top of the hill under the fairy-thorn tree. Sean placed a hand on the marker where Steve's dad was buried.

'I know he wasn't your real father, but he loved you very much, Steve, and I know he was very proud of you … strict, mind you. I remember the stick across me arse when we rolled in drunk after celebrating our getting into Garda College.'

'At least we were too drunk to feel most of it. He wasn't so bad, at least he cared. I just wish he had cared enough to take Bree too.'

'We can't always do the right thing, Steve; my daddy was a drunk and I followed in his footsteps. I sorely regret the way that I behaved, and my children hate me now because of it, but I can't change what happened and neither could he. Yer mammy said that she thought Bree had been adopted so they weren't to know. Please don't hate them for something that as a parent they did wrong, it's a bloody hard job as I think yer are finding out now that you have Romany to look after. Come on, I hope yer mammy has made colcannon, I love her cooking, so I do, her coddle is just deadly.'

Steve laughed and patted his stomach. 'Don't I know it? I have put on so much weight since being here, I haven't done much running either, and I was going to start again in the morning.'

'I won't offer to get up early and join yer, I like me sleep too much. Anyways, me knees are knackered now after ten years on the force rugby team.'

They laughed in happy companionship as the doorway of the farmhouse came into view and the last rays of the sun hit the windows and bounced back into his eyes. Steve smiled to himself. Blinded, that's exactly what he had been until Meg had opened his eyes to what life might be like. Her love had made him strong, not weak; that is how he had coped with Bree and it is how he will cope with Sara Dyson.

CHAPTER 25

"People don't want to hear the truth because they don't want their illusions destroyed."

Friedrich Nietzsche

Romany woke up with a start. She heard voices murmuring downstairs; she looked at her phone, it was gone two in the morning. She listened to the adults talking downstairs, surely her mum and Steve still weren't up. She thought of sneaking downstairs to get a drink, they were probably half drunk on the wine from dinner. She smiled to herself, that way they wouldn't miss a little glass for her. After all, she was sixteen and she had been so good lately, her exam results were due in tomorrow, and she was nervous for the results. She had missed a fair amount of school when she had been attacked by Bree and left in a coma after the arranged riding accident that had nearly taken her life. If she couldn't find any wine, she knew where a bottle of vodka was kept, she could always add a bit to her squash and that way they would never know. She tiptoed down the stairs, avoiding the one that she knew would creak and slipped past the living room into the kitchen. She had forgotten Sean was staying and she could hear the deep resonance of his voice but not what was being said. She heard Steve reply and when she heard her mother's name, she pricked her ears up. She had never been one to eves-drop on the adult conversations as all she had ever heard were her parents arguing. That seemed so long ago now, before the divorce, and her mum was happy now with Steve; for the first time in ages, she smiled all the time, and apart from his mental health being affected (which was understandable after that nut-job sister of his tried to kill them all), he had been making great progress lately. She was happy too; everything was more relaxed since Steve had come into their lives, she felt safe and loved, so when she heard Sean's next sentence she nearly gave herself away by dropping the bottle of vodka that she held in her hand from shock.

'But I don't understand why she thinks that you have a relationship … did yer sleep with Sara. Steve? Is that what this is all about, a woman scorned and all that? I am yer oldest friend and yer can tell me anything and it won't leave this room. Is that why she is threatening to tell Meghan?'

Before she heard Steve's reply, she quickly placed the bottle back in the cupboard and crept her way back upstairs. So, he had been cheating on her mum? The pig, he was no better than her dad. What could she do with the knowledge she had? Whatever she did it would hurt her mum. She thought Steve was different, she looked up to him … she loved him, he was her dad. He had become more to her than her own father. She turned her face to the wall and tears rolled onto her pillow, wetting where her face lay, brushing the tears angrily away she flipped her pillow over and closed her eyes. Why did it have to be her? She had seen the way Sara Dyson looked at Steve, she had watched her brush against him when they went into the station to make a statement. Meg had been oblivious, but everything made more sense now.

Eventually she dropped off to sleep and when she awoke Steve and Sean had already left for work. She lay in bed; turning over she could hear her mum singing and the sound of Bridget washing up. She looked at her phone, it was already ten o'clock and her results would be posted online in fifteen minutes so she had better get herself washed and dressed. She felt sick and knew that she couldn't face her mum's positive attitude this morning. Pulling on her jeans and t-shirt she crept down the stairs and headed across the fields to where she knew the police were working. She was angry and tears pricked at the back of her eyes as she thought about Steve and Sara together. She wiped them away with the back of her hand. 'I will confront him, that's what I will do, and her the bitch ... I will ... I will.' She slumped to the ground, letting the tears fall again. She closed her eyes and thought about her mum and life without Steve in it and how it had been before he came into her mum's life. 'Oh why the fuck did I go down to get a drink.' She turned herself around and watched as the farmhouse door opened and her mum gave her a wave. She couldn't put it off any longer, she needed to find out her results.

She needed to get at least five C grades to get into art college. She barely dared to look. She brought up the site on her phone and the school logo came into view. She scrolled past until she saw in bright red writing *GCSE exam result*. Clicking on the link, she waited as the site slowly found the correct page. One thing about Bally-Bay, the internet was crap, she thought. 'I could use that as an excuse if my results are rubbish. That way I can put mum off for a bit.'

Only Romany had the password; it was given to her by the school to access her results, so she was quite safe. The phone vibrated in her hand, her friends were messaging, and texts were pinging to her as she tried to concentrate on the task at hand. She closed her eyes as she clicked on the link. 'Please let me get what I need to get into college.' She opened one eye and scanning the list she counted two A's, three B's and a D ... yes, a result!

She stood up, she knew that it would make her mum happy and she had no plans to spoil her day but the burden she carried was great. Heading back down the hill, Meg watched her daughter's slumped shoulders. From the doorway she could see her unhappiness, it hung about her shoulders like a cape and she prayed that her results weren't the disaster that she obviously thought they were, and that perhaps it could be salvaged.

Meg tentatively reached for Romany as she arrived at the door and enfolding her in her arms she started to say, 'It doesn't matter, love,' thinking that her sadness was a reflection of her grades but she whispered, 'I passed, Mum, it's ok … I passed.' Meg, not understanding her daughter's forlorn expression, hugged her gently to her and held her tight.

'Well done, darling, you have worked so hard to catch up, you deserve to pass. All out now for art college!'

Walking inside together, Meg quietly said, 'Come on, let's get breakfast, we can have a cup of tea to celebrate.' But Romany, mumbling something about telling her friends, fled to the quiet of her bedroom. Meg shrugged her shoulders. 'I don't think I will ever understand teenagers,' she sighed and headed to the kitchen for that long-awaited cuppa.

Romany flung herself on the bed; if she carried on moping her mum would ask questions and she wasn't prepared to tell her the truth so she needed to confront Steve first and find out just what he had been doing with Sara Dyson. All she knew was that her mum was going to get hurt. Washing her face, she then quickly texted her friends at home and headed down to the kitchen for breakfast. She felt quite sick but knew that if she didn't squeeze in at least a slice of toast that her mum would be suspicious. Plastering on a smile, she opened the door to see Steve and her mum sat at the table.

'I thought you had left for work?' she spluttered.

'No there isn't a lot to do until geophysics finish and I thought I would have breakfast with yer mammy for a change; Sean has gone on ahead. I also hear that congratulations are in order?' Steve stood up and stepped forward to pull Romany into a hug. She stiffened in his arms and pushed him away. He held onto her arms, but wondering what was wrong and covering it up, he gently kissed her cheek. 'Well done love, Mum and I are so proud of yer.' Hastening out of the door, he called a cheery goodbye and waved as he left. Meanwhile, Meg had put on the kettle for more tea and poured

Romany a glass of juice, so had missed the little scenario played out a few minutes before.

Slumping down at the table, Romany picked up her juice and started to sip it and Meg, totally unaware of anything amiss, continued making tea.

Sean greeted Steve as he arrived at the site. He scanned the area but saw no sign of Sara and breathing a sigh of relief he smiled at his friend. He had been so grateful last night when Sean had believed him about Sara. He was beginning to question his own sanity; after all that had happened over the last year, it wasn't surprising. They would need to talk again to enable them to catch Sara at it so to speak. They had decided the only way to fight back was to catch her on tape and to let her think that Sean was still enamoured and that Steve was just jealous. It had got too late last night and the details of how they would achieve this had not been discussed.

His thoughts back on the job, he turned to follow Sean into the portacabin and plonking himself at a desk he waited for his large friend to bring him up to date.

'Coffee?' Sean poured them both a cup and placing it on the table between them he said, 'I think yer are gonna need this, the geophysics boys were busy last night and sat and translated their findings so far into something that even a moron like me could understand. Things are not looking good, there is an area they are looking at again today, right in the very top corner ... a very open area.' He hesitated so that Steve could understand the seriousness. 'They think that they have found a large pit or chamber area, it is huge, and this is apart from the single graves discovered down the wall area where we thought that we would find bodies.' He picked up the report left for him by the geophysics forensic team and read from it.

'The part of the cemetery we are looking at covers twenty-five thousand square metres and they scanned up to six metres below the surface. Using ground penetrating radar techniques (GPR), they mapped the landscape. The tomography and electrical imaging covered four profiles – west, east, south, and central. On certain sections of the cemetery, anomalies were located and indicated. But a large void was located at a depth of three to ten metres, it is believed to be a manmade cavity below the surface and is estimated at fifty metres in a south to north direction and twenty metres in an east to west direction. The information received so far constitutes the site as a prominent target for future investigation. In addition, three-dimensional resistivity imaging techniques for detection of graves at small depths is on-going.'

'I will be honest, Steve, it's not looking good, that is a bloody big void and I am not looking forward to what we might find in it. Tomorrow we will start on that site with the diggers to see exactly what we are dealing with. Maybe even start this afternoon if the geophysics give the ok.'

Steve whistled. 'I knew that we were going to uncover a lot but I can't imagine what we are going to find. Where is Sara?'

'Don't worry, I sent her off to Dublin for the day and I told her to stay over so we can finish our talk tonight and set up a plan; so you can relax. I sent her off to make sure that all of the paperwork has been filed properly for the exhumations. I don't want any more delays. I am still concerned that one of the girl's parents may change their mind and that would throw all of the permissions up in the air. We would have to get a court order and as it's a cold case investigation you know how long that could take, and if the judge is friendly with the Bishop and church? Then that's that. I don't know about you, but I am beginning to feel that the sooner we get this over and done with the better for everyone. The lads are reporting some hostility from the locals already, so word is getting out.'

Steve sighed. 'Well let's go and take a look at what we are talking about and see where to go from there. The diggers are in place; we have borrowed one from Aidan Doyle, the farmer who has lent us his field, and I can get another from my home if necessary. I am sure one will be all that's needed. Anyway, I don't know if Daddy's has been used or even started for a few years. I know Mammy lets the person that rents the field use all the equipment, so it could be good.'

They both stood and as they started to walk towards the gap that had been made in the stone wall that enclosed the cemetery, for easier vehicular access, Steve told Sean about Romany's reaction this morning.

'Ah you know kids, especially teenagers, you don't know how they are gonna be from one minute to the next. It's all those bloody hormones.'

'You don't think she could have heard us talking last night, do you?'

'Nah! She was sound asleep, even before Meg went to bed. I'm telling yer, it's just teenagers, you will get used to it. On and off like a bloody light switch.'

The day was busy and taken up with looking at images and discussing data with the forensic team. Josh, the lead on the geophysics, came to find them late afternoon.

'Well we have finished,' he told Sean. 'I certainly don't envy you tomorrow. I will get the rest of this data written up tonight so that you can see clearly what you are dealing with, but to give you a heads up; as-well as the large void that was discovered yesterday, today we have identified over two hundred and seventy single, individual, man-made cavities at a depth of two to three metres, that we believe to be grave sites, running along the side of the east wall and two smaller voids further in at the central point. All will need to be investigated and I shall put that in my recommendations. We just have a few sites left to investigate over against the west wall of the building itself, but as these are all marked clearly as graves with head-markers, we should be able to finish that whilst you start over in the other corner without interfering with you.'

'Thanks Josh, get the team back to the B&B for your meal and thanks for all the work. See you in the morning; I will be staying at Steve's again tonight.'

The two men locked the port-a-cabin door and heading out across the fields towards the farmhouse, Steve turned back and as he did a small, figure ducked back down behind the wall. Steve shook his head as if to clear the vision that he had just seen, of a glimpse of red hair and a child's sad green eyes staring into his.

'What's up, man?' Sean looked back towards where Steve was still staring. 'Did yer see something?'

'Nah! I don't know ... I thought ... Nah it was just an animal or something ... my imagination playing tricks as usual ... I'm a bloody wreck, I tell yer.'

Sean smiled and pulled Steve's arm. 'Come on, nothing that a good hot meal and a night's sleep won't cure. I wonder what your mammy is cooking tonight? Oh how I miss a good home-cooked meal so I do.'

The two men walked home in companionable silence, both of them ruminating about the part that they would play in the forthcoming upheaval. One thing that they both knew, without a doubt, was that nobody, including the local community, would come out of it unscarred by what they would find.

Evening came and the two men took a well-earned beer for Steve and a soda for Sean out into the garden. The night was warm and Steve hoped that the weather would hold for the digging to take place over the next few weeks. There was nothing worse than a crime scene like a muddy bog.

'Will you call in the forensic team yet or wait until we know what we are dealing with?' Steve asked his friend.

'I am holding out a little bit as I want to be sure before I get the

Super on me back for wasting resources. I'm already in his bad books for keeping the geophysics team here for an extra day. It all costs money and has to come out of the budget. Apparently, I have spent that already and there are "real crimes to investigate." His words, not mine.'

Steve sighed and they tackled the thorny problem of Sara Dyson. 'The only person that knows besides you is Dr Evelyn Watson, the psychiatrist that I have been seeing.'

'What did she recommend that you do?' Sean asked.

'The same as you, that I come clean to the boss and tell all, but you know mud sticks and even though I know I haven't done anything wrong, I think it will finish me and Meg for good.'

'Ahh she loves yer, man, any fool can see that; you have been to hell and back together. That builds a strong bond. She would believe yer if you told her, I'm sure.'

'No, no please, we can't tell Meg. I just need to sort this myself; just help me to get rid of that bloody bitch and I know I can sort the rest with Meg.'

They again talked late into the night and decided that they needed to get Sara on tape so that they could use it to stop her. They agree to use Steve's phone to tape her and Sean would encourage her to follow him. 'It will be easy when she comes back, I will play on how I missed her and how jealous you were that they were an item. I will let slip that you jog every morning, down at the harbour ... setting the scene.'

Parting to go to their own rooms, Steve thought to himself that Sean might be confident about his plan, but he certainly wasn't. Sighing, he crept into bed, shedding his clothes across the floor. Meg turned into his arms sleepily and he held her close. Sean's idea had better work, he would rather die than lose his beloved Meg. His heart hurt at the thought.

CHAPTER 26

"Free yourself from the people who cause you drama and poison your soul. You know who they are ... they have to go!"

Steve Maraboli

The next morning Steve was in a rush. Romany had been awake early, hoping to catch him and confront him with what she had overheard between him and Sean the other night, but they passed as he dashed out of the door. She had wanted him to look her in the eye and tell her that he wasn't cheating on her mum. She would know if he was lying. His face was an open book to anyone, if they only wished to see. That is why she loved him so dearly; he had become the father that she had always wanted. Strong, steady, reliable, and kind. He was always the first person wanting to know how she had been doing and he showed an interest in her drawing and artwork. She admired him so much and to overhear that he was far from perfect was a huge blow, not only to her but the pressure of keeping it secret from her mum was beginning to show.

She had tried to behave normally around him the next morning, but she just couldn't. She had wanted to shout and scream at him and call him a liar as he held her mum and kissed her goodbye, something that usually made her smile but now, holding the knowledge that she did, it made her feel sick to the stomach. She wanted it to all be a nightmare and disappear with the morning light but when it hadn't, she had blamed the pressure of awaiting her exam results. When questioned by her mum, she wasn't going to be the one to break her heart and she hoped that Steve didn't either, good old honest Steve, the liar and not-so-good bloke. Now even the joy of her grades had been wiped away from her. After laying awake, waiting to hear him stir, she had finally drifted back to sleep and when she did finally wake she had witnessed him kiss her mum goodbye and then leave, she would have to try and catch him later.

The sound of the diggers rolling in through the gap in the wall meant that this was truly happening. Steve especially had wanted to be the first on the scene and so had arrived before Sara and Gardas Siobhan and Connor.

'Well here goes, the permissions are all in place, that's one thing I will give Sara; she is a bloody good DS and by the look of it here is the Environmental Health officer.' He waved his arm towards a man that was approaching them. 'Just in time, I wasn't going to wait on him, but I also wanted to do this properly. I don't want the boss on me back now.'

Steve looked up as a young man with a clipboard headed towards them. Handing Sean a piece of paper, he stated that he was happy that only the area outlined on the map was to be exhumed and that he was heading back to Dublin to file the records. With a wave he was gone. Steve felt a presence at his elbow, and he turned to see Sara with the largest grin on her face holding a coffee cup out towards him.

'Coffee, boss? I bet you thought you had got rid of me and just like a bad penny I turn back up. I won't go away that easily, and anyway, Sean has missed me so much that he can't wait to spend time with me alone tonight.'

Steve, playing the part of a jealous rival, snarled at her to leave Sean alone and he stalked off. She smiled with satisfaction and drinking the coffee from the cup she spat it out on the ground. She had forgotten who it was intended for, and she had made it as bitter as possible for him. Heading back over towards Sean, she watched as he supervised the digging and smiled at him in a sexy way when he turned towards her. With a big grin on his face, he headed off to survey the area that the geophysics boys were finishing up. The wall was tall and dark and as his eye travelled upwards towards the sky, he could just make out what was left of razor wire and glass embedded in the top. And running alongside the bottom were the remnants of wooden crosses in varying degrees of decay; broken and falling over in piles like a sad monument to what was below the ground. As he approached, he could hear the excitement in the voices of the men who were stood in a circle looking towards what he thought was a pile of rags. Steve looked up on his approach.

'It's a child's body, it was so close to the surface that I am surprised that it hadn't been taken by foxes. The geophysics stumbled over it as they turned to pass back over the area. Forensics are on the way. I am not sure but it looks like a baby, but something is wrapped around the cloth, or what is left of it. See a small skull peeping out of the top, but look closer, Sean ... it has a hole in the skull; it could easily have been damaged as it was so near to the surface, or it could be cause of death.'

Steve looked at Sean with hope in his eyes.

'Well at least if it is we will have proof of murder, not death in childbirth ... that's if this poor wee one's death was even recorded.'

Forensics took over, and the area where the body was found soon revealed a deep pit filled to overflowing with tiny bodies with holes in their skulls wrapped in rags. The reason for the first discovery was soon made clear as the pit had been filled and no more tiny bodies would fit into it. After watching forensics photograph and tag the position of each tiny body before being placed carefully onto a stretcher for removal to the temporary morgue, the two men looked at each other, the knowledge between them of worse to come, as the babies' bodies piled high.

Steve and Sean headed back to the portacabin for coffee. Steve had almost vomited but not before Sean had barked out orders that the wee one's remains be treated with the utmost reverence and that he wanted them to place the remains in the temporary morgue that had been placed on site only that morning. Leaving the forensic team to do their job, he ran a hand across his eyes and blinking away tears he followed Steve to the edge of the field where he was throwing up his breakfast. Catching up with him, he placed a hand on his back and joked.

'Yer always did have no stomach for this job, I am surprised that yer lasted as long as yer have. Well at least yer didn't contaminate the crime scene.'

The team gathered at the end of the day and Sean began by asking Connor and Siobhan to undertake night duties until he could arrange for more help to keep the site secure. 'Yer know when word gets out that bodies have been found where they shouldn't have, locals will be trying to get on site in droves. So be prepared for the uproar when they know exactly what we are up to and let's hope that the press doesn't get wind of it yet. I shall get security fencing and Garda here ASAP but in the meantime I am relying on my trusty team, ok? Nobody gets on site without my say so from now on, is that clear?'

Siobhan and Conner both nodded their heads. Steve saw the remnants of tears on Siobhan's face, and he placed his hand on her arm. He remembered how he had felt the first time that he had seen a dead body and smiling at the karma of it he said softly to her, 'My first one was the priest responsible for all of this. At least we know that there is some justice; we just need to find them peace now.'

She nodded gently and he could see the resolve strengthen her back as her spine straightened. Sean disappeared and Steve, ensuring that some food would be brought to the two young garda later on and that they had as much comfort as they could have under the circumstances, left.

Entering the house, he could hear chattering coming from the kitchen in the back. He opened the door to find Sara Dyson happily ensconced at the kitchen table with a cup of tea and a plate of biscuits laid out before her. He could still see remnants of a smile on all of the faces as they turned towards him.

'What the hell are you doing here?' he roared at her.

'Ah boss, I just thought that I would pop in and say hi to Meg and Romany as I haven't had a chance to yet. I was on my way to get food for the youngsters left on guard duty for the night. Your mum was just telling us what a little sod you were as a boy ... bit of a lad then, sir ... I promise I won't tell the others.' She started to laugh but to Bridget's ears it didn't sound quite right, and she certainly had not been telling her about Steve as a child. Before she could protest, Sara Dyson jumped up. 'Sorry boss, only joking, I will be on my way. Nice to see you again, Meg, I am glad that you are enjoying your stay with your family. They must be happy that there aren't any more secrets to reveal, those poor girls.' Turning she left the room.

'I will see you out.' Steve glared at her and followed close behind.

Grabbing her arm as soon as they were in the hallway, he shut the kitchen door and in a harsh whisper he said, 'Don't you ever come here again and if I see or hear that you have said anything about the case I will have you sent home immediately. Do you hear?'

'Well I can't really do much about that, can I? Your mum and Meg are already involved in the case. I could say that you are biased and let that little bit of info trickle back to the powers that be at home. Anyway, I am sure that Meg wouldn't want to know all the details now, would she, and Sean definitely doesn't want me to go anywhere. I just thought I might pop in and introduce myself to your dearest mammy ... to tell her that Magda, or is it Bree, sends her love.'

Her laughter carried her out of the door as Steve stood stunned in the doorway. Turning angrily on his heel he thought he saw a glimpse of someone moving at the top of the stairs. He shook his head to clear it; just the mention of her name caused him to jump at ghosts.

It was probably Romany. He hoped that she hadn't heard their conversation. At least if she had, it wasn't relating to any kind of a relationship between him and Sara. He would need to do something about her before she managed to tell Meg all of her spiteful lies and kill any hope that he had of getting through this in one piece.

Steve plastered a smile on his face and returned to the kitchen to a subdued atmosphere. 'Sara was needed urgently back at the site, she is going to supervise the collating of information for me. Had she been here long?'

'Ah Steve don't be cross with her, she was only teasing about us chatting about your childhood, we really had only just made tea and introduced her to Bridget when you arrived. I hope you won't give her any trouble. I like Sara, we are going to catch up for a drink when we get back home, she seems pretty fond of Sean too.' Meg smiled, already planning the outcome of her matchmaking skills.

Bridget, standing now behind Meg, caught her son's eye and gently held his gaze, almost imperceptibly she shook her head. Laughing, Steve hugged her to him and said, 'No trouble but I would prefer her to be concentrating on her work at the moment, not setting up girly nights out.'

'Ah you're a tough boss.' Meg smiled and kissing him she went to find Romany to help with dinner.

Bridget gave her son a strange look, she was sure that he would tell her if he needed to talk it through. One thing she was sure of, was that she didn't like Sara Dyson … not one bit.

Steve found himself outside deeply breathing in the fresh air; summer was definitely coming to an end and there was a chill to the air that had not been there a couple of weeks ago. He smelled the salt and heard the seagulls crying as they wheeled above the newly ploughed fields. Aiden has been busy today, he looked across and could see the tractor finishing the last few rows, the plough on behind, as he sowed the winter barley. He stopped and looking back he found himself at his daddy's grave under the Hawthorn. Dropping down in the grass next to the headstone, he laid back and closed his eyes.

Thoughts ran through his mind; he pictured his childhood and he could almost feel the way his daddy carried him on his broad shoulders. He could smell the pipe tobacco that lingered in his clothing and feel the roughness of his jacket. He was transported back in time, jiggling up the hill swaying from side to side, his small hands clasping tightly to his father's waistcoat, then lifted up high to see the Robin's nest with the five small blue eggs nestled inside of it. It sat deep inside the branches of the faery thorn tree. The thorns of the Hawthorn providing protection from predators, and the stinging nettles that grew below provided food from the caterpillars. He wiped a hand across his face to clear the image of the weathered face of his father smiling down at him, and the feeling that he had in his stomach, as he swooped through the air, up into his arms. Carried like a king on top of the world as they headed home for tea.

He looked shocked at the wetness on the palms as he hadn't realised that he had been crying. The tears silently falling down his cheeks, he had left them to dry on their own.

'I love you, Daddy ... I love you,' he whispered to the wind.

Bridget, looking out of the window, watched her son drop to his knees, as if in prayer, and she hoped that he could find some comfort in his contemplations. She went to the back door and waving into the distance she watched as her most precious boy turned and looked towards her. The sun glinting low on the horizon made her catch her breath; it gleamed above his head in a golden halo. For a moment she thought that she saw a figure standing next to him, one arm carelessly flung over her son's shoulder, the other raised in greeting. She blinked and it was gone, the brightness of the sun now hurting her eyes as the last rays dipped below the hill.

CHAPTER 27

"The human capacity for self-delusion is boundless."
Michael Shermer

The morning meeting was under way as Steve arrived, he had overslept which was so unlike him, so his morning jog had to be deferred. Sara had almost been late herself as she had waited overly long to catch Steve in his early morning run. Pretending to leave for a run herself, she had missed breakfast and her stomach was complaining loudly. 'I should have brought you a bacon roll before you joined us,' Sean said laughingly. 'Where were yer anyway? I missed our little breakfast chats, it almost makes me feel like I am playing happy families.'

'Just a coffee would be good, boss.' She winked at Sean.

'That's good then, mine is white with three sugars,' he replied.

'If you keep having all this sugar you will lose your trim figure, you have to watch your weight you know, now that you are getting older. You don't want middle age spread.' She poked his paunch. No-one could call Sean slim, he had always been big, and that is why he had been a great asset to the police rugby team in his youth.

'Yer cheeky mare.' He smiled at Sara, but it didn't quite reach his eyes. After all, he knew what she was now, and he was just playing a part. He watched her swagger away and he thought to himself what a shame it was; he had longed for someone like Sara in his life but he knew that if she wasn't playing a vicious game she wouldn't look at him twice.

They all met in the portacabin, the security team had arrived and the fencing was being erected.

'I won't keep yer long, I will in fact be brief so that you two can go and get some sleep.' He pointed towards Siobhan and Conner. 'By the way, great job; everything is as we left it last night. The team are going to tackle the other smaller pit this morning on the west side of the site before we go all into the biggest void.

'So far I can tell you that one hundred and seventy-three bodies have been recovered, all of them infants, no more than a few hours old at point of death, and they were all similarly interred and wrapped in pieces of a cloth material. Most of which was degraded too much to be recognisable, but it is to be presumed at this time that it was cotton sheeting. Fibres are being sent to the lab in Dublin along with any D.N.A. samples from each child, in the hope of matching the D.N.A. samples that we had taken from our known list of family members.' He took a huge breath. 'The worst of it is that, as far as forensics can tell, each child was bound tightly in some kind of vine or plant material and every one had similar wounds to the skull, leading to the suspicion that they were all murdered and did not die of natural causes at birth. Steve, can you please find out who is the local priest and arrange an appointment to speak to him. He may be able to identify any of the nuns that were here at the time we are talking about and where they are now. I would certainly like to ask them some questions. Sara, can you please supervise the site today and arrange the sorting of the D.N.A. samples to see if there are any matches; and yous two get yerself back to the B&B. I have asked them to keep yer some breakfast and then get a few hours kip.' He pointed to Siobhan and Connor.

'I will be updating the chief super, so yous had better wish me luck.' He pointed to the door. 'Well crack on.' Everyone except Steve shuffled out, head bowed and silent as the enormity of their task sunk in.

'Are yer ok, man?' Steve placed his hand on Sean's arm. "It is taking its toll on all of us.'

'When I looked in the morgue this morning and saw those wee bodies laid there in rows, I felt sick. I thought about how happy we had been as each of my own children were born and how fragile their little bodies were. Do yer know I wouldn't hold my eldest Michael for at least a week? I was terrified that I would drop him or break his neck with that wobbly little head; but ah! Man, the feeling when yer hold them in yer arms for the first time; those poor wee things never felt the comfort of a pair of safe arms, did they? I swear that if any of those bitches are still alive, I will see them prosecuted even if they didn't commit the act themselves, because they knew ... Steve, they bloody knew.'

Steve, at a loss for words, patted his friend's arm again and left to find the priest. He had actually been surprised that the parish priest had not visited them before now. After all, he had been informed about what was going on and the church was right next door to St Theresa's; even if only to check that they weren't interfering with any pastoral graves.

As he was about to climb into the car, he felt an arm slide through his and he turned to look into the face of Sara. Passing a hand over his face he looked at her. 'Sara, I don't need any more shit at the moment. Why don't yer take yerself off and do what yer were asked to do? '

Looking back at him with hurt in her eyes she pulled her arm back from his and said, 'I only wanted to say that I know how hard this must be for you and your family and Meg's family too of course.' Before he could take in her words, in shock he mumbled out his thanks. Maybe she had realised her errors and was trying to make amends, he thought.

'Magda said that you would take it hard, she told me to tell you to dig deep to uncover ALL of the secrets that are buried here, but especially your own grave; now that needs to be so very deep so that you can never ever get out of it.' She laughed loudly as she walked away; running her fingers down and stroking his arm as she went. 'Keep digging,' she called.

As he watched her, stunned by what she had said, a chill had entered his heart. If he didn't know better, he would swear that was his sister laughing. How? Why? Had she spent a lot of time with Bree, or Magda as she had been named, or was she using it to torture him? Yes, that's what she was doing; well it was going to stop very soon and the only grave that was being dug was her own.

As Steve turned to get into the car again, he looked around the graveyard to see if anyone had heard or seen the exchange between him and Sara but, as usual, she had been so careful. Sean was inside the portacabin, and the rest of the team were in the top area, and he could hear the sound of the digger as it started on the next void. Crossing himself he prayed that no more babies' bodies were found that day, but he knew that his prayer would not be answered. Out of the corner of his eye he saw a movement and as he glanced to where he had seen something, a glimpse of a small figure with red curls came to his vision before disappearing completely. He blinked rapidly and rubbed his eyes. He looked at his hand as if he could remember the feeling of the small hand in his. 'God almighty yer useless bugger you are so tired that yer are seeing things again,' he spoke out loud to himself. Maybe later today he would give Dr Watson a call, he hadn't spoken to her for a few weeks; possibly he needed his medicine adjusting. He thought with everything that was going on that he had been coping pretty well. He would do a lot better as soon as Sara Dyson was off his back. He hadn't had a chance to put into action Sean's plan to tape her and confront her so that he could report her and have her removed. He was waiting for the opportunity to catch her out. He would tell Dr Watson about their plan too as she had known about it from a previous session. He didn't think she would be happy with him for not following her advice and reporting it to his superiors at the time.

He drove out of the grounds and headed onto the main road out of Bally-Bay. He reflected on his childhood. Brought up in the small seaside village, he thought back to being ushered into church on a Sunday and being swiped around the ear at Saturday morning catechism by the nuns for not listening to his lessons. He was headed now to the nearest town of Mornside to meet the priest who covered Bally-Bay. As with everywhere else, cutbacks had been made and Bally-Bay no longer warranted its own priest, so the services were shared with the other parish. If parishioners couldn't travel, a small bus picked them up and took them to Mornside on a Sunday according to his mammy, who took this service once a month to seek confession and attrition.

Steve himself had not kept up his religious beliefs as soon as he had left Bally-Bay. Although you could take the boy out of Ireland, you couldn't take the Catholic Church from his soul. It had been ingrained into him so well that he had lately found himself reverting back to the old practices of crossing himself and genuflecting as he entered the church. Even earlier that morning he had offered up a prayer. He smiled to himself and wondered how he would feel in the presence of the priest. Would he revert completely back to the boy from Bally-Bay, or would the detective take over? It would be interesting.

He parked outside a large gothic building, it was much larger that the small parish church in Bally-Bay, and he looked up at the beautiful architecture; one thing about the Catholic Church, it knew how to spend money. Inside was just as stunning with beautiful painted friezes, stained glass, and gold leaf as far as the eye could see. He swallowed down his disdain and headed to the back of the church where a robed figure had appeared.

'Father Murphy?' Steve called out. The figure turned, his soutane swishing against his legs, and he headed towards Steve with a smile on his face and a hand outstretched in greeting, ready to shake the detective's own.

The smile soon left his features as Steve introduced himself and reported the reason for his presence. 'Walk with me, my son.' The priest gave instruction and Steve followed as he led him out of the church through a small arched wooden door that was intricately carved. 'Even the back door is beautiful,' Steve thought as they passed into a small walled garden that adjoined the church. It was obviously a resting place for previous clergy as here and there grand marble obelisks or carved stones showed through the tumbling roses and flora. The scent was heady, and Steve sat on the bench offered by Father Murphy with gratitude.

The priest turned to Steve and said, 'I want you to know, Detective, that I have been instructed by the Bishop to help your investigation in any way that I can.'

Steve frowned and looked the priest up and down. Before him sat a man in his late sixties or possibly seventies, his hair thick on his head and white as snow; his face weathered and open, and upon it a warm expression. Steve knew that before their conversation had ended that expression of kindness and helpfulness would be gone.

'Did you know Father Benedict?' His first question threw the priest.

'Yes, I did, sadly.'

'Sad for who, Father? The girls that he abused or the ones he murdered?'

Father Murphy sighed deeply. 'I knew a facet of the man, a good priest, always he was there for his parishioners and a comfort to them in their sorrows. He struggled with his own demons and I wish a thousand times a day that he had sought help from his brothers in the church.'

'Well, Father, I am digging up the consequences of his struggle and I can assure you that demons were definitely involved; but as for seeking help? Well then I don't believe that he could be helped; as far as I can see he was completely insane, and the church were accountable for leaving him in a position where he could perpetrate his crimes.'

'I understand your anger and we must pray for his and his victim's souls. As I said, if I can help in any way I will. I have been authorised to show you any records in our archive that you may wish to see but they will not be allowed to be removed from the church or copied.'

'Well Father, we will surely have to agree to disagree on the subject of paedophile priests and leave it there. But when it comes to the matter of murder and serial killers, I believe that is my domain. What I have come for today is records of the sisters who were at St Theresa's from nineteen seventy till its closure in the nineties. Tell me, Father, why are priests celibate when they so easily break their vows?'

'Detective Ryan, I can only tell you what pope Benedict XVI said. *"The abuse of faith has to be resisted precisely. Celibacy is not a matter of compulsion; someone is accepted as a priest only when he does it of his own accord."*

'Maybe all Benedict's struggle with this part of their faith, as did Saint Benedict who beat himself with Hawthorns to overcome temptation. I thank the lord I have never felt the need for such extreme measures. Now, shall we go find the records that you wish to see? Most of the sisters that served at St Theresa's are either dead long ago or have gone on retreat where they cannot be reached, I'm afraid.'

'How convenient for the church.' Steve let Father Murphy know that he wasn't as stupid as he thought and that he knew they had been deliberately moved when the investigation was opened; whisked away into the night as soon as the application to open the graves at St Theresa's hit the Bishop's desk weeks ago. Steve followed the elderly man back into the church and along a passage to another arched wooden door. On opening it he led him into a beautiful wooden panelled study that smelled of lemon furniture polish. A large desk with a leather insert on the top gleamed and shone and it was mostly from it and the tall bookcases behind him that the lemon scent emanated. He turned and asked Steve to take a seat, directing him to a chair, he then seated himself behind the desk and turned his attention to a pile of folders on the right-hand corner of the desk.

'I see that you were prepared, Father, even though I never made an appointment before coming here.'

'As I said to you, Detective Ryan, the Bishop asked me to make available to the investigating team any records for St Theresa's.'

He picked up the first folder and turned it for Steve to view. The folder, old and musty, had ornate writing on the front partially missing in places, but stated *Staffing Sisters of Saint Theresa's, Order of St Benedict*. Here goes that name again, Steve thought, it haunts me whichever way I turn. The names of the sisters in alphabetical order listed on the first page were dated underneath the title '1971'.

The first names to appear were of two nuns whose names Detective Steve Ryan wished to never hear again.

Sister Francis De Lyon – Abbess

Sister Marie Claire – Nursing Matron

Stamped in red next to most of the names on the list was the word 'deceased'. Steve ran his finger down the list, every name the same. Picking up the second folder from the pile he repeated the action with the same results. Year after year after year; until frustrated he picked one from the very bottom of the pile. The date on the front read 1983. Opening the file, he scanned the list, amongst the names a couple stood out, some of which he remembered himself from school. Running his finger down yet another list of names with either deceased or retreat next to their names, one stood out simply because it was different to the others. It stated:

Sister Monica Joan – Ex-Communicated

The word struck a chord with Steve. Why did he know that name? He needed a moment to think. Leaving the folder on his lap, he picked up another from the very bottom of the pile dated 1990. The list was very short, and he knew that this was the year that Bree had murdered Father Benedict and Sister Francis; also that Sister Marie Claire had died from a heart attack upon finding the bodies. Two other names on the list claimed to be on retreat.

'If they have been on retreat since 1990, Father,' Steve said, pointing to the names of the sisters that weren't dead or elsewhere employed, 'then they have been away for a very long time; surely some of the sisters are working in other schools or homes or even within the order now ... today.' Steve could barely contain his anger at being fobbed off by the priest.

'You have to understand, Detective Ryan, that most of the sisters were left traumatised by the events at St Theresa's and a couple of years later, of course, a fire destroyed most of the records.'

'How bloody convenient for the church. I suppose if I ask to see any records pertaining to the girls that gave birth to children over that time period, or records of the babies' adoptions, I presume you will tell me that they went up in smoke at St Bloody Theresa's.' Steve threw the files back onto the desk. Father Murphy stood.

'Please keep a civil tongue in the house of our lord, Detective Ryan. I must ask you to leave now. I am sorry that your search was fruitless.'

Steve looked the priest up and down. 'Now if I come back with a warrant, would yer still be this obstructive, Father? But then again, I know the answer to that one, don't I? You have made the position of the church very clear on this.' He hesitated before delivering the last blow to Father Murphy. 'It's a good job we have duplicate records at the Dublin station then; and this is not **my** lord's house, he lost that privilege a long time ago.' Holding his hand in the air as he left the room, he said, 'I know … I know, Father. I will rot in purgatory for my sins, but most of you buggers will be burning in hell any way.'

Steve's anger abated a little as he came in sight of the car. He did have access to some records in the Dublin station but just like these ones he doubted very much if they would do him any good. He shouldn't have lost his temper; he will be in trouble now. He used to be able to let things go, be more professional, but ever since Bree or Magda, whatever she called herself, came into his life, his whole world had turned upside down. For years he had been working on auto pilot, calm and confident in his role as a policeman working his way up through the ranks, steadfast Steve, but that was before!

He wasn't sure of anything anymore … maybe he never had been. It was all thanks to a wall that he had built around himself over the years to stop him feeling anything. Meg had knocked the first brick down and Bree had taken a wrecking ball to the rest. Sara Dyson was currently trawling around in the rubble, just in case she found something whole to smash. Perhaps he had better let Sean know to expect a call from an irate Bishop or the Superintendent. They were probably all having lunch together right now at some exclusive golf club, so he didn't think it would be long before he got the call.

He sat in the car and made the call to Sean explaining that Father Murphy had been no help whatsoever and that before he came back, he was going to have a rummage through the old files back at the station in Dublin. Just in case they missed something. He also had a name rattling around in the back of his mind that nagged at him, but he couldn't remember at this moment what it was or why.

'Bloody hell, man, you know how to upset them ok, don't yer? I thought that yer would be the better man for the job as yer had grown up here and understood the church. Obviously I was very wrong.' Sean let rip at Steve, he had to hold the phone away from his ear. 'Sorry Steve, it has been bloody awful here, we have recovered another two hundred and sixty babies' bodies, all as before, wrapped and skulls smashed in, in the second void. We haven't even got around to the huge pit in the middle yet. I will see yer later … I am just as frustrated with this case as you so when I get a holy shit show from the boss, I will give it back some, I can tell yer.'

'Jesus, sorry Sean, the church's co-operation would make our job so much easier if we could get some names or records. I will see what I can dig up. By the way, does Sister Monica's name ring a bell?'

'No, I can't say it does, but I sure remember that Sister Francis, she was a right bitch when I was singing. Always at Father Benedict's side, I smiled when I knew she was dead.'

Steve could hear Sean mumbling and knew that he was saying a Hail Mary and crossing himself for what he had just said and thought.

'Ah yeah, I forget yer were a choir boy; it's a good job Father Benedict preferred girls, the bastard.'

The two men laughed as they said their goodbyes, the laughter helping each of them to break the tension.

CHAPTER 28

"If history teaches anything, it is that self-delusion in the face of unpleasant facts ... is folly."

Ronald Reagan

Steve pulled into the carpark, at least he was going downstairs to the archives; he hoped to avoid any encounters with the Superintendent at this time as he knew he would eat his head off if he caught him. He found two young Garda sat at a desk finishing the job that poor Collum O'Brian had been working on when he was killed by Bree, placing any leftover paper files onto the computer and destroying the paper copies.

Steve smiled as two young faces turned towards him.

'Hi, I am Detective Ryan and I have been working with DCI Sean O'Dowd on the St Theresa's case. I popped back in just to see if the files were still here, I need another look at something in their records.'

'Ah sir, we finished those just last week. I can put it all on a stick for you if you wait a few moments, or I can email it to you if that is easier,' the young girl spoke then smiled at Steve. The young man scowled which made Steve chuckle as he was obviously jealous that he was getting her attention.

'Thank you, I will wait whilst you download it.'

The task was quickly done, and Steve was in the car heading back to Bally-Bay, congratulating himself at his escape and that he didn't have to trawl through all the musty paper files to find what he needed. 'I should be home early for a change. I could take Meg down to the pub for a meal and an early night.' He smiled to himself at the thought of the night to come. His romantic life had been suffering lately and Meg was a saint to be putting up with all of his late nights and exhaustion. Even at weekends he was so knackered and involved in the case that he couldn't relax or pay her much attention.

He would put this case to bed and whisk her off somewhere quiet and make it up to her. She would get used to being married to a copper, he thought. Hang on, did he say married? The thought of spending the rest of his life with Meg had been rumbling around in his thoughts for a while. He had never felt this way about anyone, and he definitely had never thought of marriage to anyone else. It had slipped into his mind as easily as the time that they spent together. There was just one problem ... Sara Dyson; she could ruin everything, that was for sure.

Pulling into the lane that led to the farm, he approached the house. He could see a dark blue car parked outside but no sign of the little hire car so Meg must be out. As he approached his anger soared as he recognised Sara's car ... how the bloody hell dare she?

He rushed into the house to be met by his mammy sitting at the kitchen table with a pot of tea and sat on the opposite side with a huge smile on her face was Sara.

His fists clenched as he tried to hold back the anger but suddenly he grabbed her by the collar and hissed into her face. 'What the fuck are you doing here? I told you before to stay away from my family.'

Bridget, not realising what was going on, paled.

'Son ... son please let her go ... please!'

'Yes Steve, do what your mammy says like a good boy. Don't you want her to know all about us? I am sure she will be thrilled to learn that she is going to be a grandmother.'

Steve's hand dropped from her shirt front. She stood rubbing her neck, smiling up at him. At least if he marked her in front of witnesses it would be evidence against him.

He raised his hand as if to strike her. 'You bitch, you fecking liar; how can it be? It certainly isn't mine.'

Before she could reply, Bridget felt herself falling, she slumped across the table and Steve, letting Sara go, rushed towards her.

'Mammy, oh Jesus, Mammy!' He looked up with such hatred in his eyes that Sara became afraid; she had seen that look once before on Magda's face and she knew then that she had pushed Steve to his utmost limits. The Diabhul had risen, and he wasn't going back quietly.

'Get out of me sight before I fecking kill yer.'

Turning, she ran for her life as Steve's screams hit her ears. Cradling his mother in his arms he managed to find his phone from inside his pocket and dialled 112. Hearing it ring he waited for someone to answer. The rest was just a blur. The ambulance arrived and a short time later so did Meg and Romany, just in time for the ambulance crew to declare Bridget dead. Seeing Steve sat on the doorstep, a broken man, sobbing, Meg's heart broke too. How could she ever comfort him when she was still reeling from her own loss? Flinging her arms around him, Romany joined them; they silently stood together and watched as they took his mammy's body away. The sound of the door to the ambulance slamming brought him to his senses and storming to his car he screeched off down the lane, heading towards the village and St Theresa's, leaving Meg and Romany standing in the driveway just staring after him. Meg, pulling herself together, managed to dial Sean's number to warn him of what had happened.

Fury and pure hatred burned in Steve. His thoughts irrational, he could almost feel the heat in his stomach as the bile rose up. He felt sick ... suddenly a calm feeling came over him; it was as if his body had been taken over by an entity other than his own consciousness. He felt calm now, distracted; he pulled into the site entrance and headed to the portacabin, ignoring all greetings from team members.

They stood looking after him in confusion. Steve was always the first to have a friendly greeting and to bring cakes and coffees to everyone. This was definitely out of character. They watched and followed with their eyes as he tracked his way across to the other detectives. Sean and Sara were having an animated conversation at the bottom of the portacabin steps. Something was definitely wrong, you could practically feel the air pulse as he strode past them, his face a blank.

The team watched in horror as Steve grabbed hold of Detective Sgt Sara Dyson and shook her like a rag doll. They couldn't hear what was being said as they were too far away, but they could see DCI O'Dowd tackle DCI Ryan to the ground and sit on his back until he calmed. DS Dyson recovered herself and ran to her car and drove away from the site. By now a crowd had gathered and Sean, lifting Steve gently to his feet, half carried and half pushed him inside the building. All of the fight seemed to leave Steve in one go, like a deflated balloon he practically collapsed into a chair.

'Steve what were yer thinking? Oh Jesus, Mary and Joseph, what were yer thinking?'

'She killed Mammy, Sean ... that bitch killed my mammy, sure as if she had murdered her.'

Steve slumped even further as if he could disappear.

'Jesus! I am so sorry about yer mammy. Meg rang me. What happened?'

'She told Mammy her filthy lies ... she said she is pregnant ... well it isn't fecking mine. Oh Jesus, Sean, tell me yer didn't? Please tell me she isn't carrying your child? I grabbed her, the lying bitch, and Mammy just keeled over ... one minute she had a pot of tea on the table and the next that bitch had killed her. I held her in me arms as she took her last breath .'

Sean moved to comfort Steve, but he brushed him away.

'And you can feck off too if yer shifted that bitch.'

Sean, at a loss, shrugged his shoulders and gestured with his arms and in that moment he knew that Sara had done what she intended to do; destroy his best friend and ruin a forty-year-old relationship. He hoped that she was lying and that she wasn't pregnant. He had been just as used by Sara as Steve, and the shame he felt in that moment knew no bounds. His own selfish reaction to a woman that flattered his ego and left him believing that she was on the pill had compounded what was already a terrible situation. How fecking stupid could any man be in this day and age? Was he not an adult, responsible for his own contraception? He wanted to batter himself with his own fists.

'I suggest that yer go home to Meg, Steve, and stay there. I will do my best but yer know that I will have to report this to the chief. I am so sorry about yer mammy and everything else. I promise yer that I will have Sara sent back to England within 48 hours.' He patted his friend on the shoulder and left him to go outside and soothe the gossiping amongst the crew, which he knew had witnessed everything, including Steve's attack on Sara. 'Jesus Christ why did he have to lose it now? Just as they were going to sort it out and in front of everyone.'

Talking to the small crowd that had gathered outside the door, he explained that Steve's mother had died and that he blamed Sara. They all uttered sympathetic noises and said that they knew it wasn't like him at all, but that he did go beyond what they all felt was appropriate behaviour for a senior policeman, let alone a man to a woman. Making them all reassurances that Steve would probably be suspended from duty for a while, at least, but that also it wasn't up to him, or them, to make any disciplinary assumptions. The feeling amongst them was that he was genuinely a good guy, so whatever had happened to banjax him, to make him lose his shit big time, must have been the Diabhul's work.

He stepped back as Steve came down the steps of the temporary building and, head down, steered his way through the crowd, they parted to allow him to pass towards his car. Some of them called out their condolences as he passed. Sean grabbed his arm and whispered that he would join him later at home to let him know the outcome of his conversation with the chief, and where he stood. Steve shrugged his arm away and didn't reply. He climbed into his car and left in the same hurry as he had arrived, with a cloud of dust trailing behind him. He didn't care about his job, about Sean, Meg, or anyone; it wouldn't bring his mammy home.

CHAPTER 29

"There are days when I am haunted by a feeling that is blacker than the blackest melancholy. I have contempt for humanity. I despise the people I have been fated to call my contemporaries. I feel suffocated by their filthy breath."

Friedrich Nietzsche

As Steve approached the bottom of the lane to turn onto the main road back to the farm, a small gathering of vans and people were starting to mill about. What the … Shit, it's the press. I wondered how long it would be before they sniffed out a story, or they had a leak in the team. After all, hadn't Sean said they had recovered another load of babies' bodies today? The last thing that he needed now was the press poking their noses in and finding out about the incident between him and Sara today, or worse, about her allegations. He knew he could depend on Sean to keep quiet, but the rest of the team …

He pulled out onto the main road, quickly having to swerve as Aidan Doyle in his tractor was heading his way. The figures ran after him, calling out behind him. 'Are you part of the investigating team? Is it true that you have found children's bodies?'

Aidan, assessing the situation, waved to Steve and pulled his tractor across the road behind Steve, blocking the journalists and allowing his escape. Steve swore under his breath; he would have to pull over and call Sean. More shit to add to the pile. He was sorry for his friend, after all, most of it he had either brought over with him or added to himself.

After turning up towards home, he stopped away from the house

THE DETECTIVE

and walked up to his favourite spot high on the hill where stood a bent and twisted Hawthorn tree. Its branches bowed by generations of the salty winds that came in from the sea, and beaten by the harsh winter storms that rolled in from the Atlantic.

He could hear his daddy telling him that he should never come here after dark or he would be stolen away. 'It's a Faery tree, son, a Sceach Gheal, and at night under the fullest of moons the little people will dance around it, and any little one still awake, or outside, will be stolen away to live under the hill with the Sidhe. Oh, and another thing, if yer hear music, pull yer covers over yer head and don't dare look out the window or they will know yer are awake. No, yer must never harm a Faery tree or yer will anger the little people as sure as God is in his heaven …'

He also remembered hearing his mammy say, 'Now then, Jim, don't yer be scaring the wee boy. He will be up all night with nightmares.' On hearing his daddy's chuckle, he would snuggle down, sure in the knowledge that his daddy would keep him safe.

He reached the top of the hill, he was becoming quite a visitor lately, the grass was well trodden where he had been over the last few weeks. Oh, how he wished for those days again. He didn't want to be here telling his daddy that his mammy would soon be joining him under the tree, and that he was to blame. If he hadn't shouted at Sara or grabbed her … perhaps his mammy would still be alive. He knew also that what Sara had told them played a large part in his mammy's reaction and consequent death. Touching the headstone, he cried like a new-born baby. He howled at the injustice of it, then he sobbed as he asked his father for his forgiveness.

Drained and tired, he dragged himself up and started walking down towards the farm, unaware of several pairs of eyes that were watching him descend. Romany sat in her bedroom window watching Steve return. She was unsure what had happened earlier, but she believed that Sara Dyson was involved. Maybe Bridget caught them kissing, or worse? She loved Steve as a father, but she still thought that he had cheated on her mum. She was sorry for Bridget's death, she really liked her; she reminded her of Magda, her own grandma.

Meg held herself back. She wanted to run to Steve to hold him, and comfort him, but she knew that from what Sean had said on the phone he would shrug her off. He walked like a zombie towards the house, she was so concerned for him, he was so fragile. She hoped that her strong man could pull through this last blow, intact. She had some questions about why he had attacked Sara Dyson, but she didn't want to bother him yet … but he had been acting strangely whenever her name was mentioned. Maybe Sean knew more about it than he was telling her. All she could do for now was to be there for him, in any way that she was needed.

Sara Dyson crawled down low on her belly up to the brow of the hill. She had a clear view of the farm from there and she watched as Steve fell to his knees, sobbing on his father's grave. She smiled to herself. Bree would be proud of her; she had him really rattled now. He was going to get just what he deserved soon enough. As he stood and walked down the hill towards the house, she stood up from her hiding place, sure that no-one could see her, and headed back over the fields towards the gap in the hedge to the lane where her car waited. Romany looked up at that moment and she saw a flash of red. Her eye travelled to the figure making her way across the field. So, she came to watch the damage … the cow, she hated Sara Dyson … she was about to take away everything that was good in her and her mum's life!

The house was quiet as Steve walked in. It would never be the same again with mammy gone. He headed straight up the stairs, he fell onto the bed and immediately fell asleep with exhaustion. Meg stood in the doorway, and she could hear his steady breathing, she closed the door gently again; she walked back downstairs; everything else could wait. Sleep is what he needs right now; after all, the reality was a nightmare that he would wake up to soon enough.

Sean, upon ending the call from Steve, swore loudly. The crew had gone back to work and Gardas Siobhan Thomas and Connor O'Brian had just arrived back on site after a sleep, ready for another night shift.

'The press are at the bottom of the lane, boss. We nearly knocked some down as we turned in. They jumped us as we slowed to turn.'

'Yes, I just had a call from DCI Ryan. Have yous two seen DS Dyson?'

'No sir,' they both replied together. "Err … is it true that DCI Ryan attacked her, sir?'

'Ah I see the jungle drums are working. I want no gossip about other colleagues on this investigation, is that clear?'

'Yes sir.'

'And the last bloody thing I need is the press getting hold of it, got it? Right, I want you, Siobhan, to contact forensics to see if they have got the DNA samples done from the first pit and if there are any matches to our girls on the board. If so, can you please update the information, maybe set up a new board with matched babies to girls' names. Connor, I need you to go visit the geophysics team over in the graveyard, before they leave for the night. Can you please bring back their findings for today and a list of bodies from the temporary morgue and any findings that they may have so far? Please warn them the press are waiting for them and that I will have the balls off any of them that so much as looks at them. Then, when yer get back, help Siobhan. So crack on; I am going to lock myself in the cabin now to update the boss.'

Sean watched as Gardas Connor O'Brian and Siobhan Thomas hastened off in different directions. They were both efficient and eager to learn. If one thing came out of this sorry mess it would be that he made sure that they were recognised for it. He turned on his heel and wearily climbed the step to do the task that he had been dreading all afternoon.

Settling himself into a chair he dialled the number. The conversation went as he expected. Of course he was in the dog house as it was on his recommendation that Steve and Sara joined him on the investigation; but to be fair the chief recognised Steve's good work and excellent record, also the pressure of his mother's death as the pre-cursor that led to the incident with DS Dyson. Stepping outside, he took a deep breath of air. The next task was to ensure that Sara Dyson was returned home as quickly as possible and then he could pass the news onto Steve of the Chief Super's decision. Either way, none of it was going to be easy for him.

He climbed into a car and headed towards the lane to the B&B, hoping to find Sara Dyson there. As he approached the press, he speeded up, making them jump out of the way or get run down. He would get some more security placed down here to keep them back. 'Another bloody thing to add to me list,' he sighed.

The Kittiwake B&B was appropriately named. It sat high on the cliffs looking out to sea. The gulls whirled and cawed above his head. He had only spent one night here since his arrival. He had either stopped with Steve or been too busy to bother. He admired the place and thought oh if only this were a holiday, what a spot! He had forgotten his childhood and had been a city boy for so long that the pale was where he called home. His eyes roved across the bay to which the place was named and onto the small fishing harbour. His kids would love it here. What was he even thinking, his kids were now teenagers and they didn't want to know him! He couldn't blame them; he had been a terrible father to them and husband to his wife. The demon drink had owned his soul at one point. Sighing at what might have been, he entered the building, up the few steps and into the grand entranceway. Climbing the stairs wearily he found the room number that he was looking for and rapped loudly on the door. He heard a shuffling behind the door and the sound of the lock being turned before it cracked open a small amount. A wan face with tear tracks down it turned towards him. Sara flung herself into his arms only to find them not open.

'Oh Sean ... Sean, what a mess. Steve tried to kill me ... I don't know why. I think he is jealous of you and me.'

Sean pushed her away from him and staring into her eyes he said, 'We can do this out here if you want, Sara, or somewhere a bit more private. Me personally I would prefer everyone to hear what a whore yer are, and how yer have been crucifying a good man, a good friend, and causing the death of the loveliest lady in Bally-Bay. On some mission to destroy him over some bloody slight or knock back. In fact, I think yer got away light. I would have killed yer meself.'

Sara stepped back and allowed Sean to pass, she sneered as he followed her into the room. 'Aw what a shame, did the Irish fat boy loser find out his mate had been shagging his girlfriend? I want charges pressed against Steve Ryan and I want him sent back to England; he is a disgrace as a police officer. He attacked me in full view of everyone for no reason.'

'No reason yer say? Have yer not been threatening and persecuting him since before yer left Cambridge and on top of that yer went to his home and terrified his mammy to death. What, no tears for Sean now? Yer are the one that is a disgrace to the force, and I shall make sure that yer never serve as an officer again. The Chief Superintendent here and the Chief Inspector in Cambridge are aware of yer lies and frankly a campaign of sexual harassment against Steve Ryan and yer are no longer on this investigation. I want yer gone on the next flight home. I will take yer badge please and yer will report to your commanding officer back in Cambridge where yer will be officially suspended whilst further investigation into the incident today, and yer behaviour here and back home, takes place.'

Sean left Sara staring at him as if he had struck her, he snatched her badge from the shelf by the door and opening it he turned and said, 'Yer had better be gone by this time tomorrow or I will take yer to the airport meself and throw yer on the plane.' Then slamming it behind him, he left.

Climbing into the car he headed out of Bally-Bay, winding down the window he gulped in the fresh air and it tasted salty. Trying to get the taste of deceit from his mouth, he headed past the press and was happy to see that they had been pushed away from the entrance to the driveway leading to St Theresa's and the cemetery where they were working. Two large police officers touched their cap at him as he passed. He was glad that at least one thing on this bloody investigation was working correctly.

Turning into the lane that led to the farm he took a deep breath. This was not going to be so easy as dealing with Sara Dyson, he knew that Steve would put up a fight, but he had a job to do now and the best thing for everyone was for him to take time off and let the powers that be decide his fate.

Meg opened the door, and he could see by her pale face that things had not improved since he last saw Steve. 'How is he doing, Meg?'

'He's in the shower, Sean, he has had a little sleep. I hope it will make him feel better.'

'That's good, I could do with a cuppa tea while I wait if yer don't mind?'

'Of course, I will just pop up and tell him you are here. Romany, pop the kettle on, there's a love.' She called as she ran up the stairs. Sean was just settling down with a mug of tea in front of him when Steve appeared in the doorway, followed closely by Meg. 'Come on, love,' she called to Romany, 'let's leave the men to talk.' Kissing Steve on the cheek, she pulled Romany outside. 'Come on, love, I don't know what's going on but I don't think I want to know either.'

No, I don't think you do, Romany thought to herself, but I think I know … some of it anyway.

Sean looked up at his old friend. He looked rougher than he had ever seen him look. Gesturing to the pot of tea and picking up another cup, he started to pour the tea into the mug. 'Sit down, Steve, we need to talk.'

CHAPTER 30

"The bravest sight in all of this world, is a man fighting against the odds."
Franklin Knight-Lane

Sean had left by the time the girls came back and Meg sighed with relief. She knew that Steve was in trouble, but at the moment he needed to be left alone, to grieve, and deal with his own personal issues. She knew that he was suffering way beyond what had been happening at home, and even his mammy's death had only added to a problem that was already there. She wished she knew what was going on. He had been acting strangely ever since they had arrived in Ireland, and she didn't believe that it was just a case of bad memories from the past. Sean was as much help as piece of string, she knew that he was covering for Steve and she needed to know the whole story before she could help him.

Steve heard the door go. He was in no mood to talk to Meg. He had been told by Sean that he was officially off the case until an internal investigation had taken place. He also told him that he had been brutally honest with the chief super as he felt that honesty was their only weapon against Sara's lies. He had disagreed. If they all knew the truth then it wouldn't be long before Meg knew, and he still wasn't ready to share that information with her. He stood abruptly, meaning to leave the room before Meg came to find him, but as he stood something jangled in his pocket. Putting his hand inside, he touched something cold and hard and pulled out the stick with the records from St Theresa's on that he had collected from Dublin earlier in the day.

He brushed past Meg and Romany with hardly a greeting and holding up the stick he mumbled something about work and left them stood there unsure of where to go next.

'Come on, Romany, we can start dinner.'

'I'm not really hungry, Mum.'

'Ah don't you abandon me too, come on, help me make some soup. That will be light and I can take a bowl up to Steve later.'

The two women gathered ingredients from cupboards and fridge and set to chopping vegetables and making supper. Meg found it therapeutic, and Romany found some comfort and camaraderie in working together with her mother. She washed the board and knives that they had used, whilst her mum removed all of the vegetable peelings. 'Oh, I had better not put them out in the compost bin, Bridget won't need them any—' Suddenly it was all too much for Meg and falling to her knees she sobbed into her hands. Romany flew to her mother's side and drew her into her arms, letting her mum hiccough and cough her way out of the collapse. She held her tight and whispered, 'It's going to be ok, Mum; you can't always be the strong one, we all loved Bridget.'

'Damn onions!' Meg choked out a sort of a laugh. 'They always make me cry.'

The women hugged and cried together, holding on to each other as they had always done … just those two against the world. It had always been just them, even when Meg was married to Romany's father Barnaby, thought Romany, but she had a secret burning inside of her, itching to get out. Her mum was upset enough, she certainly wasn't going to be the one to add more pain. It just wasn't fair … that bitch Sara had destroyed everything that she loved, as sure as Bree had first time around.

Steve plugged the stick into his laptop and page after page of documents came up. Scanning through them his eye alighted on a list of staff names for the year that he wanted – 1983 – it was the same document that he had been shown by Father Murphy when he visited him. Except this one had more information ... in fact, he thought he had his answer staring him in the face. Next to Sister Monica Joan's name he read ex-communicated from the church for inappropriate behaviour towards a child at St Theresa's, Bally-Bay. Of course, hadn't Bree mentioned to Dr Padraic O'Neil when she was in St Philomena's that a Sister Monica had helped her by teaching her to read and write?

The best part for Steve was the information next to the original record and it gave the best information of all – Sister Monica's real name and an address for her family. It would be sheer luck if any of her family were still living at the same address, but it was a start. Thank God that it jogged something in his memory. Not that he would ever forget any part of the interview with his sister after her arrest. Poor Dr Padraic O'Neil had been one of her victims, even though he tried to help her and even got her freed from St Philomena's mental health facility. I suppose it is some kind of poetic justice that he became one of her victims, as against everyone else, including his own wishes; he persuaded the panel to release her. He hadn't known she was his twin sister then, how he wished for that innocence again.

Picking up his phone he started to dial Sean just as Meg entered the room with a steaming bowl of soup. 'I'm not hungry,' he snapped.

'Please darling, try to eat something.' Placing the tray on the small bedside table, she watched as he slammed the lid down on his laptop.

'I told yer I'm not—'

'I know, hungry... I heard you.' Sitting on the bed next to him, she picked up his hand, turning it over she smoothed his palm with her fingers. 'Will you speak to me, Steve? Please tell me what is going on? You have to eat sometime, to build up your strength. You will have to deal with the arrangements for your mammy tomorrow. Please darling, I love you, I am here for you … please talk to me.' She laid her head on his arm and tears flowed. 'You helped me when my parents died, please let me return the favour. I feel so helpless.'

Steve's heart ached. He longed to hold Meg in his arms and just tell her everything, but he couldn't, not yet. Sean had told him to come clean. He said that he knew that Meg would stand beside him, but he had his doubts; once she found out about the kiss and the lies that Sara had been telling. Worst of all she would never forgive him for raising his hands to a woman, he knew that … no matter what she had done. He couldn't even forgive himself. He turned her tear-stained face towards him and kissed her eyes and her cheeks. He held her face in his hands as gently as a cloud.

'Mo Gra' Thu' A Mhuirni'n,' he whispered as she fell against him. They kissed harder and fell back against the covers, grasping at their clothing as they went. Their love making was a comfort to them both and Steve held on to the thought that it might be the last time that he held his love in his arms.

He woke early. The sun had not risen yet and slipping out from under the covers he grabbed a t-shirt and joggers and headed downstairs. He knew that Sean would be up already, and he had forgotten to ring him last night with the information he had found. Maybe Sister Monica, or Susan Monahan as she was now known, had some answers to what exactly had been going on at St Theresa's. He looked at his watch, it was six thirty. Sean would definitely be up now, if he had even had any sleep. He was pretty shorthanded after losing Sara and Steve. Romany awoke. She slipped out of bed onto the landing and listened as she heard Steve talking on the phone. Was he calling her? She couldn't hear what was being said as Steve had shut the kitchen door so as not to wake Meg. She slipped down a couple of steps just as Steve pulled open the door, she jumped back, rubbing her eyes as if she had just been on her way to the bathroom half asleep.

Steve spotted her and whispered, 'Morning beautiful, I am just off for a jog. Tell Mammy if she wakes we will talk when I get back, ok? I have put the coffee on.'

He set his watch and turned the lock on the front door. Stepping outside he took in a lungful of air, the salty tang hitting his throat and he smiled, after last night's love making with Meg, and his conversation with Sean this morning to confirm his feelings, he had decided that the only way forwards was to tell Meg the truth. He was pleased, a sense of relief already on his shoulders as he jogged down the lane. Romany watched him from the bedroom window, she saw which direction he was headed then scrambling into some clothes she followed him.

Sara Dyson sat in the B&B cradling a cup of coffee in her hands, her flight to England was booked for this afternoon and a taxi would pick her up to take her to the airport at noon. She felt a bit sick and hoped that the coffee would settle her stomach. She had lied about being pregnant, she was going to pretend that she had lost it later on. It was just to annoy Steve, but she had been feeling sick in the mornings for the last few days ... come to think of it, she was late with her monthly period, but she had put that down to all the stress.

Her ears pricked up when she heard Sean's voice out on the terrace speaking to someone. She peered behind the curtain and could see that he was on the phone. She listened and heard her name mentioned, it had to be Steve then She would get him later, it was her word against his and she intended to win this battle. She heard him mention a jog and laughing as he told Steve to bugger off. Running up to her room she dressed in her work-out clothes, throwing on a sweatshirt she headed out of the door just as Sean finished his conversation.

She knew where Steve ran, she had followed him enough times; this morning she would be waiting for him. If she really was pregnant, she could keep pretending it was his and by the time they found out after the birth, and she was forced to give DNA, his relationship with Meg would be completely destroyed, and Sean too. As a bonus, his career would be in tatters as well, the misconduct inquiry would be on her side if she was having his baby.

She smiled to herself as she made her way down to the harbour, to his favourite spot. He would stop and rest on the wall before jogging back home. She knew his routine well.

She spotted him doing his stretches. Hopefully she could get close enough before he saw her. She silently crept along the harbour. He had his back turned and his headphones in; so didn't hear her approach.

'So you think that you have won, don't you, Steve Ryan? Don't forget I have friends on the team back home and I will have plenty of time to gain sympathy from them before you return, especially when I start to show,' she sneered.

He turned to face her just in time to see Romany pounding down the wall behind Sara. She couldn't understand the confusion on his face, she expected him to be angry with her she was hoping for a few more bruises to photograph as evidence against his attack. As it was, yesterday's confrontation had left barely a mark on her, it looked worse to the others than it was. His grip on her front had only been shirt, not flesh. She was determined to press charges and was about to tell him when a noise behind her made her start. She turned awkwardly as Romany screamed at Steve and pushed on, reaching towards Sara. Taken aback at Romany's presence as she lunged at her, Sara's foot caught in a mooring rope, and she toppled backwards over the wall to the rocks below.

Steve heard a sickening thud as she hit the ground. The tide had been out for an hour now and the rocks below were sharp and exposed. He leaned over the wall to look, Sara's body lay nestled between two fishing boats and blood pooled around Sara Dyson's head. Romany screamed by his side.

He folded Romany into his arms and taking out his phone he dialled 112 for the second time in two days.

CHAPTER 31

"Sometimes it is better to lose and do the right thing, than to win and do the wrong thing."

Tony Blair

Sean received the call from Steve and his face paled. He turned to find the team looking towards him. They had been in the middle of a briefing and a new DS had been dispatched to temporarily help out for the week. A young fella called Josh, he barely looked old enough to be out of school, let alone made DS, Sean thought, or maybe I am just getting old. The chief super's words still rang in his ears from his conversation last night. 'What the hell is going on down there, Sean? It's a bloody holy shit show, with the press onto it and the bloody English faction determined to sabotage any credibility the force has left with the public; behaving like teenagers, acting the maggot. I want it wound up in two weeks, do yer hear me?' On and on he went. Yes sir! Thanks for asking, I'm just grand, he said to himself when the call had ended. What would he say when he heard this latest news, God only knew?

Turning now to face the team, he stated in a voice with no emotion that sadly he had been informed that there had been an accident and Sara Dyson had been hurt. Siobhan gasped and before the mumbling had time to grow, he asked them to carry on whilst he went to assess the situation. Reluctantly climbing into his car, he thought this is the second time his friend had wanted him to get him out of shit; well, he wasn't sure that this time he could help him; it would be out of his hands entirely. As he drove off, he wondered if

Meg had been informed. The call had been brief and to the point, with no detail; so what had really happened was still a mystery to him as much as anyone else.

Heading to the harbour he wound his way down the hill and into Bally-Bay. The blue lights drew him to the right place. He could see a crowd gathered, some standing on the wall trying to peer over the heads of the others, and amongst the locals he could see some were press. Like bloody vultures, he thought, never far from a crime scene. It was as if they knew exactly where to go, an instinctual honing in on a crime scene, like a sniffer dog in heat.

Pushing his way through the gathering crowd, he made his way to where Steve sat with his arm around Romany in the back of an ambulance. Stopping on his way to make himself known to the officer in charge, he was a familiar face to Sean, not one that he would wish to see on any case. DI Paul Hunt should have retired years ago, not only was he old school, but he was incompetent to say the least, bumbling along through life till his retirement. He probably copped this one as they thought it was a suicide and the others were all busy solving real crimes.

'Both of them yours, so I hear?' he said pointing to Steve and then over the wall of the harbour. Sean peered over the wall to get a look at the crime scene below and immediately took it in. Forensics in white suits were below in the harbour just in the process of lifting Sara Dyson's body onto a stretcher and he could see the dark tell-tale mark on the rocks. He also noticed that the tide was on the turn and soon their crime scene would be under water. He didn't believe that Sara had jumped and killed herself, so the only other scenario was that she fell, or worse was pushed. Turning around, he watched as Romany was holding an oxygen mask to her face and taking deep breaths and Steve, staring into space, just looked stunned. If she was pushed, then which one of yous two had done it? he asked himself as he headed over to speak to them. Before he could speak to Steve, he realised that Paul Hunt had reached the same conclusion and Steve was being led away and placed into the back of a police car. He turned and shouted back to Sean to look after Romany and to tell Meg he was sorry.

Pulling out his phone he made the call to Meg then walked across to a now hysterical Romany as she realised that they had taken Steve.

Meg arrived at a scene of utter chaos and, after handing over Romany and offering advice to get Steve a good lawyer, Sean left the scene to concentrate on his own team and headed back to the site outside of the village.

Pulling up to the portacabin, he entered the building. Siobhan and Conner were busy still collating the DNA evidence that had been returned that morning from the bodies of the babies and were in the process of matching them to mothers on their list that had already offered up their DNA for familial matching. At least they were still alive, he thought, and their baby's remains could be returned to them for proper burials. Most of the babies had been matched according to Connor as he pinned the last result to the faces on the board.

'All matched except two and of course we haven't received back the DNA results for the second void dig yet, they hopefully will arrive this afternoon, sir.'

Siobhan looked at Sean as she placed a steaming cup of coffee in front of him on the desk. 'I hope that's bloody strong. Because I need it to be.' He rubbed his hands over his face.

'I made it as strong as I could, sir.' Siobhan smiled at her boss. 'I have a message, sir, from the site crew and geophysics; they need you to come take a look at their findings as soon as. Is there any news for us, sir?' She looked at him hopefully.

'Oh Siobhan, it's a right bloody mess I can tell yer. Sara Dyson is dead … it looks like an accident, but Steve was at the scene, and he has been taken in for routine questioning. Please keep that to yerselves as I don't want it getting out just yet. I will drink this and head over to the site to see what is happening there. How's the new DS settling in? Josh isn't it, is he ok?'

Siobhan blushed. 'Sorry sir, I think I upset him by calling him Josh, he insists on DS Hall. I won't make that mistake again sir, he ate me head off, it made me feel like a right eejit.'

'Yeah it was brutal, sir,' Connor agreed and Sean scowled.

'As I made clear to both of yer, we are a friendly bunch on my team. If yer aren't, and are up yer own arse, then yer aren't part of **my** team; perhaps our young DS Hall didn't understand that, and if he did then he can bugger off back to the pale.'

Siobhan blushed and Conner chuckled, they both admired Sean for his dogged work ethic and his kindness. They also liked Steve and whatever had happened, they didn't think that the gentle man that they had got to know over the last few weeks had it in him to harm someone, let alone kill them. Although, as they were to say to each other later in the day, things had become quite tense since DS Dyson turned up.

Steve sat in a room with no windows and a small table with four chairs. He felt strange. The boot was on the other foot and now he knew what it felt like to be a suspect. He hoped that Romany would tell her mum what had happened, but he wanted to protect her, even if that meant lying. He wasn't quite sure if Romany had made contact with Sara, it had all happened so quickly. One minute she was arguing with him and the next she was gone. All he could remember was Romany screaming at them both and he would never forget the recrimination in her eyes as she screamed his unfaithfulness at him. He had tried to explain that he was innocent, but he could see that she was convinced. The gist of it was something she had overheard between him and Sean.

Oh God, he placed his head in his hands. He was glad Sara was dead; did that make him evil too? Was he insane like his sister? All he knew was that she had managed to do what Bree hadn't, and completely finish him. He would be nothing now without Meg and Romany; he also knew that he had blown any chance that he might have had. Everything was going to come out and he will look like a first-class shit!

He heard the door open, and his mammy's old friend and solicitor John Blake followed closely by DI Hunt entered the room.

'I would like a moment with my client please.' John Blake turned his old face to DI Hunt; he wasn't up to facing down the steely glance of the old man and turning he left the room. 'I still got it,' the old man chuckled. 'Now then, young man, what have you been up to? Before we start let me say I am sorry to hear about your mammy, Steven. I was going to call you to arrange an appointment for the reading of the will. Have yer had chance to arrange a wake yet? No, I don't suppose yer have with all that's happened. Yer better tell me all about it; now I suggest that yer start from the beginning? And if yer want my help I suggest yer be truthful too.' The old friendly face gave off assurances that all would be well, and Steve had known him as a family friend for years. If he could trust anyone it would be John Blake.

Steve held nothing back. He explained how his mental state had been shot from the aftermath of the case and revelations about his twin sister. 'Yes yer mammy told me about that, what a sad mess.'

He went on to explain how his relationship with Meg had been affected, because of his mental health, and that they had decided to have some time apart and how in a weak moment he had kissed Sara Dyson. How from that point on she had stalked him and made allegations, blackmailing him with telling Meg and his boss that he had raped her. How she had been obsessed with him, stating that they had a relationship. When she was rejected by him, she began a campaign of harassment. He told of his escape to Ireland when Sean had asked him to help on the follow up to the St Theresa's investigation, and how she had used Sean to try and make him jealous. How he thought that he had left it all behind in England and then she had managed to follow him out here and had started harassing him again and threatening to tell Meg. Right up to the pregnancy allegation in front of his mammy which had led to his anger and mammy's death. He paused in the telling of his sorry tale and, taking a deep breath, he finished by explaining that whilst out on an early morning jog with Romany, Sara Dyson had confronted him on the harbour wall and subsequently fell to her death. He had decided not to include or mention the fact that Romany had been involved in an argument with her and had lunged towards her. If he had to be honest, he couldn't say if she fell of her own accord, only that he remembered her catching her foot in the coiled ropes on top of the wall before she fell.

'Did you arrange to meet Sara Dyson this morning, Steven? Have yer told me the truth, was she carrying yer baby? Yer know that it will come out at post-mortem and that fella out there ...' he nodded towards the door, 'will be on it like a dog with a bone especially when he finds out about the connection yer had to her. I think the best we can do is stick to exactly what you have told me; that yer were having a conversation with a colleague and she fell whilst talking to you, when you were out on a run with Romany. Will the girl say the same thing? I strongly suggest that yer keep quiet about the other stuff for the time being.'

'I swear to you I never touched Sara Dyson, so, if she was pregnant, it wasn't mine. I am willing to give a DNA sample to prove it. I don't want Romany questioned, she is vulnerable and only a child, she suffered a terrible accident a few months ago and is still recovering physically and mentally.'

Steve looked towards John who patted him on the shoulder. 'Just stick to what we agreed, and I will hopefully have yer out of here in no time.' He opened the door to allow DI Hunt into the room.

Looking at the policeman opposite him, Steve re-counted exactly what had happened on the harbour wall that morning and held his breath and waited for the inevitable.

'Well lucky for you, Detective Ryan, two fishermen from across the harbour witnessed exactly what happened and have given statements which bear out what you have said, but with one difference – that yer were shouting at each other. Is that true were you arguing or was the young girl, Romany, arguing?' He leant back in his chair and Steve knew that how he reacted now would mean whether he walked out of the door and home to Meg or if he heard the sound of the cell door closing behind him. Mustering up some courage he straightened in his seat.

'No, we weren't arguing, Romany called out for me to hurry up as she was starving and wanted her breakfast, she was a little way off and ran up to us. She had been looking in the rock pools over the wall. That's when Sara caught her foot in the rope; it must have happened as she turned when Romany called. It was all so quick … she just fell.' The lies tumbled out of his mouth. He would do anything to protect Romany and he needed to get home to talk to her.

'Well that seems to tally with what the fishermen said, you are free to leave, for the time being, but I may need to speak to you again. I suggest that you stay in the area and, at some point, I will want to talk to the girl. Perhaps you could bring her in with her mother tomorrow morning to make a statement.'

Steve let out the breath that he had been holding and, trying not to leave with too much haste, left the room with John Blake following in his footsteps. He picked up his phone from the desk and asked John for a lift home.

Dropping Steve at the farm, John Blake turned with a last word of caution. 'My advice, son, if yer still want it is that; I suggest that you tell Meghan everything and, Steven … be prepared, the Garda won't let this go and they will find out eventually. Tell Meg to call me if you need me and I will ring with an appointment for you to come to the office for the reading of the will. Now go, make arrangements to bury yer mammy; I'm sorry again about her death, she was a good woman.'

CHAPTER 32

"If you give up, you're not worthy ... The truth is, everyone is going to hurt you. You just got to find the ones worth suffering for."

Bob Marley

Dusk was just settling and a chill hit Steve as he climbed out of John's car. Reluctantly he opened the door to the cottage, and he could hear a murmuring of voices coming from the back of the house. He opened the kitchen door to find Meg sat at the table with her Aunt Sian and Uncle John. They stood as he entered the room 'Steve ... we didn't hear you come in; would you like a cup of tea?' Meg, so formal in front of her family, gave nothing away.

'I will just pop up for a shower first, I stink of the cells, and I need to wash it away. I have been in these clothes after a morning jog, all day.' He tried to smile but it just wouldn't come. He acknowledged them all with a nod of his head and disappeared up the stairs.

Now would be his chance to catch Romany. They needed to get their story straight and he needed her to know the truth, whatever she thought she heard between Sean and him needed clarification as she had obviously been under the impression that he had been cheating on Meg. Tapping on her bedroom door, he didn't wait but entered quickly. He saw a figure laid in the bed asleep.

Sitting on the side of the bed he called her name softly and shook her shoulder. She jumped and then, when she saw his face, angrily turned away to face the wall.

'Please Romany, we need to talk and quickly; I am sorry that you had to witness what happened this morning. I promise you that Sara just turned up; I wasn't nor have I ever been having any kind of relationship with her. Things have been going on that I have found hard to talk about with your mum and I promise that as soon as we have spoken, I will go downstairs and tell her everything, I will hold nothing back ... but I need to know, love ... did yer push Sara this morning?'

Romany looked back at him in horror. 'No, no, I didn't. I thought that you did?'

'Oh god what a mess ... no, I never touched her, love. She just fell. When yer shouted she turned around to see and fell ... I swear that's the truth. The police want a statement from yer in the morning and that is exactly what I told them and yer need to tell them exactly the same. Don't mention any argument. I told them that yer came with me jogging and Sara turned up; we were talking and yer called out to me because yer wanted to go home for yer breakfast and, as she turned, she caught her foot in the rope and fell. Two fishermen witnessed it, so it ties in exactly with what they say happened. God, love, I wasn't sure if yer touched her or not. It was all such a blur. I'm so sorry, love.'

Romany turned to Steve, her anger had dissipated and tears flowed down her cheeks. Steve scooped her into his arms. 'It's ok, love, it was just an accident, a horrible accident. Just tell them what I said, and it will be an end to it.' He gently patted her on the back and turning her face to his he wiped away her tears and brushed her hair from her face.

'I thought that you ... and she ... were, you know? I heard you and Sean talking ... I heard you say you kissed her.'

'I know, love, but I will explain, I promise. As soon as I get out of the shower I will bring yer downstairs and yer can listen while I tell yer mammy everything, ok?'

'Well not as soon as you are out the shower. I think you had better put some clothes on first. I might throw up if I see you naked.' She smiled and Steve patted her hand.

'That's my brave girl."

He left her room, closing the door quietly behind him. He went into the bathroom and closed the door. He could hear Sian and John leaving and murmured condolences spoken about his mammy. Leaning his back on the door, he slid down it to the floor. Head in his hands he took in a breath. Thank Mary, Jesus and Joseph that Romany hadn't pushed Sara Dyson. Hopefully with her statement tomorrow confirming what he had said, it would be an end to it. He was quite relieved it was finally going to be over, he just had to tell Meg everything; there was no point him holding anything back now. The sooner he told them the truth the better ... he should have done it sooner, maybe then he wouldn't lose them, as he was sure that he would do now. He wouldn't blame Meg if she left, after all, she had done nothing but be honest with him and he had thrown her trust back in her face, by deliberately, not exactly lying, but by keeping everything from her. He didn't deserve her love.

Climbing into the shower, he let the water pound over his head then he turned it to the cold setting. When he could bear it no more, he turned it off and climbed out of the shower. Wrapping a towel around his waist, he looked into the mirror. Staring back was a complete stranger. 'Who are yer and what have yer done with Steve Ryan?' he whispered. Brushing his teeth, he moved to the bedroom to dress. He could hear Meg washing up and Romany talking to her. He needed to hurry; now that he had decided to tell everything he couldn't wait to start. Pulling on a sweatshirt and joggers he ran down the stairs and entered the kitchen. Meg and Romany turned to him, startled. Meg started to speak, her eyes held all of the anger she felt, the disappointment and disgust.

'Please, before yer say anything, I need yer to come and sit down so that I can explain everything to yer.'

'Explain? How can you explain your distance from me, your unexplained absences, involving my daughter in whatever sordid little game you were playing with Sara Dyson? Go on, Steve, explain that!'

He stretched out to pick up her hand and she withdrew it quickly.

'Please Meg let me tell yer, please … I'm not asking for anything else, I just need yer to listen. I will answer any questions afterwards but please let me tell yer it all, I need to tell yer it all.'

'It's a bloody pity that you didn't tell me before this terrible accident happened.'

Pulling her into the living room he made her sit and he sat Romany next to her.

'Are you sure you want me to be here? Isn't this just between you and Mum?' Romany asked.

'No love, yer can leave at any time but I would really like yer to stay if yer could. It started way back just after Bree … as yer know I wasn't coping well with the aftermath of what had happened and the fact that she was me sister. Meg, you and I were having relationship trouble and we stayed apart for a few days. Romany was still recovering from her injuries, and I had my head messed up big time; I felt terrible for not protecting yer both and guilty about what had happened to Bree. I was also experiencing panic attacks and blackouts. Sara Dyson witnessed me having one and, concerned for me, or so I thought at the time, came to my flat. I had just got out of the shower, and I heard the door, I grabbed a towel and went to open it. I thought it was the pizza that I had ordered but it was Sara. Basically, she told me that she had feelings for me, and she kissed me; I being the idiot that I am, and I have no excuse, kissed her back. One thing led to another, the towel fell, and before I could make a complete eejit of meself, the doorbell rang and it was the pizza … saved by the pizza man. I apologised to Sara. I told her that I loved you and I felt such a bloody prawn that I sort of pushed her out the door. I was meeting you that night, Meg, and I wanted to make a fresh start. I had booked up counselling and I know that I needed to deal with whatever was going on with me so that I could be the man that yer deserved. I am not making excuses, I promise.'

Meg started to speak, but Steve held up his hand. 'No please; just hear me out. That is only the start of the bloody stupidity.'

He went on to explain how Sara set him up by following him into the toilets at work and flirting when colleagues were near, how he had rebuffed her over and over again.

'Then things turned nasty; she started to threaten me, saying that she had my DNA on her clothes from the pizza night and she would tell the boss and you, Meg, that I had raped her. When Sean called, it was as if I had been thrown a lifeline. I stupidly thought that she would go away and get over herself because I was in Ireland. That at last I was far away from her. Suddenly, she had turned up at the investigation site; she had wangled her way over and was crawling all over Sean like a rash, trying to make me jealous. I tried to warn Sean, but our old school rivalry kicked in and Sean thought I really was jealous. By then, she had a hold on Sean, she threatened to hurt him and I know that he was still recovering from his marriage breakdown. All I was doing was trying to protect the ones that I loved. The final straw came when I came home to find her with mammy the day she died. We argued and mammy just keeled over because … she told her she was pregnant with my child.'

Meg gasped and Romany held her hand tight. 'Steve … oh my god … did you … are you?' She was lost for words.

'No, no I swear, I just lost it then; everything that she had been doing to me, all of the hateful things, and she had killed Mammy. It all came out in a burning anger. I raced down to the site. I was blinded with this anger. I didn't care in that moment if I killed her in front of everyone, which apparently I would have done if Sean hadn't stepped in. He had been helping me set her up, to get proof. I was supposed to tape her on my phone when she threatened me. Sean was going to let slip that I was out jogging in the hope that she would follow me, and I tape the conversation. That is what you overheard, Romany. I had confided in Sean that night and he was helping me get proof. That is why you followed me that morning isn't it, to catch me cheating?' Romany nodded, her head drooping.

'I didn't actually expect her that morning. I was on suspension because of the incident, and she was meant to have gone home. Sean had told his boss and there was going to be an enquiry. She appeared just a few minutes before Romany arrived and she had just started her usual nasty tirade. To be honest, I was too weary to listen anymore, so I wasn't really taking any of it in. Then I saw you running towards us, I didn't know why, but as soon as she realised someone was coming and she would be overheard, she turned sharply, caught her foot in the rope and fell ... that is the God's honest truth. I never ever touched her; I swear. If she is pregnant, it isn't mine and I will give a DNA sample to prove it. I actually think it might have been Sean's. We may never know. I am just sorry that I didn't tell yer sooner. I wanted to protect yer both. We had all been through so much.'

'Exactly, Steve, but we had all been through it together! What were you thinking? Did our relationship mean nothing to you; did you think that we weren't strong enough to get through it? I told you that I loved you and would be there for you, wasn't that enough? How could I have proved it anymore? Sara Dyson was a very sick woman and she needed help. I don't think I know this man that you have become, this man that hurts women. This man that I loved would never have raised a hand to any woman, no matter what the circumstances. Come on, Romany, we are going to Aunty Sian's to think, I don't want to look at you right now. Don't try to stop me,

Steve, I need to be on my own.'

Meg stood and Steve looked helplessly on as she picked up her keys and handbag and grabbing Romany's hand she walked out of the door. Romany looked back with an expression of regret on her face. Steve smiled at her reassuringly and suddenly they were gone.

CHAPTER 33

"It is during our darkest moments that we must focus on the light."
Aristotle Onassis

Steve awoke the next day with a pounding head. His mouth tasted like the inside of a toilet bowl and as he flung his legs over the side of the bed the world spun. He thought that he could hear banging, but he wasn't sure if it was in his head or someone at the door. Getting himself into a standing position was a challenge of its own and he lifted the curtain and peered hazily out of the window. The light hurt his eyes and blinking he could see Sean moving his great meaty fist to once again pound on the door. Opening the window, he asked him politely to stop and staggering back he pulled on his joggers and holding onto the door frame made his way down the stairs one painful step at a time. Stepping towards the door, he held on tightly to the frame and turned the key, only to have it pushed back against him and Sean's loud voice shouting at him. 'She said that's what yer would do, bury yerself in a bottle of Jamesons! God yer stink like a bloody brewery. Let's get yer cleaned up, fella, and get some coffee down yer."

'What do yer want, Sean, and stop feckin shouting, will yer?' Sean laughed and Steve flinched as he turned to climb back up the stairs. Crawling on his hands and knees, they got him into the bathroom and sat in the shower. Sean turned it on full pelt and laughed as Steve flinched. 'Ouch ... ouch Jesus, Mary and Joseph, that hurts; are yer driving nails into me head?' Laughing, Sean let the water pour over his friend for at least ten minutes whilst he went back downstairs and put some strong coffee on and made a pint of orange juice with some paprika and ginger stirred in. Dragging Steve clean and fresh back downstairs, Sean stood over him whilst he drank it. Steve started to reach as soon as the first of the liquid hit the back of his throat, but gulping it down he managed to drink it all without vomiting. A warm sensation grew in his stomach, and he welcomed the glow.

'I think yer ready for some coffee now and maybe some eggs and toast.' Sean thumped Steve on the back and he almost threw up.

'No ... no food.'

Sean sniggered and put a black coffee in front of his friend. 'We will see how yer feel after that has gone down.'

Steve's hand was shaking as he picked up the mug of coffee but as its warmth spread through him, he began to feel better.

'Meg rang me this morning. She told me that you had confessed everything to her and asked me to accompany her to the station for Romany to give her statement. Yer will be pleased to hear that she told it exactly as it was and DI Hunt is happy as a pig in shit, he can go back to his desk and write up his accident report and drink his coffee. I have talked to the boss, and we have all agreed that in light of the accident the case against Sara Dyson, lodged with professional standards, will be dismissed for the sake of her family. Nobody wants to tarnish an officer's name unnecessarily; which, Stevie, me boy, lets yer off the hook. Yer will have to have a talk with yer boss when yer get back home but in the meantime yer are back on the case with me.'

'Well that's just grand,' Steve said sarcastically. And Sean gave his deep chuckle.

Sean stayed with Steve for a couple of hours and during that time he spoke to him about his mammy's funeral. 'I know yer are not religious, but yer mammy loved the church, God rest her soul. Did yer want me to talk to Father Murphy on yer behalf and do yer want help to organise the death certificate etc, will yer have a wake?'

Steve shook his head. 'Top of me to-do list for today.'

'Well, I will leave yer to it, I will come back tonight, and shall I bring us a takeaway?'

Steve groaned at the thought of food and Sean, chuckling, left him slumped across the kitchen table.

Steve had a busy day organising his mammy's funeral. He balked at meeting Father Murphy again but knew that it was what she would want. Everything sorted, he made his way to the pub down in the village. Many people remembered his mammy and daddy, they had been a huge part of this community for many years. Steve had not spoken to most of them for years, but he wanted to do the right thing.

Ordering an orange juice he downed it quickly and leaving a couple of hundred pounds with the landlord he was assured that his mammy would be remembered and have a good send off.

Heading for home he saw Meg's Aunty Sian's pretty cottage, the same little path leading to the door that almost a year ago he had visited for the first time when he had suddenly pieced together the puzzle of his birth and of his mother's deceit. Turning up the hill that led out of the village, he decided to look in on Sean and the crew to see how things were going; he also needed to turn over the stick with all of the records on for St Theresa's. He hoped that Siobhan or Connor could track down Sister Monica and that he could pay her a visit. Parking up he realised that it was getting on for late afternoon and Sean would probably still be over on the site. He decided to pop his head into the portacabin first and give the records to Siobhan and ask her to try and track down Sister Monica AKA Susan Monaghan; that's if she was still alive or wanted to talk to him. He entered the room and a young man in a suit too big for him was slouched in a chair by the desk.

'Yer can't come in here, now bugger off.' He stood and came towards Steve aggressively. 'Bloody press think yer can just walk in anywhere.' He went to grab Steve's arm and force him back out of the door. Siobhan watched on in horror and Connor had a big grin on his face as Steve twisted the man's arm slickly up behind his back and held it there as he writhed and swore. 'Now that is no way to speak to a senior officer, DS Hall.'

'Welcome back, sir, would yer like a coffee?' Siobhan giggled out and Connor just roared with laughter. Steve eventually let the spluttering DS go.

'Sorry sir. I didn't ... know who yer were.'

'Even so, we frown on actually expelling the press physically, as much as we would like to. Anyway, have yer got nothing to do? Go and find Sean, I mean DCI O'Dowd and see if there is any paperwork ready to be picked up from the site team, I want to catch up. Well, crack on.' Steve made a gesture with his thumb in the direction of the door and winked at Siobhan at the same time.

DS Josh Hall looked stunned and furious that he was being humiliated in front of the two garda and being made to go back to the site when he was just going to creep off to the pub early. He had seen a really pretty barmaid that he had been chatting to last night and he wanted to see if she was working again. Who the hell did he think he was anyway? He rubbed at his shoulder, it still hurt from Steve's grip on his arm. Still rubbing his shoulder, he made his way over towards Sean.

'Ah I see yer have met DCI Ryan already? Did he send yer to get me? I wasn't expecting him back till tomorrow. He was always the best at unarmed combat and disarming an attacker when we were at training college. I see he hasn't lost the touch.' He laughed as Josh scowled. 'Right I will leave yer to sort out here and see yer back in the office in twenty with the day's findings please.'

Sean chuckled to himself as he watched the young DS pick his way through the squelching mud towards the men and the digger that was working over the other side, and smiled in satisfaction as he stepped into a really wet bit that oozed up over his fake crocodile skin shoes. The young DS that had been sent down from the pale had started off on the wrong foot with everyone on site. We will soon knock yer airs and graces off of yer, he thought as he watched the hapless young man slip and slide across the site, the mud now clinging to the tapered trouser legs of his smart suit. Shaking his head he turned, and in his trusty wellies he stomped his way over to the building being used as a base.

Sean sat in the chair behind the desk, thanking Siobhan for the cup of coffee waiting for him. He took a sip. 'I wasn't expecting yer in till the morning. I also saw that yer met our young Josh. He is a right pain in the arse, but we will soon whip him into shape, ay Siobhan?" He raised his mug of coffee at the garda, and she smiled. Connor and her were becoming very fond of both Sean and Steve, they had earned both of their respect from day one, and they knew that they could learn a lot from this experience, more so than from any text books.

They had known that they were great detectives from the beginning and that they were both passionate about their job and compassionate too. They would stop at nothing to bring peace to the families involved. Josh, coming in from a different perspective, would see that eventually, and forever be grateful that he had been able to work with these men. At the moment he just thought that he had been sent to the middle of nowhere with the culchies and he couldn't wait to get back to civilisation. If he continued with his attitude, it would be his loss, an opportunity to see these two in action was not to be missed, they are legends, she thought in her hero worship of the two detectives, and I'm in for the ride!

Steve told Sean about his day and the progress with organising the funeral. 'By the way, Siobhan, Connor, I left some money behind the bar so that anyone can toast Mammy tonight if yer want to go along.

I'm sorry, with everything that has happened, I couldn't cope with a full on wake. It would do me head in to have all the neighbours popping round with casseroles and condolences.'

'I'm sure yer mammy would understand, have yer thought about where yer are going to put her?'

'No, I hadn't thought about that, but she certainly won't be going in Bally-Bay cemetery, that's for sure. It's bad enough that I got to go talk to that snivelling excuse for a priest Father Murphy, again tomorrow and John Blake has asked me to visit him later. Maybe he has some instructions from mammy that I don't know about in her will. She can always go up on the hill with Daddy. I know the land is still sanctified by the church because Mammy had to have permissions and all sorts just to get daddy buried in his spot under the Faery thorn.'

Josh came stumbling back into the room, mud splattered and looking sorry for himself.

'Take yer bloody shoes off, Josh, we don't want mud in here on the carpet now.' Sean winked at Siobhan who smirked as she watched him trying to remove his shoes with one hand and getting more covered in mud. She snatched the paperwork held in his hand before it became illegible with mud stain and handed it to Sean.

'Here yer go, sir, it looks like today's findings update.' Sean took the paperwork from Siobhan and quickly glanced through it. His face fell and any humour that had been in the room left as if it had been sucked out in a vacuum. He looked at them with sad eyes as he soberly asked them all to stay for an update.

'Steve, yer have missed a wee bit for a few days but the gist of it is we have started work on the new void … the largest of the lot. We were quite unprepared to say the least for what we found. We knew that we had over two hundred girls unaccounted for, but the numbers of bodies recovered so far have far exceeded that amount.

We are actually at double that amount, and the men have said that they would like to continue into the night to finish the job. I have given permission for that to go ahead, and I plan to come back later this evening myself to watch the removal of the last of the girls' bodies. And yes ... they are all young females recovered so far, as I have had verification from the forensic team to that effect.

'I suggest that we meet early tomorrow morning, say 6 a.m., here for a team briefing. Thank you everyone, get a good night sleep. I have a feeling that we will have a busy day ahead of us tomorrow. The press are still at the bottom of the lane. I have been given permission by the press office to give a statement which I intend to do in just a moment. But a word of caution, if I hear any of the details pertaining to the way that the babies and girls' bodies have been found leaked to the press, I will hunt yer down and kill yer with me bare hands. Got it? Good.'

CHAPTER 34

"A mother's love for her child is like nothing else in the world. It knows no law, no pity, it dares all things and crushes down remorselessly all that stands in its path."

Agatha Christie

Sean and Steve left together to return to Steve's family farm. 'I will stop and get some takeaway and if yer don't mind, Steve, I would like to discuss the case with yer tonight. God, I have missed having someone to run things by and I want to catch yer up with what we have discovered so far. I need some advice about where to go next as I know that if it were left up to the powers that be the whole bloody shenanigans will be swept under the carpet. After all, who gives a fuck about girls that died twenty years ago.'

'Well maybe these pariah's might be interested about the girls, but for all the wrong reasons.' Steve pointed to the press waiting at the bottom of the lane.

'Bugger, I was going to give a statement … ah they can wait till the morning. If any of them are still here at 6 a.m. then they deserve a little nugget of information. We aren't going to keep it quiet for much longer. Already I have noticed that some of the questions have been a bit more direct and a little closer to the knuckle than I would like but crews gossip, and ears are big.'

'I don't think the locals would talk to them, Sean, they are just as eager to hide it as we are because of the shame it will bring here. They might gossip amongst themselves but not to the press.'

As they passed by a camera flashed in Steve's face and voices began to call out questions. 'DCI Ryan, are yer responsible for Sara Dyson death?' 'Were yer having a relationship with her?' 'What about you DCI O'Dowd? Was it a threesome and whose baby was she carrying?'

Sean pushed his foot onto the accelerator and sped off. 'Feck … feck , feck, I wasn't expecting that. How the feck did they get that information? Somebody has been leaking and I will cut their balls off,' Sean spat. 'We haven't even had the autopsy report on Sara yet, let alone DNA results.'

Steve remained silent. 'I didn't push her, yer know that, don't yer?' He looked across at his friend.

'I didn't think yer had, but like you I was worried about Romany for a while.' Sean swallowed. 'I was a bloody eejit. I thought I could have something that you had with Meg and now neither of us has any of it.'

Turning into the lane to the farm, Sean realised that he hadn't picked up a takeaway for their dinner. 'Well I hope that yer fridge is well stocked, I'm starving, and we forgot to get any dinner. I hope yer got some bloody beers too. I want to be back on site in an hour or two.'

Opening the fridge door, Steve pulled out one of several casseroles sitting on the shelves. 'Thank God for community spirit, it looks like the Diabhul and his wives dropped by with their condolences; at least we won't starve.' Shoving the dish into the oven, he opened two bottles of beer and handed one to Sean. 'Oh god I'm sorry, I forgot yer can't drink.'

'Give me that bloody bottle, just don't let me have any more.'

Sitting at the table and shrugging off their jackets, they pulled the files towards them. Opening the first file, Steve was pleased to see that a lot of the babies had been matched by DNA to girls either still alive or with family contacts, from their original list. Those still alive had been shocked, according to Sean, as they believed that their babies had been adopted. By returning them to their mothers, they could arrange proper burials for the mites. Only two babies from the first two open pits were still unaccounted for. Sean interrupted and, pointing his finger towards something that Steve had missed, he whispered, 'Look at the DNA results.'

Scanning the list, Steve halted suddenly at a sentence on one of the pages. He looked up, startled, into the face of his friend, and reading out loud he said, 'Results for babies A&B familial DNA evidence match. Oh Jesus, Mary and Joseph, are yer saying the two babies not connected to our list of girls are twins?'

'That is exactly what they are saying.' Sean nodded to his friend. 'I wanted to discuss this with yer as I have kept this knowledge to meself and yer need to read the latest findings that emerged today. The forensic team promised to finish the job tonight and remove the last of the bodies from the large void. Once all of the bodies have been removed for analysis, they will take them all back to Dublin. And hopefully we might be able to find their families and give them the burial they deserve. That is why I am going back after dinner to watch them lift the last one out. I think I owe them that. I need to witness what has happened to them to give them justice.'

Steve, in a sombre mood, lifted the casserole from the oven and plated some up for Sean and himself. He continued flicking through the files and poured through the forensic evidence for each individual body. 'Well, they all seem to say the same, cause of death, strangulation. The hyoid bone is broken in each and every one of them and the pelvis shows that they had all given birth recently. I should think that we can assume that the bodies recovered today will show the same.'

'This goes further than the abuse of girls, this is the work of a serial killer.' Steve took a swig of his beer. 'I wish that bastard was still alive so that I could kill him meself.'

'Well we have the records from Dublin and we also have Sister Monica's name, I asked Siobhan if she could try and find a contact for her. I would like to speak to her to find out exactly what she knew. I will come back with yer tonight and in the morning first thing; but after that I have an appointment with John Blake for the reading of Mammy's will and one with Father Murphy in Mornside. If it wasn't mammy's wishes I would not have a bloody priest anywhere near her.'

Sean and Steve had suddenly lost their appetite and pushed the un-eaten food away from them. Swigging on their beer, Sean broached the subject of Meg.

'She has gone to stay with her aunty Sian. I told her everything and she basically called me a selfish prick, which I know I am, but I was trying to protect them from Sara.'

'Come on, Steve, it's me yer talking to and yes yer are a selfish prick, yer always were to be honest. Where were yer when I needed me mate? When my marriage went down the shitter and I lost everything, including my kids. Yer were wallowing in self-pity as usual. Poor Steve saw terrible things and he couldn't face life ever again. So let's run away and hide in Cambridgeshire and pretend that everything is ok. Yer mammy needed yer too when yer daddy died but still yer stayed away. What happened to yer all those years ago was a terrible thing, but now yer need to man the fuck up and apologise to Meg until yer eyes bleed. Do yer hear me? Yer don't deserve her, she has stood by yer and been there for yer and she has suffered a great deal too. Yes, yer are a selfish prick!'

'Well say it like it is why don't yer.' Steve was angry now with Sean, but it lasted for only a few minutes; suddenly deflated, he sighed. 'Yes yer right, I know yer are. I am everything yer said I was, always a coward ... I should have faced an Diabhul a long time ago, instead I let him rule my life. I'm sorry, Sean ... about yer family I mean ... and everything else.'

'Yeah, yer had everything I always wanted Steve and still yer couldn't see it. Come on, let's get back to site, at least this is one thing that we can put right, and not fuck up.'

Sean stood and flinging his arm around his friend's shoulders he said, 'I don't think it's too late with Meg yer know; it just depends how hard yer grovel. Yer might need some knee pads.' He chuckled as they made their way out of the door.

The lights around the site had an eerie glow as they lit up the men now working late into the night, their white suits were stained in mud but still bright enough to shine in the darkness. The sound of the machinery echoed out into the night. Sean and Steve, pulling on a suit and wellies, made their way over to the forensics team leader. Greetings being said, Sean asked for progress.

'I think we are coming to the end now; we were about to remove the last body from this void ten minutes ago, what is holding up the process is a small collapse over in the corner. All of the wet weather has turned it into a bit of a nightmare and I think lines were lost. This was a poorly marked grave but marked all the same. What we have found though has put a new slant on things. The grave was much older, the body recovered was of a female, approximately ten or eleven years old. She was wrapped as before in cloth, but this cloth was not the same cotton variety of the others, but of a much richer cloth, possibly silk. I won't know until I have done more tests. The worst part is inside the wrappings was the body of a foetus, not much more than second trimester. I will need to do more tests of course but I think we can assume that they are mother and child. Oh, by the way, the name on the grave marker said Magda Reilly and was dated 1958.'

Steve gasped and Sean put his arm out to steady him. 'Come on, I think yer need to sit down.' Shaking Sean's arm from his, Steve reached across to grab the forensic detective. 'Where exactly was the grave? Can yer show me on this map please?' He pulled a screwed up copy of his original map from his inside pocket, holding it out for him to see, looking at the paper he smoothed it out.

'Oh well yer already have it marked, X marks the spot,' he said, pointing to a red cross on the map with the initials M. R. next to it. Stunned, Steve couldn't speak; Sean thanked the team and set back off across the site, he practically dragged Steve with him. Steve hadn't said a word and Sean was worried that was worse than him shouting or swearing.

Stumbling into the building Sean placed Steve in a chair, he put the kettle on and bustled about making them coffee. Placing a steaming mug in front of Steve he watched as he wrestled with his words.

'She held my hand … I saw her … that day, I mean; when I came to the cemetery. She pulled me towards her grave, to show me … then she just disappeared. I thought how much she looked like Meg … and Bree … I thought she was just a local girl, but she showed me … I could feel her hand in mine, Sean as … as if it were real.'

Sean looked towards his friend as if he had lost it completely. 'Come on, we will go get some sleep and come back in the morning. I think we both need some sleep.' Dragging Steve out of the chair, he headed for the door. Steve, as if in a trance, followed.

'She held my hand, Sean … she held my hand,' he muttered.

CHAPTER 35

"It's no use to go back to yesterday; I was a different person then."
Lewis Carroll

Arriving back at the farm, Sean and Steve fell into their beds and grabbed a couple of hours sleep. Steve didn't think that he could ever sleep again, but after lying under the covers for a few minutes, he fell from exhaustion into a deep sleep. Sean on the other hand lay in bed for a while thinking about what Steve had revealed to him. He knew that Steve's mental health had suffered with the actions of his sister, but he wondered if it was more than that. Removing the barriers that he had so carefully built around himself for years had obviously had a huge impact on him, and he feared for his friend. Was he right to have involved Steve in this investigation? He hadn't realised how fragile he had become and the business with Sara Dyson had pushed him to his limits and beyond. Sean had seen too much of life to have any kind of belief in the supernatural, what men did to each other whilst of this earth was enough for him. He knew exactly how to deal with that, but he also knew that where Steve was concerned, he was out of his depth in understanding how he could help.

Waking later, fully clothed across Steve's spare bed, Sean was disorientated for a few minutes. His thoughts soon pulled him back to last night and the discovery of the young girl's body and Steve's revelations. He made his way to the bathroom; it was barely light and looking at his watch he could see that it was nearly five a.m. Just time to freshen up and a coffee, he thought, before the briefing and press statement. Stripping quickly, he jumped into the shower and heard Steve bang on the door. 'Coffee's on, hurry up and don't take all the hot water, I want a shower too.' He leapt out more refreshed than he had felt in days. He could see an end to the investigation and to be honest he would be bloody glad when it was over. Dressing quickly, he joined Steve in the kitchen. 'God yer look like shite,' he said.

'Well some Jackeen was hogging me bathroom.' Steve laughed and pointed to a cup of coffee waiting on the table. 'I won't be a minute.' He made his way back upstairs to the bathroom to shower and dress.

The two men climbed into the car. 'Are yer ready to talk to Father Murphy? Promise me that yer will be polite. We might need his permissions at the site, so please try and keep him on side.'

'Ay I promise, I will try to stick to the business of mammy's funeral, but I can't promise to keep me hands off him, if he says one more time about how we need to forgive Father Benedict's fecking discretions. Anyway, are yer ready for the vultures?' Steve pointed to the crowd of press gathered at the site entrance.

'Jesus they must have bred in the night. I'm sure there are way more than there were yesterday.' Sean breathed in exasperation. Pulling into the entrance, he stopped the car and walked back towards the crowd of gathering press. Cameras flashed and people shouted, calling questions to the detective. Steve stayed put, he didn't trust his temper lately if anyone threw him a curved ball about Sara Dyson.

'Ladies, gentlemen, if you would all look this way I will give a short statement concerning our investigation. No questions will be answered at this time, and I ask that yer respect the families involved.

'A few months ago, an investigation that myself and DCI Ryan were working on led to documentary evidence and information concerning crimes that may have taken place at St Theresa's over a period of forty years or more. This led to our team of forensic scientists and geophysics team looking at a number of un-marked burial sites within the grounds of the original cemetery of St Theresa's. As some of yer are aware, before its closure St Theresa's was used as a mother and baby home and Magdalene laundry. As yer are also aware, several of these homes run by the Catholic Church have since been investigated for claims of abuse and in 2015 a commission found the claims to be worse than at first thought. We are ourselves at this time investigating claims of abuse and even murder of some of the girls sent here to give birth and their babies. We have recovered bodies buried in pits in the grounds and our investigation is still ongoing. Our forensic teams are busy taking samples and looking at causes of death. My investigation team are collating information from records, a list of names of any girls that may have been resident here over the period of time from nineteen seventy till its closure in the early nineties. Most of these records are incomplete and many staff from this era are either unavailable or have since died, so our information sources are limited. I would like to stress that all physical remains have been treated with the greatest respect and have been removed from site for proper internment at a later date. I would thank yer to allow us to do our job.' Sean finished, handed back the microphone, and turned on his heel whilst behind him questions flew, one hit his ears: 'What about DS Dyson, wasn't she part of your team?' Sean spun on his heel.

'DS Sara Dyson was part of my team, a colleague and a good police officer. Sadly, she had a fatal accident, and I would ask that yer respect her family and her colleagues who are obviously still very upset about her death and are mourning at this terrible time.'

Climbing into the car beside Steve, he breathed hard, started the car, and drove quickly up the lane with questions ringing in his ears from the mob gathered behind them. 'Hopefully that will keep them quiet for a bit, but I won't hold my breath ... I wish they would drop the Sara Dyson questions though.'

'It's only natural when an officer dies on the job, there are going to be questions. I just don't want them digging too deep and neither do you. I wonder if Sara's autopsy report is in, and the DNA results are back yet? It will prove that I never touched her; if she was pregnant, it wasn't mine,' Steve stressed.

They walked into the building to find Siobhan and Connor already there. 'No sign of Josh yet, we will give him a few minutes.' Sean thanked Siobhan as she handed him a cup of coffee and one for Steve.

'I banged on his door this morning, but he was back from the pub pretty late last night and a little worse for wear by the sound of it, sir.'

'Well, we won't wait any longer then. What have we got come in overnight?' Connor handed Sean two folders, one held the results of the autopsy and DNA results for Sara Dyson, and the other was an address and telephone number for Miss Susan Monaghan. It was in a suburb of Dublin's west side. Hastening to the back of the room with Steve on his heels, they both sat down. They looked at each other across the desk. Sean, his hand all but shaking, held the folder with Sara Dyson's results.

'Well go on then, let's see the results.'

Reading from the sheet of paper in front of him, Sean, with a relieved look on his face, shared the coroner's findings. 'Accidental death caused by a head trauma received during a fall from the harbour wall onto the rocks below. She was in her second trimester of pregnancy, approximately sixteen weeks, and no DNA matches from samples given, to the foetus. See, it couldn't have been mine, she was still back in England when she got pregnant.' Sean sighed with relief.

'Well, I have a pretty good idea who might be the father … there was a young DC back in England who was pretty fond of her. I think she used him to try and pretend the baby was mine so that I wouldn't be believed; she could have completely ruined my career, and as for Meg and I? We would have been finished; she knew that, if I had to wait for it to be born before I could insist on DNA testing.'

'Well yer done a pretty good job of that all by yerself without any help from Sara Dyson. He is releasing the body to her family,' Sean stated.

'At times I hated her so much that I could have killed her meself. That morning included, but I don't feel guilty about her death … is that wrong of me? She deserved what happened to her, for all of the heartache she caused to my family. Mammy died because of her, and Romany had to deal with even more trauma when she was only just making a recovery. Sara knew who she would hurt with her behaviour, and she didn't care that it wasn't just me. Though I still, to this day, don't know what I ever did to deserve her hatred of me.'

Turning to the folder in front of him, Steve realised that he would be quite close to where Susan Monaghan lived when he visited Father Murphy. 'I might just call in to see her later, catch her unawares so to speak, rather than give her a ring. I am surprised that she is still living so close by. I would have run as far away as possible. I also have some questions for Father Murphy concerning our girl Magda from 1958. He must have been very young then, but he might know something. He might be able to shed some light on who she was'

'Don't forget the reason for yer visit, Steve, yer need to look after yer own for a while and sort yer mammy's funeral. Yer need time to say yer goodbye's, yer know … and to grieve,' Sean whispered the last bit under his breath because he knew that his friend was putting his own feelings to one side so that he could deal with the case. Both Steve's personal and working life were an emotional rollercoaster at the moment and he seemed to be stuck at the top of a bloody great drop. He also knew that the downward trip when it did come would be fast and very furious. Sean hoped his friend didn't crash!

CHAPTER 36

"I can be changed by what happens to me, but I refuse to be reduced by it."
Maya Angelou

Steve looked at his watch. 'Time to get moving. I am meeting Father Murphy at nine, I will be back as soon as I can; but I also have an appointment with John Blake this afternoon and the funeral home.'

'Take yer time, Steve, after all, no-one is going anywhere, please just do what yer need to do. In the meantime, I will be talking to the chief super and putting in a request for church records to be made available for the ten years previous to our 1970 timeline. That will send a rocket up the Bishop's Cassock. It's time that we knew exactly what went on here and just how many more girls suffered at the hands of the church. I know it won't go down well with the chief's friend, the Bishop, but I can always say that the press have already got onto it, and that it would look bad on the force if they think we are covering something up. Especially as they have just had a huge inquiry into the same thing in the Bessborough home in Cork; they couldn't even find the bodies or any records there. In that I suppose we have an advantage. I don't think they cared who knew.'

Shutting the door on the portacabin, Steve's thoughts turned to his mammy. He wanted it to be over and done with as quickly as possible and her body laid to rest with daddy under the Sceach Gheal on the hill.

Walking back into the church at Mornside, he was greeted by Father Murphy. 'DCI Ryan, I am sorry to hear about your mother.

Bridget was a good parishioner and helped out at many of the fundraisers that we regularly have. She will be sorely missed by many in the church and her community in Bally-Bay. I have a few dates next week that you can choose from that you could have the funeral on. If you would follow me, we can dispense with the formalities. Is it with Absalom that her body rests? They are a good firm and will treat her with the greatest of respect, as she deserves.'

Steve faltered, he had neglected his mammy, what with everything that had happened he really hadn't thought where she would be taken or even if last rights had been read. He hoped that she wouldn't be horrified at him and would understand. Sean was right, he needed to ensure that she had a respectful sending off; even if he didn't believe in the afterlife, she did.

'Actually, she is still in the morgue. Well I think that's where they took her. I have been a bit busy, a colleague died on the same day too and the investigation has kept me so busy.'

'Did she not receive absolution, Steven? Dear God forgive yer.'

'Oh I don't need forgiving, Father Murphy, but you might.' Steve chose a date for the Tuesday of the next week, for the funeral. Counting days in his head he decided that three working days would be enough for him to arrange everything else.

'Talking of forgiveness, Father, can yer tell me when did yer first arrive in this parish?'

'I came here in nineteen seventy, before that I was with Father Peter in Bally-Bay. His health was not good. I went straight from the Seminary to him from nineteen sixty-six till I was given my own parish here in nineteen seventy and Father Benedict moved to Ball-Bay, under Father Peter's wing so to speak.'

'Would that be after the trouble that Father Benedict had in Dublin with allegations of abuse of young girls? Then the church moved him to another parish so he could continue with his predilection for young females? It is about one of the graves that we have come across near to where all of the pits have been found that I want to ask yer about. I was hoping that yer could shed some light on who Magda Reilly was? The grave marker gives her internment date as 1958. That name has cropped up in other investigations.'

Father Murphy visibly paled, his eyes looked haunted as he fought to regain his composure.

'Now don't yer dare pretend that yer don't know who I am talking about, Father, your expression says it all. The thing that I am having trouble with is the fact that Magda Reilly couldn't have been one of Father Benedict's victims as he didn't arrive in Bally-Bay till … what was it yer said … 1970, and as yer told me yer were not resident at the date in question with Father Peter. So, who the hell, Father, was Magda Reilly?"

'Yer have crossed the line, DCI Ryan, yer were never given permission to disturb the graves inside the marked boundaries. Yer must stop digging the site immediately … I will have to speak to the Bishop about this, until then yer will stop all excavations.'

'The grave was right on the edge, Father, and it caved in whilst the area next to it was being excavated. Yer didn't answer me question, Father. Who was Magda Reilly?'

'I think that yer had better leave now, DCI Ryan. I am sure that the Bishop will be very displeased with the liberties that yer have been taking with the site and I am also sure that he will let yer chief inspector know when he hears what yer have been doing.'

'But what exactly have we been doing, Father? Our job, that is what a Detective does, and I like to think that I do my job well. Put it this way, when I get a sniff of a lie, I don't give up till I find the truth. If in the process secrets that the Catholic Church wishes to stay buried are discovered, then I will not hesitate to reveal them. If it concerns the abuse of children and babies, then I promise yer as a good upholder of the law, I will leave no stone unturned until I bring the perpetrators to justice. I can assure yer I will keep digging till I find out exactly who Magda Reilly was and her significance in this investigation.'

Steve turned on his heel and left Father Murphy standing in the church, his face suffused with all that he wanted to say to the detective. Again, Steve felt his anger rising. He walked quickly to his car and headed off towards the address in his phone app to hopefully get some answers from Sister Monica/Susan Monaghan.

He followed the directions to a street on the outskirts of Dublin. It was a neat and tidy road with houses lining both sides of the street. Following the numbers down he arrived at number seventy-four, a neat little terrace with a bright red front door. He parked outside, climbed out, and lifting the knocker in his hand he noticed how the brass shone in the afternoon sunshine. Looking at his watch he realised he would have to be quick here or he would be late for his meeting with John Blake. Rapping hard he stepped back and waited for the door to open.

The woman that answered took Steve by surprise. Her build was slim and her blond hair shone as much as the door knocker. She certainly didn't look the sixty plus years that he knew her to be, if his timeline was correct. He looked up into a pair of sparkling blue eyes and introducing himself. He was surprised when she reacted with, 'I have been waiting for someone to come and speak to me. Is it about St Theresa's? I saw it on the news last night. I am so glad that the terrible secrets of that place are being discovered, and that the world will know what evil lived there.' Stepping inside to be seated on a sofa in a nice, neat room, he found it hard to believe that Susan had anything to do with what had happened at St Theresa's, but he had learnt over the years that looks could be deceiving, and he would never have made it as a copper if he took anything at face value. He thought he saw something familiar in the woman, but it had been a long time since he had attended the school in Bally-Bay.

Susan offered tea or coffee and, declining, Steve got to the point straight away.

'As you already know, I am here to talk to yer about St Theresa's. I won't beat about the bush. Were yer aware of the abuse going on at the time? Did yer witness anything untoward?'

'I was very young, and St Theresa's was my first ever order. I had trained as a teacher and my role was to teach the village children and give lessons to some of the younger girls in the home. One girl in particular, she was about seven or eight at the time, came to my attention. She was always around helping in the laundry area and around the kitchen. She was so much younger than the other girls who were there for the duration of their pregnancy. She was not old enough to be there, so she seemed out of place. She was often singled out by all of the sisters, but one in particular, Sister Francis, was the vilest of all the nuns; she punished her for the slightest thing.

'I asked Sister Francis one day why the girl didn't attend the school. I could see she was of an age to go to school; a little late, I thought, in fact, and she was a smart little thing. She had the reddest curly hair and the brightest of green eyes. Her eyes will always haunt me, Detective Ryan. She had endured such suffering in her short lifetime, you could clearly see it in her eyes. I was told in no uncertain terms to mind my own business. I befriended the girl and secretly taught her against Sister Francis's wishes.

'One day, she obviously felt that I had earned her trust; she confided in me that Father Benedict had touched her in a sexual way and that he had been abusing her for a very long time. I could only assume that she had been born at the home, maybe her mother died giving birth. I know a lot of the girls did as they were so young, and their treatment was simply appalling. They certainly didn't receive proper midwifery care.

'They came and went in the night secretively. Now of course you are discovering what happened to some of them." She started to cry and, giving her a few moments, he allowed her to gather her thoughts.

'Bree, as she called herself, learned quickly and over the few months that I was with her she learnt to read and write and do maths, way above her age level. She was so starved of any kind of attention, or kindness, that she soaked it up like a sponge. She denied the abuse as soon as she had uttered the words and said that she was lying, but I was suspicious. For months I searched the records looking for a name and birth mother's name that fitted with her age, trying to understand if she had been abandoned there in that hell hole, but to no avail.' She broke down in tears again and Steve offered to get her a glass of water.

'No please, Detective Ryan, I must continue, this has haunted me for many years and I need to speak … please.' Continuing with her story, she told how she was discovered with Bree in the orchard by Sister Francis, a place where they would often escape to for her lessons. 'Poor Bree, we were just sitting and reading quietly to each other … she so loved the books that I was able to sneak to her now and then. I never saw her again after that day, she was hauled off by Sister Francis and I was sent to my room. The Bishop arrived that same afternoon and I was excommunicated from the church and sent away all on the same day. I tried so hard to tell the Bishop what had been going on, but they turned it around and accused me of secretive, inappropriate, and lewd behaviour with a child. Of course this wasn't true; then they threatened me … to keep their terrible secret or that they would prosecute me if I said anything to anyone. They put me in a taxi and sent me away on a train to Dublin. I live with the shame of that day every day of my life, Detective Ryan. It is a relief to finally tell someone. They had me over a barrel. I would never be able to work as a teacher again or with children if they did what they threatened. I was young and terrified, for years I looked over my shoulder waiting to see a Garda come to arrest me. I made a life and I retired from teaching only last year.'

Shaking, she quietly whispered. 'What happened to Bree? Is she one of the bodies that yer have found?'

Steve ignored her question for a moment and asked one of his own. 'Tell me, Susan ... may I call yer Susan?' She nodded in assent. 'Does the name Magda Reilly mean anything to yer? Have yer ever heard the name spoken or seen anyone with that name whilst at St Theresa's?'

'No, I can't say I have, but Bree said that Father Benedict called her Magda ... as he abused her ... and said she was a whore. Oh my god, poor Bree, I abandoned her that day and I will never forgive myself.'

'Bree, as yer call her, Susan, is in fact, as I have discovered during my investigations, my twin sister and her real name, given to her by my mother on the night of our birth, in St Theresa's in 1974, was really ... Magda. But she is not the Magda I am searching for. I don't have any more questions for yer at the moment if yer think of any particular names or incidents that yer witnessed I would be grateful if yer gave me a call, and I will send someone to take a statement.' He stood to leave.

'Wait, Detective, what happened to Bree?'

'She is alive, but completely insane; her mental state has been caused by the abuse that she suffered over the years. Not just by all at St Theresa's, but also later by a male attendant at the institution that she was sent to. She killed Father Benedict and Sister Francis when she was only seventeen, in the church at Bally-Bay, after she had suffered sustained and terrible torture and sexual abuse at their hands. Sadly, she was then placed in the mental health facility where she eventually received some help but by then it was too late ... the damage to her fragile mind had been done. She was released from the facility sixteen years later. Only to then set out to find her real mother and seek revenge for her own suffering. She went on to kill ten other innocent people. Oh how I wish that yer had been brave enough to take her with yer, or go to the authorities.'

'So do I, Detective Ryan … so do I.' Susan collapsed in her own misery into a chair. Looking at her with disgust, Steve left Dublin. He was pretty frustrated as he knew the key to the whole investigation, and what had happened to his sister, was finding out who the original Magda Reilly was. Susan Monaghan had really just confirmed what he already knew, from statements that his sister had given at the time of her arrest. She knew nothing more than he himself. Father Murphy on the other hand … Steve knew that he was hiding something from him, something that tied the whole thing together.

CHAPTER 37

"All women become like their mothers, that is their tragedy. No man does. That's his!"

Oscar Wilde

Steve arrived for his appointment with John Blake with moments to spare. The ride back from Dublin had been fraught with roadwork's and hold-ups along the way. Sitting himself in a chair, he visibly slumped, tiredness had finally caught up with him and he looked up into the face of his old family friend. 'Come on then, let's get this over with.'

John started to read from Bridget Ryan's will; nothing was unexpected, she had left the farm and all of its contents to Steve, being the only living relative. 'Obviously this was written before the revelations about yer sister, Steven, and I have a letter here that she wanted yer to read after she had gone. I will get yer to sign a couple of papers and yer can be on yer way. I will arrange for the transfer of the property deeds and get them to yer when they are done.' Smiling at Steve, he said, 'She was a good woman and she wouldn't want to see her son suffering. My advice, son, is to take yerself home, shut the door, and think seriously about yer next steps. Whatever is making yer unhappy, sort it out.' He patted Steve on the shoulder and said that he would attend the funeral of his dear friend Bridget on Tuesday.

Gripping the envelope in his hands, Steve made his way back to the car. He would call in to the farm for a cup of tea and read it in peace and quiet.

Sitting at the table of his childhood, he felt a sort of comfort in its familiarity. Sipping his tea, he poured another cup and placed it across from him. 'Well Mammy, as yer always told me, a good cup of tea can make everything seem better. Perhaps it's appropriate that yer join me whilst I read yer letter.' He passed his thumb over his name written on the front then tugged on the envelope and pulled out some sheets of paper, he unfolded the pages and read on.

My darling boy,

I firstly want to apologise to you for the way that you found out about Magda; I should have been brave enough to tell you when you were younger. Maybe because you were a Garda, you could have found her and saved her. I know I will never forgive myself for forgetting about her and just enjoying the husband and baby that I had. All I can say to assuage my guilt is that I didn't know; I thought that she had been adopted. That doesn't make it right and telling you would also have compounded my shame at the circumstances of your birth and I didn't want you to think less of your daddy. He loved you as his own and he couldn't have been prouder of his son. I was so afraid that you would hate me if I told you. I have left everything to you, as it should be, but after finding out about Magda, I would like to make a small request. Please forgive me and make sure that your sister has whatever she needs. It is all that I can offer her now and I know how inadequate my apologies are in the circumstances; but I need you and her to know that they are heartfelt.

Thank you, Steven, for being a son that any parent could be proud of, or ever wish for. I often think of us all on the farm when you were small as you came home from the fields, high on your daddy's shoulders, waving to me as I waited to hold you in my arms; all warm and dirt smudged; the sun glinting off your hair. I hope that you can also experience that same joy one day with your own child. (Hopefully by the time you are given this I am ancient, and you have a dozen children! Well one or two anyway.) I love your Meg and Romany, please go on and have a wonderful life together. Try not to be so stubborn, when you need help … ask for it, and put this all behind you, please, and move on. One last and simple request is that you place me under the Hawthorn with your Da.

Your ever-loving Mammy xxx

Steve crumpled, just like the paper in his hands. There was never any need for forgiveness, she was but a child herself and was bound as tightly as the poor babies' bodies, wrapped in the thorns of the church and the secrecy, silence, and shame, of an outdated societal moral code. He was only sorry that he had not had any time to tell her so.

That, he blamed Sara Dyson for. He would of course check on Magda, his own guilt would allow him to do that, but he would never, ever, visit her again. He knew that if he wanted to keep hold of his own sanity that must never be allowed to happen. His thoughts turned to Meg. He was glad that his mammy had not lived to see what a disappointment her son had been in that direction. How stupid and self-centred he had been to think that he could control everything on his own. Well, he was paying the price now. His love was lost to him, and his career too, when he returned to Cambridge, it was most likely over. He was still waiting to hear whether he was to have a hearing with professional standards. He was grateful that he was being allowed to finish this investigation with Sean. He thought that was because his Chief Superintendent knew what he had been through and because he grew up in Ball-Bay he was the best man for the job.

He finished his tea and poured himself another; Sean and the investigation could wait a little longer. He was spending time having a cup of tea with his mammy. He smoothed out the crushed paper and started to read her words again. 'Such a shame that I never spent time with yer while yer were alive, Mammy ... I'm the one that should apologise; but it's too late now.'

He came too, his head and cheek resting on the table, a noise had woken him up. He shook his head to clear it and listened ... silence, he must have been imagining it. He looked out of the window and he could see that it was dark, fumbling for the light switch and his watch, he could see that it was gone eight p.m. He startled as he heard a scratching noise at the door again. Heading to the hall, suddenly the door flung inwards and Sean, loaded with a case of beer and bags of takeaway, almost fell inside.

'Oh hi, I couldn't get the bloody key in the door with me hands full. I thought yer might be a bit hungry by now.'

Steve smiled and shaking his head, he laughed. Reaching for the beer, he took it through to the kitchen.

'I wasn't sure if yer would make it back to the site tonight; so, I thought I had better bring some sustenance.'

Placing the bags on the table, Sean noted the pot of tea and the second cup, gone cold long ago, and wondered if Steve had a visitor. He hoped that Meghan had been around to see him as he had called and spoken to her today and pleaded with her to talk to Steve and sort things out. He had to admit, at this moment in time he couldn't see that happening, although he didn't want to let his friend know of his doubts. He was stupid, but at the end of the day he really hadn't done anything wrong except to ask for help from his colleagues and to confide in Meg. He understood that Steve didn't want to lose her, but he had probably done that now anyway. Getting some plates down from the rack, Sean laid the table. 'I got loads, I'm starving. I haven't eaten all day, what about you? How did things go with Father Murphy?'

Biting into a spring roll, Steve sat down. He had not realised how hungry he was too. Then he related the day's events to Sean.

Meg looked out of the window across the bay and realised just how much she was missing Steve. She could hear Romany and her aunt Sian in the kitchen below her and the rattling of cutlery as they got ready the evening meal. Meg had gone for a lie down; she had been feeling so drained and tired lately. Suddenly the smell of food drifted up to her. She recoiled and ran for the toilet. The bitter taste of bile rose in her mouth, and she swished it away with water from the tap. It must be everything that had happened, she wasn't herself. Tears came easily and she didn't want Romany to know just how much she wished she had stayed. Poor Steve. She had been angry with him at first, unsure if he had been sleeping with Sara or not and for allowing Romany to overhear his conversation and how she had worried about how to tell her mum. Never mind, she would stay for Bridget's funeral and then she was taking Romany back to England. She would be starting at college soon and she herself had a whole house to sort out after swapping with Becky and the boys, all of her stuff was in storage awaiting her return.

Things were quiet at the site over the next few days. The sounds of machinery that everyone had gotten used to had stopped. Inside the temporary building the team were working on building a file of girls that they had matched to families, their bodies were being released slowly for burial and each one would be followed by a news team. Sean and Steve were preparing themselves to attend as many as they could and to meet the families. They wanted to reassure them that their girls would not be forgotten and that they were all victims of a terrible crime. As such, the cases now would be treated as murder.

Steve himself needed the distraction from thinking about his mother's funeral the next day. He had heard nothing from Meg. He hoped that she would come. He had texted her a million times and he had asked Romany to please get her mum to attend the funeral, if nothing else. The day drifted by, and the work became laborious for everyone when awaiting results had held them up, they all decided to call it a day.

'We hope everything goes ok tomorrow, sir. Connor and I would like to say we are so sorry about yer mammy." Siobhan looked across at Steve as he gathered his laptop and jacket from the back of the chair.

'It is much appreciated; I thank yer both. I will see yer tomorrow afternoon.' He turned to catch up with Sean, leaving Siobhan and

Connor with surprise written on their faces. No-one expected him to carry on as if nothing had happened, but if that was how he would cope then his team would support him one hundred percent. It was just that they could all see that it would end in disaster for Steve who they knew was in denial, and grieving. They knew that something had happened with Sara Dyson too, but that was nobody's business but his. They just knew that this gentle man was broken.

CHAPTER 38

"Grief never ends but it changes, it is a passage of time, not a place to stay. Grief is not a sign of weakness, nor a lack of faith; it is the price of love."

Unknown

Steve pulled back the curtains in the bedroom. The sky was grey and rain clouds gathered. Looking up at the hawthorn, he could see the pile of dirt and the hole in the ground waiting to receive his mammy's body later that morning. It had been dug yesterday by Absalom & Keilty, the funeral directors, they had also retrieved Bridget's body from the morgue and arranged viewings for her large circle of friends. They had practically taken over all of the arrangements for Steve. The women were struggling with the disgraceful way that Bridget's son Steven was dealing with her wake and funeral. The arrangements were sparse and by all that they had heard he didn't really want Father Murphy to give her a proper burial. If the gossip was to be believed, he was just happy to throw the poor woman into a hole in the ground. She had even had no absolution, or last rites according to some. The women were horrified.

He pulled the curtains closed and sat on the bed. Sean had disappeared earlier, promising to return to support his friend and say his goodbyes to Bridget. Steve, at a loss as to what to do, made himself coffee. Standing in the kitchen in his jogging bottoms, he was surprised to hear a knock at the door. Three women who he had known since childhood as good friends of his mammy stood on the step laden with plates of cakes and sandwiches. Not understanding why, he stepped back and went to close the door behind them.

'Steven James Ryan, yer mammy would turn in her grave, even though she isn't even in it yet, at the thought that the good people of Ball-Bay were not fed and watered at her own funeral. The shame that she would feel would be terrible and shame on you for not giving yer mammy the best send off. We will not allow yer to bring shame to her name and we will not allow people to remember Bridget Ryan as the poor wee woman that didn't have a proper funeral.'

The women barged into the house past Steve and began rummaging through the kitchen cupboards for cups and plates etc., tutting to themselves every so often. Steve, grabbing his coffee, made a run for the bathroom. He would just hide up here until it was time to come down. The women were right of course, he should be ashamed, and he was, but not about what they thought of the funeral arrangements, but about all of the times over the years that he had made excuses not to come back to Bally-Bay to see his parents.

Sean arrived back to a kitchen full of bustling women. He cheerily accepted a cup of tea and a piece of cake, he placed two onto a tray and took them upstairs to Steve.

'I see the Ma'ithreacha have arrived, thank god! I was a bit worried that yer mammy would have a poor send off.' He laughed. 'Come on, get this down yer and we will get ready to go. Are yer having the service at the church first or just at the graveside?'

'I couldn't stand Father Murphy preaching for too long, but I owe it to Mammy to at least let him give her a religious send off, just at the graveside. The house has been taken over too; I have hidden up here hoping they would go away.'

'Steve, let them do this, it's for yer mammy; they were her friends and it's their way of paying their respects to her memory.'

'Nosy old bags in the house yer mean, telling me off, saying that I should be ashamed of meself.'

'Well they have a point, don't they? Ignoring it won't change anything or bring her back. Now stand up and be the son that she loved and let's go and say goodbye to a wonderful mammy and woman. Ok?'

Pulling him upright, Sean drew the curtains. He could see that the funeral car had arrived, plus several other cars were pulling into the farmyard. Father Murphy was stood in the hallway as they came down the stairs. Steve faltered as he held out his hand towards him. Sean gently pushed him in the back. It was going to be a hard job to keep Steve on track today and he hoped that they could get through the ceremony without any trouble. He scanned the sea of faces looking for Meg; if she came, his job would be so much easier. Stepping outside into the fresh air, Steve noticed a familiar little white car pulling up the driveway. Ignoring all of the people waiting to offer him their condolences, he pushed his way through the crowd. Meg stepped out of the car; she wasn't surprised that so many people had come to pay their respects to Bridget. She was a lovely and kind soul who had not allowed the difficulties that she had encountered in her life to mar it. She felt someone brush her arm and say her name quietly in her ear. She looked up into Steve's blue eyes. They held a multitude of questions, surprise, and gratitude.

'Thank you for coming, Meg.' He hugged her tightly and then Romany. 'Please will yer come be at my side? I don't know if I will be able to hold back any punches from Father Murphy without help.' He smiled tentatively down at her and thought how pale and wan she looked. Romany stepped up and grabbing hold of Steve's hand she urged her mum to do the same.

'Of course we will; won't we, Mum? But I can't promise not to punch Father Murphy myself.' She smiled reassuringly at Steve and watched as her mum took his other arm. Making their way across the farmyard, he saw Father Murphy talk to the undertakers and lead the way across the field and up the hill where she was to be laid to rest. Steve, holding tightly onto Meg and Romany, followed. Behind them was Sean and not far behind him came a sea of faces, some familiar to Steve and even Sean, but all there for one purpose: to say goodbye to a beautiful woman.

How he got through the day he didn't know, but with Sean and Meg's support he managed to stand at the door and say goodbye to the last person to leave. He had even managed to thank all of the women involved in supplying a huge spread and kept the tea flowing all afternoon. The kitchen had been left gleaming and Sean had disappeared back to site for a couple of hours. He surprised himself that he didn't punch Father Murphy and even managed a begrudging thank you.

Romany popped her head in the kitchen doorway. 'I'm going back with Aunty Sian; I will see you later on.' She ran up to Steve and kissed his cheek. 'At least neither of us punched Father Murphy. Well done.' Kissing her mum too she whispered, 'Talk to him for god's sake, you are both miserable as hell, or I might have to move in with my father.' She watched as the horror of that statement hit home and she laughed at her mum's face, then quickly ran out the door.

Left alone for the first time all day, they looked at each other shyly. Steve's face had always been an open book and his longing and love for her showed on it. She wasn't ready yet to forgive him so she cautiously pulled a chair out and sat at the table. Steve started to talk; he wanted to tell her again how sorry he was, how much he needed and loved her, but before he could say a word Meg, said, 'I'm going back to England; the flight is booked for Friday. Romany needs to start college and I have a whole house to sort out.'

'Well, I guess there is no more to say, but thank you for coming today a mhuirni'n, Mammy would have wanted yer there.'

Shocked by Steve's reaction, Meg had hoped that he would have fought harder for her to stay. She knew that he was going through a lot, and he had been through a lot. Well, so had she! Romany too;

maybe this was for the best. She had a life back in England that she needed to return to. She had put her own life on hold whilst helping Steve ... perhaps it was time to put herself first.

Unknown to Meg, it had been a deep blow for Steve to hear that she was leaving Bally-Bay. He longed for her to stay, but he understood her decision to run away back home. He loved her enough to let her go. What use was he to her now? She was better off without him. Standing abruptly, not wanting to prolong the agony, he gently kissed her cheek and showed her to the door. He watched the small white hire car as it disappeared into the distance. Returning to the kitchen, he took out a bottle of Jameson's and poured a large glassful then swallowed it down. Today he would allow himself to wallow in his agony, tomorrow he would see.

Sean found him passed out on the sofa, the bottle of Jameson's almost empty. He would forgive him today but tomorrow he needed his friend in his professional capacity. Things were happening back at the site, and he needed his help. Covering him with a blanket and placing a glass of water by his side, he stumbled up the stairs to bed.

CHAPTER 39

"I know not what may be coming, but be it what it will; I'll go to it laughing."
Herman Melville

Getting Steve up the next morning was more of a task than Sean wished to acknowledge. Leaving him in the shower, and with a mug of coffee in his hand, he rang Meg. 'Steve tells me that yer leaving Friday. I just wanted to say goodbye and to apologise for holding back from yer about Sara Dyson and what she was doing to Steve. I thought, well I hoped that he would come clean and tell yer himself. He is so bloody stupid and a right pain in the arse, always has been. Always got to be the one to do the right thing, no bending of the rules for Steve, and thinking he can handle anything that the world can throw at him by hisself; telling everyone he is grand. I am sorry, Meg, I know he loves yer something fierce; he just needs to get over hisself. Thanks for yesterday and safe journey home.'

Returning to the house, he hoped that he could change her mind about leaving. 'I don't think I have met two more stubborn people in me life.'

'What, who?' Steve wandered out of the kitchen, mug of coffee in hand.

'Come on, I will buy yer breakfast at that little café by the harbour. I want ter talk to yer away from work.'

The two detectives climbed into the car and Sean whisked them down the lane and out onto the road leading to the seafront. He looked up as gathering storm clouds could be seen blackening up in the distance and he knew that what he was about to tell Steve would cause gathering storm clouds of his own.

Steve settled for a light breakfast of scrambled eggs and toast whilst Sean went all out for a full Irish breakfast with fried potatoes and soda bread toast as extras. Steve looked at his friend's plate piled high and was unsure if he would keep anything down if he had to watch his friend consume the lot. He was beginning to feel a little better as he sipped the coffee and nibbled on some toast. 'Jesus, Sean, yer are a heart attack waiting to happen. I need to sort yer diet man.'

'Well I just get hungrier now I'm not drinking; talking of which, yer can talk; yours is just liquid lately.' The two friends smiled at each other. Sean could see a small spark of the old Steve coming back to life.

'Well what did yer need to take me away for our breakfast date for; are yer going to tell me or stuff yer face all day?' Laying his knife and fork down and taking his time to respond, Steve knew that whatever Sean was about to confide in him wasn't going to be good news.

'When I left yer this morning, I popped back to site to see if we had any more news from forensics.' Sean pushed another piece of toast into his mouth before continuing. 'Some of the results have come back on the body of the child marked Magda.'

He hesitated long enough for Steve to say 'Spit it out, man.'

'Ok but I don't quite know how to tell yer. The forensic guys have been busy matching DNA and have come up with a match from the data base. The foetus buried with her was not her own, no familial match was found, but she did match to another un-related case as a familial member that we happened to have DNA for.'

'Well go on, what is all the fuss about for Jesus sake? Don't tell me I got another bloody sister … no she can't be mine, my mammy wasn't even born.'

'Steve, it's Meg! The match is to Meg's family. They think that the child in the grave was Meghan's Aunt. Sian and Magda … Meghan's mammy's older sister.' Steve just stared at Sean, the toast dropped from his fingers and he laughed in disbelief.

'No … no … that can't be right … how could that be true? There must be some mistake … oh Mary mother and Joseph, how am I going to tell her that?'

'The thing is, Steve, her Aunt Sian must have known this all along. There is more to tell yer yet. The twin babies' bodies that we found in the pit, the ones that we couldn't match to any of our girls on our list.' Sean hesitated before saying, 'They have come back as related to Meghan too!'

Sean watched the news sink in, and Steve's face said it all. Picking up his knife and fork he continued eating. Ever practical, he said, 'I think yer had better get something in yer stomach, because knowing you yer will heave it all up again later. Better to have something to come out than nothing.'

Steve threw down his napkin in disgust and stood up to leave.

'Look I know that yer are upset, but I want to talk to Father Murphy myself, to see if I can find anything more out about Meg's family first. I want to see the records of births and deaths as I am puzzling as to why both sisters would be called Magda. So pull yer neck in a bit and let me see what I can find out. Either way, I want to know who was responsible for Magda number one's death in 1958 and I think Father Murphy knows the answer.'

'I want to come with yer.'

'I don't know if I can trust yer to behave. Father Murphy will never talk if yer keep raging at him like yer do. If I let yer come, only I talk to him whilst you look at the births and deaths records in the church for nineteen fifty-eight. Got it? Now let me finish me bloody breakfast in peace.'

Dropping back into his seat, Steve sighed. He knew that Sean was right this time; and if they were to finally solve this case and make sure that all of the wee ones were decently buried and recognised, he had to do as he was told. Keeping calm was not one of Steve's virtues and it often worked well within the team, the two detectives bounced off of each other. Sean laid back and Steve impatient and eager to get going. Lately though his stamina had been letting him down, so he knew that he needed to step back and let his colleague take the lead on this one. It was too close to home.

Sean drove as he was sure that Steve would be over the limit still. It also gave Steve time to read through the reports that Sean had brought with him. Pulling into the church car park at Mornside, Sean again turned to Steve.

'I have rung ahead and Father Murphy is expecting us, he promised to have the records ready for yer to see. Now look for any births in Bally-Bay around that time and note any deaths as well. We may very well find our answers today, God willing.'

'God will have nothing to do with it, he hasn't so far.'

'Now that is why I get to talk to the priest.' Sean wagged his finger at Steve but with a light-hearted smile.

Father Murphy was already coming down the steps to greet them by the time they had stepped out of the car. Holding out his hand, he directed them inside, showing Steve to a small musty-smelling room, he could see several archive registers laid out for him to look through.

'I hope you find what you are looking for, DCI Ryan. I have put the dates requested out for you to look at on the table. DCI O'Dowd, if you would follow me, we will go to my study.' Sean followed the old priest to the same room that Steve had been taken to before. Sitting in a chair behind his desk and indicating that Sean should sit, Father Murphy looked at Sean before stating, 'I don't know how I can help you, DCI O'Dowd, I have already told DCI Ryan all that I know about Bally-Bay.'

'Yes, he told me that yer left there in nineteen seventy?'

'That is correct, Detective.'

'He also told me that Father Benedict then was sent to Bally-Bay under the care of Father Peter, the same year.'

'That too is correct ... yer see, I have told you everything I know.'

'Well yer see, I find it hard to understand how yer could not know what was happening at St Theresa's. We know Father Benedict was responsible for most of the bodies recovered there, but what yer are unaware of is that our forensic team have now confirmed that some of the bodies date back to when you yerself were there. Can yer explain that? Father Murphy?'

Father Murphy looked shocked. 'I can't break the vows of the confessional ... I can't ... sweet Jesus, I really can't.'

'Would this be about a confession that was made to you, Father?'

'Well not exactly, it's about a confession made to someone else, but it would still break the confessional seal if I told you. The punishment for breaking the seal is ex-communication.'

'We can talk about it here or I can arrest you for withholding evidence, Father. We could also make sure that we passed all of the news hounds ... yes I like that idea we could put yer in handcuffs too and let slip that yer were involved in our case of child abuse and murder. Now what do yer say, Father?'

The priest looked at Sean with a horrified expression. 'I think I need to make a telephone call, please excuse me.' Father Murphy more or less jumped from his chair and ran out of the door. Sean sat and twiddled his thumbs; he knew that he would soon be back. The Bishop wouldn't want anyone living to be connected to the horrors at Bally-Bay, the dead could take the blame. As far as Sean was concerned, they were all equally guilty, whether they perpetrated the crime or stood by and did nothing.

Father Murphy returned. 'I have been instructed to help you with your enquiry, as the persons concerned are both long dead. The Bishop felt that nothing could be gained by keeping silent. The lord has heard their confession in person now and punished them accordingly.'

'Well that is mighty gracious of his Grace.' Sean smiled as Father Murphy didn't acknowledge his little joke. 'Now please, Father Murphy, explain to me why there are murdered children and babies' bodies connected to St Theresa's in unmarked graves in the cemetery there and who the bloody hell was Magda Reilly? I warn yer, me patience is wearing very thin so yer better tell me the truth.'

Father Murphy gave a huge sigh. 'It was back in nineteen seventy. I was just settling into my own parish, enjoying the freedom to make it my own and life was good, when one day Father Benedict turned up. I wondered immediately if something was wrong with Father Peter, so asked him into the church. He was behaving in a strange manner, and he claimed that he wanted to talk to me, but he was adamant that he didn't want confession. He said that what he told me had to remain a secret, but he was frightened that he would be blamed and that is why he wanted to talk to me as I knew Father Peter well. He started by asking if I had noticed Father Peter visiting any particular graves in the cemetery. He also asked if I knew any of the parishioners that were named Magda Reilly. That is the first time that I heard the name, but it wasn't the last. He went on to tell me that Father Peter had, during confession, relayed to him a tale and that he was unsure what to do.'

'Well go on, Father, you have kept their secret far too long, it's time now for yer to let the authorities know.' Sean smiled encouragingly at Father Murphy.

'I am grateful for yer understanding, DCI O'Dowd. Detective Ryan would have hung me just for being a priest by now. Well, as I said, he was unsure whether to break the seal of confession as a terrible sin had been committed, one of murder and breaking a vow of celibacy. The Bishop was contacted and under the Church's confessional seal he told the Bishop and I that Father Peter had been having an affair with a woman in the village, it had been ongoing for a few years. Her name was Noreen Sheila Reilly, she was married to a local fisherman called Michael. He was often away at sea for days or even weeks on end and Noreen was lonely. I believe that is how the affair started; she had two daughters at the time. The eldest, Magda, I think was Father Peter's and her other daughter was called Sian. Noreen looked after Father Peter and the rectory; she was his housekeeper. Apparently, the eldest daughter used to help her mother sometimes and this one day in particular she caught them together in flagrante delicto so to speak. Apparently, she ran and Father Peter gave chase, she fell and hit her head on a gravestone. She was carried home but never recovered and died. Her mother said she had a fever and that is what she had died of. Of course, in the nineteen fifties, this was not an uncommon occurrence.

'Unbeknown to Noreen, Father Peter confessed to killing Magda with a rock, to stop her talking. According to Father Benedict, he confessed this to him. Within the year, Noreen gave birth to another baby. No-one knew if it was Michael's or Father Peter's but the timing was right to be his. Not long after that, Michael was drowned, lost at sea.'

'So yer are saying that Noreen Reilly gave birth to a baby that she called after her dead daughter Magda, and the father of this child was most likely Father Peter?'

'That is correct, Detective, that is what Father Benedict told the Bishop and myself. Now you can understand why I couldn't tell you without permission and break the seal of confession.'

'That is how a completely insane priest like Father Benedict was able to carry out the atrocities that he did at St Theresa's, without anybody stopping him. Yer were all afraid that he would tell what

Father Peter had done and instead he did far worse. Jesus, Mary and Joseph I could bloody well murder yer meself.'

Leaving the priest sat at his desk, Sean stood and made his way to the car park. Steve was stood at the side of the car, waiting for him. 'Wait till I tell yer what I found in the records, it explains a lot and I think I know who the first Magda was.'

'Yes, I know; is it to do with Meg's grandma having two daughters called Magda by any chance? I just got Father Murphy to confess what he knew. I will fill yer in on the way back to the site. It's time to lay it all out on the table and fit the pieces together; I think our jigsaw is complete.'

CHAPTER 40

"And sometimes, against all odds, against all logic, we still hope."
Unknown

Steve and Sean arrived to find the site being packed away, the fencing being taken down, and lorries arriving to remove the site buildings. Diggers were filling in the pits where the bodies had been discovered. 'At least the press have buggered off; we are yesterday's news at last,' Sean commented as they found the way clear to turn into the site entrance unhindered by flashing cameras and reporters trying to catch them out.

They climbed into the portacabin to be met by Siobhan and Connor still working hard on matching the last few bodies to the records and making contact with families to confirm the release of their loved ones' bodies. Sean noticed someone was missing. 'Where the heck is bloody Josh, skiving as usual I bet? If I wouldn't get done for assault, I would clithera his bloody arse. Obviously his mammy didn't do it enough.'

Siobhan, trying not to giggle, told Sean, 'He said that he was going to the site to organise things.'

'He couldn't organise a piss up in a brewery, he hasn't been any help at all and I don't think he has learnt a bloody thing from this case.'

'That's where yer wrong, sir; he has learnt that pretty barmaids at the local pub are more important than working,' Connor laughed.

'When he does return to the B&B, tell him I want him to return to

Dublin. He is no longer needed. And that's with immediate effect. I will let the super know he will be back with them in the morning, the useless piece of shi—'

'Now Sean, ladies present, yer got a bad dose of swearing.'

'Sorry Siobhan,' Sean apologised and she smiled at him.

'I have five older brothers, sir; there isn't anything I haven't heard before.'

'How are we doing on the girls now, will yer wrap it up tomorrow do yer think?'

'Yes sir. Siobhan has just finished her list and I am waiting for the last two return calls from family members that I have been unable to contact. They know what is happening though and so it will be a big relief for them to have their girl's bodies to put to rest properly. Will we be returning to Dublin soon too, sir?'

'Yes Connor we will, Steve and I will catch yer up tomorrow on what we have found out today after we have decided what to do with the information. In the meantime, get yerselves an early night and meet back here tomorrow at eight a.m. I better make sure that they leave us this last building for a couple more days. Thanks both of yer for an excellent job. Yer have been focussed and professional from the beginning, even though some of the work was gritty and sometimes boring, you both worked hard to do it with respect. I will be passing my compliments onto the chief. I don't think that either of yer will stay Garda for much longer. I think I might be looking for a new DS soon ... oh and, Siobhan, yer make good coffee.'

Watching the young garda leave, Sean asked Steve to get a clean board and pen and start making a timeline whilst he made a call to the chief super, and popped down to the site to see how things were going.

Steve took the information from the records and printed the pictures he had taken off of his phone. Starting with Magda Reilly (1), the girl in the grave, he put her name on the board and wrote underneath it 'nineteen fifty-eight'. Next to that he wrote Magda Reilly (2) and again underneath, 'nineteen fifty-eight.' Standing back and puzzling, he wondered how there could be two Magda's from nineteen fifty eight, he was still waiting for Sean to fill him in on the whole story.

He walked back into the room, Sean was sat at the desk. 'Well this one has been a killer I will say. Whenever it comes to wee ones, I hate it. What has made it worse is that Father Benedict could have been stopped at any time ... bloody Church.'

Sean relayed the sorry tale that Father Murphy told him about Meg's grandmother. 'That explains the two girls named both the same, one died and one was born all in the same year. Jesus I will need to tell Meg and her aunt. Oh God, I just remembered that she is leaving for England tomorrow.' Steve's face lit up with a thought. 'If I tell her I need to speak to her and it's really important, so important that she needs to delay her return ...'

'Now yer talking, we can break the news to her family tomorrow and yer can bloody well talk to Meg. I'm unsure yet where the twin babies fit in. Maybe her family will finally tell the truth too. Her aunt Sian must know something.'

Steve picked up his pen and wrote 'Magda and Sian' on the board and underneath, 'twins'.

'So, what are we thinking here? That Father Peter killed Magda (1) and of course we know that Bree killed Magda (2). And Bree herself was Magda number (3). So that leaves Father Benedict responsible for all of the other bodies that we have found.'

'Jesus, that is a lot of girls and babies, but what about the older bodies that we found over by Magda's grave? Do yer think Father Peter might have been responsible for those as well as Magda? Perhaps he taught Father Benedict everything he knew concerning young girls, the sick bastards.' Sean made a face.

'I think yer might be right, as we still don't know why the bodies of Father Benedict's victims were wrapped in thorns. Wasn't the foetus found with Magda (1) wrapped in the same way? The only thing that I can think of is that it was buried at a later date in her grave by Father Benedict. To be honest, Sean, I don't think we will ever know or understand what went on here. I just know that an Diabhul dwelt in this place for a bloody long time.' Steve sighed. 'I am going to give Meg a call and hope that she will answer. If not yer might have to do it. I am looking forward to finally putting the last piece of the puzzle into place tomorrow.'

Sean gathered all of the forensic reports together. He wanted to personally speak to all of the victim's families, five hundred and seventy-two in all. He felt sick at the thought of all of the suffering that they went through, their faces swam before him. He hoped that hisself and Steve had brought the families some closure, and answers to what had happened to them. He couldn't really bring them justice as everyone concerned was dead, but he hoped that he had given them some recognition.

Steve returned to the room. 'She has agreed to delay her flight tomorrow and she is expecting us in the morning about eleven. That should give us time to gather all of the forensic evidence and anything else that we have. Did Father Murphy give us a statement?'

'I don't expect him to, do you? That's why I taped our conversation, he can't deny what he said now…'

'Oh well done, Sean, yer sneaky bugger.'

The two men left and headed home 'I think I deserve a drink,' said Steve.

'Only one beer allowed. I will keep yer on the straight and narrow with me if it kills yer … me too.' Sean laughed and Steve joined in.

'Oh well, it looks like another casserole tonight out the fridge. We might need a beer to wash it down if Mrs Clancy made it. Mammy always said she could kill soda bread just by looking at it.' The men roared with laughter.

CHAPTER 41

"Little by little we let go of loss, but never of love."
Unknown

The next day dawned clear, a late summer sun shone across the fields where Aidan was finishing his harvesting. It looked like it had been a good crop this year. Steve and Sean arrived on site as Siobhan and Connor were just unlocking. Stepping up into the portacabin for perhaps the last time, they all set about sorting out the last of the paperwork. Connor finished his last two calls and time soon came for them to leave for their visit to Aunt Sian's cottage in the village. 'I'm not looking forward to this at all.'

'Would yer like me to take the lead?' Sean enquired.

'No, I want to be the one to tell them what we have learned; it's only right that I should do it. I hope that this doesn't add to Meg's feelings about me, and that she doesn't hate me even more for digging up the past. I know I am going to upset them all, but they need to face the truth as much as I need to tell them.'

'For a start, Meg has never hated yer, why don't yer use this time to really talk to her and see if you can get her to give yer another chance. Now we have nearly finished up here, there are only the reports left to write up. Oh, and I forgot a little thing about a possible professional misconduct enquiry … nothing to worry about.'

Steve snorted his coffee out. 'Oh, only a little thing then. Come on, let's get this over with; I can't stand it any longer.' As they were climbing out of the car, Steve thought about the first time that he had visited the cottage. The neat garden with flowers spilling over the path still led to the front door. The flowers continued up and over it and the perfume hit their noses as they rang the bell. It was answered by Meg who hastened them inside and then led them to a formal living room.

'Would you like some tea or coffee before we begin?' she asked.

Steve looked at how pale she was, standing in the doorway. Before he could say anything, they were joined by Sian and John. 'Perhaps it is best that we get this over with, love.' He grasped her hand, it trembled in his own as he gently led her to a seat on the sofa where John and Sian were already seated. Romany hovered in the doorway. He encouraged her to come and sit by her mum. He whispered in her ear as she passed, 'Yer mammy might need yer to hold her hand, love; I have some bad news to tell.' Quickly she slipped onto the sofa arm and held onto her mum's hand that had so recently been held by Steve, just moments before. Meg had to admit that it felt good to hold onto Steve again, even for a brief moment. It brought a comfort and a strength to her, she needed to talk to him, and she was so pleased that he had rang and asked her to delay going home. Looking up at him she could see how much pain he was in and understood that what he had to tell them wasn't good news.

Steve cleared his throat then began by talking about his sister and his discoveries from her case that led himself and Sean to continue the investigation into missing girls and babies at St Theresa's when records that were recovered during his sister's case showed lots of anomalies. He started with the initial discovery of the grave Magda Reilly with the date nineteen fifty-eight. He explained how his sister had been named Magda and that it had been a name that cropped up over and over in the two investigations.

Steve talked to them about the discoveries in the cemetery and the horrific findings of the bodies of hundreds of babies and murdered girls, which they believed Father Benedict was responsible for; he in fact they now knew was not only a paedophile, but a serial killer. The only one that didn't fit the timeline was Magda.

Luckily for the investigation, paper records of all of the girls that went through the gates of St Theresa's were mostly still intact and due to a fluke in circumstances were taken to Dublin when the building burned down in the nineties. These records are what they used to lead them to investigating more. A few telephone calls to the families of the girls named on the list revealed the huge number of girls that had simply disappeared, according to their families.

Steve stopped, took a deep breath, and continued. 'We have managed to match, via DNA samples, most of the girls and babies' bodies recovered. In the process of excavating the pits where the bodies were buried, we disturbed the grave of Magda Reilly. The body inside that grave was of a girl child, approximately aged ten years old, and buried with her was a foetus, approximately sixteen weeks old. We have since found that they were unrelated and believe the baby to have been placed there at a later date by Father Benedict as it had the hall marks of the other burials on the site. However, a DNA search showed that there was a match to DNA for the girl from the other case.

Sian started to weep. Meg, still unaware of the significance of what Steve was saying, looked confused. John, angry now, jumped up. 'I told yer to leave things alone. What use is it to bring this all up again? It hurts everyone all over again. Why couldn't yer have left well alone.'

Sian, sobbing, said, 'It's alright, John. It's time that the whole sorry story came out ... all of it ... do yer understand?'

'If that's what yer want, love; if that's what yer want.'

Steve nodded to Sean. 'I think it would be easier if we played the interview that Sean taped yesterday with Father Murphy. I will answer everything afterwards.'

Sean pushed the button on his phone and the clear voice of Father Murphy could be heard. As they listened to his confession of guilt in covering up what had happened all those years ago and how he himself was also complicit in allowing Father Benedict to continue his appallingly evil lifestyle, Sian rubbed her eyes and seemed to slump further into the sofa cushions. As the tape recording came to an end, Meg sat forward onto the edge of the sofa.

'So let me get this straight; what you are saying is that Magda was Sian and Mammy's older sister and she was murdered by Father Peter because she saw Grandma and him together? Dear God, Aunty Sian, is any of this true?'

Sian, wiping the tears from her face, answered by nodding her head. 'I was barely five years old at the time. I thought that my sister had died from a fever, that's what I was told, and it wasn't long after that Mammy gave birth to Magda. I didn't question why she had the same name. I just thought that I had my sister back … my Magda. I didn't know that she had been murdered. That is not the end of the story though, is it, Detective Ryan?'

Sian stood and made her way to the dresser standing in the corner of the room; pulling open the drawer, she removed something, holding it in her hand tightly she turned and walked towards Steve. She placed the object into his hand and sat back down on the sofa. Understanding dawned on Steve's face as he looked at what she had placed in his hands and the last tiny piece clicked into place. Sian nodded at Steve as if to say 'go ahead … tell them the truth'.

'The twin babies' bodies found in one of the pits also had two DNA matches. The first was a match to each other, which established that they were siblings. The second a match to Meg's DNA, indicating it had a familial significance … possibly cousins.'

Sian sobbed out the story of how at twelve years old she had given birth to Father Benedict's babies; the aftermath of years of abuse that she had suffered at his hands. She was so very young and very ill afterwards and she was told that they had both died. She never forgot them and didn't know where exactly they had been buried but she would often visit the cemetery and she made a sort of a grave with a circle of stones where she would leave flowers. Originally, she had placed two little ducks on the grave, but over the years one had disappeared.

Steve held open his hand and said, 'Yer tried to retrieve this the night I came by the cemetery, didn't yer? I thought the figure I saw climbing the wall was familiar and the next time I came back the duck had gone.' Steve knelt down before Sian, and taking her hands in his, he said, 'Yer can give them a proper burial now and yer will always know where they are and have a place to visit and talk to them.' He placed the duck in her open palm and curled her fingers around it.

The shock on the faces of all of the family was clear. Steve walked across to Meg. 'I am sorry to bring such sorrow onto yer shoulders. I would love to speak to yer later. Could I pick yer up and take yer for a drink?'

Meg looked up into his blue eyes, she saw such empathy within the way he looked at her and also something else, a spark of life that had been missing for a long time. Perhaps finally by solving this case and bringing justice to all of the families involved he had finally found peace. She hoped so as he wasn't the only one to reveal a secret tonight.

Steve and Sean said their goodbyes to Meg and her family, handing Sian a card. Sean told her to ring him with any questions that they might have once the revelations had sunk in. 'I promise that I will keep yer informed of when we will be able to release the babies' bodies for burial; I assume that you wish yer sister's remains to be returned to yer for re-burial and not returned to St Theresa's?'

Sian nodded. She didn't seem to be able to speak. She was already thinking about how she would explain everything to her son William, and daughter Cassandra. After Steve and Sean had left, Meg made a cup of tea for everyone, then asking Romany to come for a walk with her they left her Aunt and Uncle to ring and talk to their children.

Stepping outside, the salty air from the harbour blew the fogginess from Meg's brain and restored some colour to her cheeks. Romany hung onto her mum. 'Oh my god, Mum, what terrible secrets to have kept all of these years. I can't imagine what Aunty Sian went through at an even younger age than me. This place is like living in the dark ages.'

'Nothing much seems to have changed over the years either. Hopefully what Sean and Steve have done here will free people to speak out and I expect there will be plenty of families just like ours trying to recover from the revelations. Mammy never told me about it. I knew that she hated Father Benedict and I will never forget the day he dragged Bree away screaming. Mammy was so brave, she tried to stop him, and she stood up to him that day. He truly was an evil man.' Meg shuddered.

'Come on, Mum, let's get you back, you haven't been too well yourself.' Wrapping her coat tightly around her, Meg hugged herself. They were still a family with secrets, she thought, but hopefully for not too much longer.

The rest of the day went in a blur, the computers and all of the boards had been packed away into evidence boxes. All that was left to do now was for the building to be towed away in the morning. Sean had decided to take the team to the pub for a celebratory dinner, which really only consisted of Siobhan and Connor as everyone else had left the site. Steve looked at his dear friend, he had been in his life for almost thirty years, and he was so grateful for it. Sean looked up and caught Steve looking at him.

'Go on with yer, I know that yer are dying to go and pick Meg up, we all know how important this is. So I am heading back to the B&B

for the last night, if yer want to take her back home, yer will be all by yerself,' he said, winking dramatically and laughing like a teenagers. Steve grabbed his coat and practically ran out of the door. 'Don't forget yer knee pads for all yer grovelling,' Sean called after him and Siobhan and Connor joined in the laughter.

Steve was actually nervous. He didn't know what else he could say to Meg to make her stay, he just knew that he needed her so much that it hurt. He pulled up in front of the cottage and waited for her to come out of the door. Inside, Meg was just as nervous. She had clothes strewn all around her room and make-up had been put on and wiped off a dozen times.

'For God sake, Mum, it's Steve, it's not as though you don't know him. Does all of this stressing about what to wear mean that you are going to get back together? I hope so cos you are a miserable old cow at the moment, and I don't want to go back to England on our own, as I might just have to kill yer.'

'Oh Romany I am so sorry, I have been miserable, haven't I? But that's no excuse for you to start speaking with an Irish accent.' They both laughed and Meg ran down the stairs, almost tripping in her hurry.

'I won't worry if you stop the night,' Romany called behind her.

She reached the car and got in. Steve leaned over and kissed her cheek. He wanted to do much more but didn't dare. They set off and Steve tried to make light conversation, which naturally turned to Meg's family and Aunt Sian. 'I promised meself that I wouldn't talk shop, but I was concerned how yer all were after the terrible news that I brought to yer today.'

'To be honest, I think Aunty Sian is relieved. She seems different, as if a huge burden has been lifted. William and Cassandra are coming down this weekend and I just can't get over the fact that it had been going on so long. I know that Mammy never knew about her sister Magda, but she must have known about Sian's pregnancy living in the same house. Poor Sian ... poor Mammy. What evil secrets to keep.'

Steve grabbed Meg's hand. 'Come on, no more talking of it tonight anyway.'

They pulled into a restaurant car park. 'This place is nice and quiet, I thought that we should find time to talk. I have a lot to say to yer, Meg.'

'Me too,' she replied.

They entered and ordered food, Meg refusing a drink and having a glass of water. Steve didn't question it, he just thought that she wanted a clear head. 'Well shall I go first?' he said tentatively, clearing his throat. Meg nodded.

'I am not really sure what to say, a mhuirni'n.' He grabbed her hand across the table. 'I suppose please forgive me would be a start.' Meg smiled and, encouraged, he went on. 'I never intended to cause yer pain or upset, that business with Sara ... I promise yer I never touched her and never thought of her in anyway except as a colleague. I am sad that she died but I am not sorry.' Meg gasped. 'She caused such misery that I can't forgive her, not for my sake but what happened with Romany too. I still don't understand why.'

'Well it might be because you are loving and kind and a big soft Irish eejit for a start,' Meg laughed. 'I want to put the past behind us. I want a clean start ... for us all ... for me, you, for Romany and ...' she hesitated, 'and the baby.' Meg let her words sink in. She sat back and watched as Steve made the connections. His facial expressions changing with every new thought; suddenly jumping from his chair, he picked Meg up and held her tight, swinging her round and just missing the tables in the restaurant he shouted out, 'I'm going to be a daddy!' Sitting her back in her chair, he looked across at Meg with such love in his eyes. 'Mammy would have loved it being a grandma.'

'We will tell him or her all about Bridget and Magda and Andrew and Jonathon,' she laughed.

'Just promise me one thing.'

'What's that?'

'That we don't call her Magda or Bree or Sara or anything bloody Irish.'

'Well, it might not be a girl.'

EPILOGUE

Over the next few weeks Detective Chief Inspector Sean O'Dowd and Detective Chief Inspector Steve Ryan attended funerals all over Ireland. Meeting the parents of the victims of Father Benedict brought some comfort to them both. Garda's Siobhan Thomas and Connor O'Brian attended as many of the funerals as they could. The girl's faces that they had placed on the board each day would impact their lives and stay with them forever. Just knowing that they had helped in some small way to get recognition for them spurred them both on to sit their sergeant's exam, egged on by the recommendation of Sean.

Reports were written and after conversations with the mother and baby homes commission, all of their investigative material was handed over to them to add to their own investigation.

Meg took Romany back to England to enrol in Art College and to sort out their house in Kingsbridge. She was lucky that her brother Jonathon and Becky had done a lot of updating since her parents had owned it. So apart from a bit of a neglected garden and decorating a new nursery, nothing much needed doing. Steve stayed behind until he and Sean had tied up the investigation and all of the paperwork was filed. He arranged for a tenant farmer who was local to Bally-Bay and recommended by Aidan to take over his parent's farm. He didn't know if he ever wanted to return to Ball-Bay as all it held for him was unhappiness, but one day he hoped to bring his own son or daughter here and show them their grandparent's graves high on the hill under the Sceach Gheal, and to tell them tales of the Sidhe; the little folk who lived under the hill.

Leaving Sean at the airport, he knew that he needed to face the music at home over Sara Dyson and he was longing to see Meg and Romany. 'Yer promise to come visit us for Christmas now, won't yer?' Steve shook his friend's large hand and pulled him close for a hug.

'Yer know life will be nice and quiet when yer go, yer always did bring trouble with yer,' Sean teased.

'And yerself will be bored by the end of the day.'

'Keep me updated about yer little talk with professional standards, I'm sure when they hear it all they won't want to make waves and it will all be over. Send Meg my love and I will see yer in a couple of months; that's if I can't work something out with the kids. I would love to have a Christmas with them, it's been a long time.'

'And although I would miss yer I would rather yer get to see them.' Walking away he made his way to the departures desk. His excitement at seeing his girls over-riding everything; he didn't want to think about his meeting in the morning with his boss. For now he was happier than he had been in a long time. Turning his back on Ireland again, DCI Steven Ryan's plane departed.

* * *

AUTHOR'S NOTE

This book is a work of fiction, I hope that you have enjoyed it. The characters are fictitious, but the story is based on real findings at mother and baby homes that did exist across Ireland between these dates in which similar allegations of cases of abuse of mothers and children were found to be factual. The Irish Government set up a commission to investigate these claims made by women who were survivors of this atrocity.

The New York Times ran an article in 2019 about the commission investigation into abuse of children and babies at the numerous mother and baby homes dotted around Ireland.

In 2015 the Irish government commissioned an investigation into the mother and baby homes, and it is still on-going. The commission were tasked with investigating practices in Irish mother and baby homes over a 76-year period from 1922-1996. The panel were asked to look at mortality rates, general causes of death among residents, burial arrangements, and adoption processes in the homes. Judge Yvonne Murphy led investigations into clerical child abuse.

Over thirteen homes were investigated; at one home alone over 800 bodies were found buried in a pit. Some had over 900 child deaths in the time-scale mentioned but only 64 burial places were ever discovered. At one home in particular 950 babies' bodies, born to unmarried mothers, were given to medical schools as anatomical subjects.

The homes took in poor and unmarried mothers who were shunned by their communities who did not fit Irish society's strict sexual, social, and moral codes. Growing public demand for full forensic searches led to geophysical underground surveys of two of the homes, and survivors of the homes are insisting that DNA samples be taken from them. The report stated:

'Many of the dead children were buried in a mysterious chambered structure underground, possibly a decommissioned sewage tank, where their remains were found. The commission found after looking into the burial arrangements of these homes that they could not understand why the babies and young children's bodies were handled in such an "inappropriate manner" and that local church and authorities bore "particular responsibility" since they were government-owned homes.'

Anger was directed at the Catholic Church but most of the homes were jointly funded by the governments of their times.

The Irish government concluded that it would cost 6-13million Euros to exhume the sites. It was announced in 2018 that the site would indeed be exhumed but the burial site remains intact today.

The commission concluded that 'an unspoken code of silence, a lack of outside scrutiny, and contemporary Ireland's reluctance to face its recent past kept the truth of the homes hidden for decades'.

Printed in Great Britain
by Amazon

21422857R00169